POPE'S *Iliad*

Pope's *Iliad:*

HOMER IN THE
AGE OF PASSION

Steven Shankman

WIPF & STOCK · Eugene, Oregon

Wipf and Stock Publishers
199 W 8th Ave, Suite 3
Eugene, OR 97401

Pope's "Iliad"
Homer in the Age of Passion
By Shankman, Steven
Copyright©1983 by Shankman, Steven
ISBN 13: 978-1-60608-808-1
Publication date 6/11/2009
Previously published by Princeton University Press, 1983

Errata

p. 59, l. 17: for *sermoni propriora* read *sermoni propiora*

pp. 89-90: line dropped. The last passage beginning on p. 89 should read, Hephaestus makes a brief speech to Hera pleading with her to obey the commands of the awesome father of gods and men and he then passes around a bowl of nectar—the "Reconciler Bowl," as Dryden put it in his translation of the scene—to all the assembled gods. Hera, "the goddess of the white arms (θεὰ λευκώλενος), smiled at him," Homer says, "and, smiling, she accepted the cup from her son's hands" (ll. 595-596).

p. 167, l. 33: for *meticulous* read *meticulosus*

p. 189, col. 1, l. 19: for Necander read Neander

p. 191, col. 1: between Pindar and Polyclitus, add Plato, as critic of Homer, 4-6, 50, 58n. 7, 123-124

FOR WESLEY TRIMPI

It cannot be unwelcome to literary curiosity, that I deduce thus minutely the history of the English *Iliad*. It is certainly the noblest version of poetry which the world has ever seen; and its publication must therefore be considered as one of the great events in the annals of Learning.

SAMUEL JOHNSON, *The Life of Pope*

Contents

Acknowledgments   xi
Preface   xiii

PART I: DESIGN

CHAPTER ONE   The Passionate Design: Books I and IX   3
CHAPTER TWO   The Passionate Design: Book XXIV   19

PART II: LANGUAGE

CHAPTER THREE   Elevation, Decorum, and Liveliness   55
CHAPTER FOUR   "*Homer* makes us Hearers, and *Virgil* leaves us
    Readers": Pope and the Ancient Distinction between the
    Oral and the Written Styles   75
CHAPTER FIVE   Pope's *Iliad* and the Longinian Tradition   101

PART III: VERSIFICATION

CHAPTER SIX   The Heroic Couplet   131

Appendix: Pope and Horace's Implied Distinction between the
    Oral and the Written Styles   165
Selected Bibliography   171
Index   187

Acknowledgments

Generous thanks are due to Stanford and Princeton Universities: to Stanford for awarding me a Postdoctoral Fellowship in the Humanities, and to Princeton for granting me a year's leave from teaching responsibilities, thus making it possible for me to complete this book. I owe additional thanks to Princeton for financing grants for travel as well as for the typing of the final version of this manuscript.

I first became fascinated with the problems of translation when I was an undergraduate at the University of Texas at Austin, where this subject was discussed—and practiced—with inspiration. I owe a general debt to many of my teachers and friends there, and especially to D. S. Carne-Ross (now of Boston University) and C. J. Herington (now of Yale).

I owe my greatest debt of gratitude to Wesley Trimpi, whose seminars at Stanford on the history of literary theory afforded me a critical vocabulary without which much of this book could not have been written. Trimpi's published work, which is exacting in its analyses of philological detail, is at the same time so broad in its range and implications that I have found it very suggestive for treating some of the problems discussed in the following pages. And his generosity, as both teacher and friend, has been invaluable. For my understanding of the philological method of interpretation I am indebted, as well, to the extraordinary scholarly and critical essays of J. V. Cunningham.

Many of my friends and colleagues at Princeton have carefully read my work. I would like to thank, for their encouragement and criticism, Ann L. T. Bergren (now of UCLA), Lawrence Lipking (now of Northwestern), and David Quint. I would like

ACKNOWLEDGMENTS

especially to thank Henry Knight Miller and Earl Miner, whose trenchant criticisms of an earlier version of this book were crucial in helping me to reformulate many problems and to reorganize much of my material. To the readers selected by the Princeton University Press and to Marilyn Campbell, who copyedited this manuscript, I also owe my thanks for their useful suggestions for revision.

My most patient critic has been my wife, Marsha Maverick Wells, who has cast her acute editorial eye, again and again, on the many stages in the evolution of this manuscript.

Preface

In the tenth book of his *Institutio Oratoria*, Quintilian reviews the works of ancient literature, discussing first the Greek authors and then those authors who composed in Quintilian's native Latin tongue. We challenge the supremacy of the Greeks in genres such as the epic and the elegy, Quintilian says, somewhat defensively, but when he then goes on to take up the genre of satire, he proudly asserts, *Satira quidem tota nostra est* (X.1.93). When confronted by the formidable achievements of Greek literature, Quintilian is proud to claim satire as a uniquely Roman invention. So Samuel Johnson, when confronted by the achievements of both Greek and Latin as well as of the modern literatures, of his native English literature is proud to assert, in effect, *Translatio quidem tota nostra est*. "To the Greeks translation was almost unknown," Johnson writes in the *Life of Pope*; the Romans have translated nothing which "seems ever to have risen to high reputation"; "the Italians have been very diligent translators; but I can hear of no version . . . which is read with eagerness"; and the French "found themselves reduced, by whatever necessity, to turn the Greek and Roman poetry into prose."[1] It remained for the English alone, Johnson suggests, through the brilliant efforts of Dryden and of Pope, to raise poetic translation to the status of great art. And the great critic considered the *Iliad* of Alexander Pope in particular to be "the noblest version of poetry which the world has ever seen."[2]

In the concluding years of the twentieth century we have no

[1] *Lives of the English Poets*, ed. George Birkbeck Hill, 3 vols. (Oxford, 1905), 3:236-37.
[2] Ibid., p. 119.

one critic who speaks with the authoritative voice of a Samuel Johnson, and certainly no one critic who will proudly and with confidence say of a modern rendering of an ancient text, "this is the greatest poetic translation ever written," for we moderns, especially in comparison with our eighteenth-century forbears, have no commonly shared conception either of poetry or of poetic translation. I shall therefore suggest what I mean by poetry and by the translation of poetry before making a claim that some may regard as eccentric. Poetry, to be savagely brief, is metrical speech. The translation of metrical speech can take one of two forms: the literal, in which one attempts to give as close a rendering of the original as possible and in which verse will most conveniently be abandoned for prose, since the exigencies of meter will of necessity force the translator either to expand or to contract the matter he is attempting to transfuse in as una-dulterated a state as possible; and the poetic, in which one's primary concern is not literalness but is rather the attempt to convey in verse, through stylistic equivalents, selected stylistic qualities of the original.

Having suggested what I mean by poetry and the translation of poetry, I would like to venture the following opinion: there is no satisfactory contemporary translation of Homer's *Iliad*, largely because our modern versions, which are often more "accurate" renditions than are their Augustan predecessors, tend to be written in a verse that is too loose with respect to meter and too colloquial with respect to diction to be capable of simulating, in English, Homer's formal and elevated style. For a poet writing at the beginning of the eighteenth century, however, formality and elevation were still within reach. But Alexander Pope's translation of the *Iliad*, despite the efforts of such scholars and critics as Douglas M. Knight and Reuben A. Brower,[3] is not widely

[3] The first book-length treatment of Pope's *Iliad* was Douglas M. Knight's *Pope and the Heroic Tradition: A Critical Study of his Iliad* (New Haven: Yale University Press, 1951). Reuben A. Brower's helpful remarks can be found in his *Alexander Pope: The Poetry of Allusion* (Oxford: Clarendon Press, 1959), pp. 85-141. The only other book-length study of Pope's translation is H. A. Mason's *To Homer Through Pope: An Introduction to Homer's Iliad and Pope's*

read today. It is virtually impossible, for instance, to make it required reading for a college course, since the paperback edition is now out of print; the student who wishes to own a copy of "the noblest version of poetry the world has ever seen" will be forced to pay nearly one hundred dollars for the two stunning volumes of the Twickenham edition. If the translation is read at all, then, it is read by a very specialized audience of admirers or scholars of the eighteenth century, or of those interested in the problems and challenges of translation. Even before the appearance of the first of its six volumes in the year 1715, Pope's translation had been a subject of controversy and, after the revolutionary changes of taste which occurred in the middle of the eighteenth century, it remains so today. The purpose of this book is to address, by attempting to recover Pope's interpretive and stylistic aims, some of the fundamental objections which have lost the translation the audience it deserves.

Probably no phrase has lost the eighteenth century more readers than the characterization of the period as "The Age of Reason." It is not a primary intention of this book to question the descriptive accuracy of this phrase, which has, in any case, been scrutinized elsewhere, perhaps most exhaustively by George Boas in his essay "In Search of the Age of Reason"[4]; as the title of the essay suggests, the seasoned eighteenth-century scholar was apparently still searching for a clear and undiluted manifestation of "The Age of Reason" in that century in which it had reportedly been found. Donald Greene, with ample justification, entitled his excellent and informative book on the backgrounds of eight-

---

Translation (London: Chatto & Windus, 1972). One of the aims of the present study is to place Pope's translation within a more detailed context of neoclassical critical and, especially, stylistic theory than has been attempted by the two previously mentioned book-length studies. The most exhaustive discussion of the sources of Pope's critical comments on Homer is Hans-Joachim Zimmermann's *Alexander Popes Noten zu Homer: Eine Manuskript- und Quellenstudie* (Heidelberg: Carl Winter, 1966).

[4] The essay of Professor Boas can be found in *Aspects of the Eighteenth Century*, ed. Earl W. Wasserman (Baltimore: The Johns Hopkins University Press, 1965), pp. 1-19.

eenth-century English literature *The Age of Exuberance*.[5] And Kenneth MacLean writes that "the frequency with which Eighteenth-Century writers placed man and his reason at the mercy of his passions, particularly his ruling passion, suggests that the age of reason might with more justice be called the age of passion."[6] I shall adopt, with some qualifications, MacLean's designation of the period as "The Age of Passion" and summarily reject the phrase "The Age of Reason." Whatever its appropriateness as a designation of the period as a whole—and I think it a problematic concept for understanding English literature of the early eighteenth century—it is certainly a misleading notion for coming to a sympathetic understanding of Pope's *Iliad*. For what Pope stresses about Homer both in his *Iliad* preface and in his notes is the poet's "unequal'd Fire and Rapture, which is so forcible in *Homer*, that no Man of a true Poetical Spirit is Master of himself while he reads him."[7] Pope—who was the first Homeric translator in English to make abundant use of Longinus' treatise *On the Sublime*—saw Homer's style as above all passionate and fiery, not "reasonable,"[8] and he attempted to trans-

---

[5] The full title of Greene's book is *The Age of Exuberance: Backgrounds to Eighteenth-Century English Literature* (New York: Random House, 1970).

[6] *John Locke and English Literature of the Eighteenth Century* (New Haven: Yale University Press, 1936), p. 38. And see *Baroque Music* by Claude V. Palisca, who writes, "If there is any common thread that unites the great variety of music we call baroque, ... it is in an underlying faith in music's power, indeed its obligation to move the affections [or passions]. ... If we want to ascertain whether we have crossed the boundary into the baroque or out of it, there is no better test than to ask if the expression of the affections is the dominant goal in fashioning a piece of music" (Englewood Cliffs, N.J.: Prentice-Hall, Inc., 1968), pp. 4-5. The great master of baroque pathos is Pope's contemporary, George Frederick Handel.

[7] *The Twickenham Edition of the Poems of Alexander Pope*, gen. ed. John Butt, 11 vols. (London and New Haven: Methuen & Co. Ltd. and Yale University Press, 1961-1967), 7:4. The Twickenham edition of Pope's poems will hereafter be cited as *TE*.

[8] The word "reasonable," it might be mentioned, did not necessarily have positive connotations for Pope. See, for example, his verbal portrait, in the *Epistle to a Lady*, of the decorous but cold Cloe, whom he describes as "So very reasonable, so unmov'd, / As never yet to love, or to be lov'd" (ll. 165-166).

pose this quality into a correspondingly elevated Augustan style. If the reader is to experience the "unequal'd Fire and Rapture" Pope attempted to achieve in English, it is necessary for him to become familiar with the resources and intentions of that style.

When applied to the subject of Homeric interpretation, the phrase "The Age of Reason" is actually a much more suitable description, in at least one important respect, of the Renaissance. The first complete translation of the *Iliad* in English is the Elizabethan version of George Chapman. Pope's translation has been invoked by more than one modern critic in order to contrast its polish and alleged neoclassical restraint with the sensuous exuberance of Chapman's Homer.[9] And Douglas Bush writes, "If Homer could return from Elysium to read all the English renderings, he would surely find in Chapman his truest son, a man who has fed on lion's marrow."[10] Yet it is Chapman far more than Pope who is tied to the long and conservative tradition of moralistic interpretation of the *Iliad*. As I shall argue, it is Chapman rather than Pope who consistently attempts to excuse or to explain away Achilles' wrath. For in those key sections of the poem when Homer portrays his Achilles as a man whose passions are violent and beyond his rational control, it is Pope (the al-

[9] See, for example, the final chapter ("Style as Interpretation: Chapman's 'Odyssey' and Pope's") of George deF. Lord's *Homeric Renaissance. The "Odyssey" of George Chapman* (New Haven: Yale University Press, 1956). Cf. also the following remarks made by Allardyce Nicoll, who evokes Pope's translation—without quoting from it—in order to contrast it with a passage he cites from Chapman's *Iliad*: "The vigour inherent in his lines is Chapman's greatest achievement. Pope chisels a cameo where the Elizabethan hammers out a vast piece of statuary" (*Chapman's Homer*, ed. Allardyce Nicoll, 2 vols. [New York: Bollingen Foundation, 1956], 1:xii). Behind such a statement one can hear the clichéd judgments of Victorian literary historians such as that rendered by William L. Long: "The poetry of the first half of the [eighteenth] century, as typified in the work of Pope, is polished and witty enough, but artificial; it lacks fire, fine feeling, enthusiasm, the glow of the Elizabethan Age" (*English Literature: Its History and Significance for the Life of the English-Speaking World: A Text-Book for Schools* (Boston: Ginn and Company, 1909), p. 260. Long's comments are cited by Henry K. Miller in his essay "The 'Whig Interpretation' of Literary History," *Eighteenth-Century Studies* 6 (Fall 1972): 60-84.

[10] Cited from *Chapman's Homer*, ed. Nicoll, 1:xiv.

legedly restrained neoclassicist) rather than Chapman (the alleg-
edly exuberant Elizabethan) who is scrupulously faithful to the
original text.

A word about organization. Geoffrey Tillotson divided his fine
book *On the Poetry of Pope* into three sections entitled "Design,"
"Language," and "Versification." The divisions were suggested
by Pope's own enumeration of "the three distinct *tours* in po-
etry," which, he told Spence, were "the design, the language,
and the versification."[11] I have followed Tillotson's method of
organization, which has the great virtue of analyzing an author's
work by using a critical terminology to which the author himself
has given sanction.

[11] Joseph Spence, *Anecdotes, Observations, and Characters of Books and Men*,
ed. James M. Osborn, 2 vols. (Oxford: Clarendon Press, 1966), 1:167. Tillotson's
book was published by Oxford at the Clarendon Press in 1938.

PART I: DESIGN

CHAPTER ONE

The Passionate Design: Books I and IX

THE MORALISTIC INHERITANCE

"It is something strange that of all the Commentators upon *Homer*," Pope writes in the introductory note to his observations on the first book of the *Iliad*,

> there is hardly one whose principal Design is to illustrate the Poetical Beauties of the Author. They are Voluminous in explaining those Sciences which he made but subservient to his Poetry, and sparing only upon that Art which constitutes his Character. . . . Hence it has come to pass that their Remarks are rather Philosophical, Historical, Geographical, Allegorical, or in short rather anything than Critical and Poetical. . . . The chief Design of the following Notes is to comment upon *Homer* as a Poet.[1]

What Pope so eloquently says of the intention of his notes is equally true of the intention of the translation itself: Pope wishes to make sense of Homer as a poet. The commentators, Pope feels, have tended to ignore the ways in which the poem enacts its meaning and have instead imposed their more specialized and distinctly nonpoetic concerns upon the integrity of the poetic text.

[1] *TE*, 7:82.

[3]

One of these concerns, as Pope says, is "Philosophy," and the name that is most clearly associated with this truancy in the history of literary theory is Plato. At the beginning of Book XXIV of the *Iliad* Homer portrays Achilles as visibly overcome with grief over the death of Patroclus; we see Achilles as he weeps uncontrollably, hurls his body to the ground and rolls in the dust, and then paces distractedly along the shore. In the *Republic* (III.338a) Plato objects to such a conspicuous display of emotion and Pope responds to this criticism by suggesting that "*Plato* spoke more like a Philosopher than a Critick when he blamed the Behaviour of *Achilles* as unmanly."[2] Pope sums up his opinion of Plato's Homeric criticism when he says that

> It may justly be observ'd in general of all *Plato*'s Objections against *Homer*, that they are still in a View to Morality, constantly blaming him for representing ill and immoral Things as the Opinions or Actions of his Persons. To every one of these one general Answer will serve, which is, that *Homer* as often describes ill things, in order to make us avoid them, as good, to induce us to follow them.[3]

Plato's criticisms of Homer are important to consider, for his implicit demand that a work of literature have a hero who at all times will be an exemplum worthy of emulation was transmitted, through Virgil and thence through Renaissance epic theory, to the Moderns in the famous quarrel with the Ancients. Jean Terrasson, for example, says in his *Dissertation Critique sur l'Iliade* (1715):

> *Achilles* is not only abominably vicious; but the two only good Qualities he seems to have, his Courage and Friendship, are of no Use nor Example at all. His Courage is only brutal Rage, and consists wholly in the Strength and Agility of his Body, which is not therefore capable of Imitation.[4]

[2] Ibid., 8:535.
[3] Ibid., 8:476.
[4] *A Critical Dissertation Upon Homer's Iliad*, trans. anonymous, 2 vols. (London, 1722-1725), 1:346. For a discussion of some aspects of the "querelle des

That a work of literature must offer imitable exempla of moral behavior is most clearly stated by Plato in Book III of the *Republic*. Socrates is discussing the education of the guardians of his republic and he suggests that, since poetry often represents heroes in a less than ideal light, the reading of such poetic passages would encourage impressionable minds to imitate models that are bad. "We should be right in doing away with the lamentations of men of note," Socrates says, "in order that those whom we say we are breeding for the guardianship of the land may disdain to act like these." Socrates continues:

> Again then we shall request Homer and the other poets not to portray Achilles, the son of a goddess, as "lying now on his side, and then again on his back, and again on his face," and then rising up and "drifting distraught on the shore of the waste unharvested ocean," nor as clutching with both hands the sooty dust and strewing it over his head, nor as weeping and lamenting in the measure and manner attributed to him by the poet.[5]

Plato then goes on to censure what he takes to be Homer's similarly undignified representations in the *Iliad* of Priam and then of Zeus himself. The only works of literature which Plato will admit into his republic are hymns to the gods and encomia of noble men. Such criteria provide a defense, of course, for the literary genre of the Platonic dialogue which, as Eric Voegelin has said of the *Republic*,[6] may be seen as encomia of the pious

---

anciens et des modernes" that are of relevance to Pope's treatment of Homer, see chapter four of the present study.

[5] Trans. Paul Shorey, *The Collected Dialogues of Plato*, ed. Edith Hamilton and Huntington Cairns, Bollingen Series LXXI (1961; reprint ed. Princeton: Princeton University Press, 1971), p. 633.

[6] *Order and History*, 4 vols., Vol. III: *Plato and Aristotle* (1957; reprint ed. Baton Rouge: Louisiana State University Press, 1977), p. 134. The above summary of Plato's criticism of Homer is, given the context of my argument, necessarily oversimplified. Plato's remarks on Homer and the poets must be viewed in broader terms as a critique of literature that has lost its capacity for analytical speculation and is enjoyed largely for its naturalistic appeal. On this problem, see Paul Friedländer, *Plato: An Introduction* (1958; reprint ed. Princeton: Prince-

Socrates; but it is less relevant to the *Iliad* and to most Greek tragedies.

In order to defend tragedy, Aristotle was forced, in fact, to counter Plato's demand that a work of literature offer impeccable moral exempla. This he did, in part, by suggesting that it is not the primary function of literature to provide ethical models; a tragedy is an imitation of a specific action that has general implications: it is plot, not character, that is the soul of tragedy. And the best kind of tragic plot, according to Aristotle, features a protagonist who is neither morally perfect nor an utter villain, but rather a character "between these two extremes, . . . a man who is not eminently good and just, yet whose misfortune is brought about by some error or frailty[7] (ἀλλὰ δι' ἁμαρτίαν, 1453a). If a poet is to represent such a character, he must obviously portray him as he performs those actions that are, if not completely villainous, at least to some degree morally culpable. An action is morally culpable if a character allows his passions to prevail over his reason, and thus the writer of a tragedy—or of an epic, such as the *Iliad*, which has a clearly tragic structure—will of necessity represent characters in states of highly passionate and unbalanced emotion.

Plato's demand that a work of literature represent a wholly exemplary hero was met by Virgil—or, at least, Virgil tried to meet it[8]—in his characterization, in the *Aeneid*, of *pius Aeneas*. The transmission of this Platonic notion to the Renaissance is

---

ton University Press, 1969), pp. 118-125 and Voegelin, *Plato and Aristotle*, pp. 132-134.

[7] *Aristotle's Theory of Poetry and Fine Art*, trans. S. H. Butcher (New York: Dover Publications, Inc., 1951), p. 47.

[8] My own view—which is in some crucial ways at odds with the standard Renaissance view—is that Virgil did his best to write a patriotic poem, one that accorded with the wishes of Augustus, and that he did indeed try to present a socially conscious epic hero worthy of imitation. But I also believe Virgil possessed, as T. S. Eliot has observed, an *"anima naturaliter Christiana"* ("Virgil and the Christian World," *On Poetry and Poets* [London: Faber and Faber, 1957], p. 130), and that he therefore could not rest content with the notion that the *imperium sine fine* was a sufficient response to his own or to man's spiritual needs. His writing of the *Aeneid* was, perhaps, more a Stoic act of will than the fruit of a profound and unqualified commitment of his soul.

stated memorably by Sir Philip Sidney who, in the *Apologie for Poetrie* (printed 1595), says that of all literary genres the epic is the greatest and really needs no defense. It is "the best and most accomplished kinde of Poetry" specifically because, according to Sidney, the "loftie image" of the epic hero "inflameth the minde with desire to be worthy, and informes with counsel how to be worthy." "Only let *Aeneas* be worne in the tablet of your memory,"[9] Sidney says before elaborating in detail that hero's exemplary traits, and you will yourself be stirred to perform similarly heroic actions. This moralistic concern with the necessity of portraying an ideal hero who could teach by encouraging the emulation of his example made Achilles a problematic figure for the writer of Renaissance epic. In his examination of four Renaissance epic heroes who were modeled upon Achilles—Ruggiero in Ariosto's *Orlando Furioso*, Corsamante in Trissino's *Italia Liberata*, Lancilotto in Alamanni's *Avarchide*, and Rinaldo in Tasso's *Gerusalemme Liberata*—John M. Steadman, for example, concludes:

> Indebted as they are to classical epic for their versions of the Achilles-legend, all four poems convert the latter into an *exemplum* of the characteristic virtues and vices of the magnanimous man; they essay, in varying degrees, to adapt Achilles' behavior to the chivalric ideal. . . . All four poems tend to "moralize" the motif by sharpening ethical contrasts, by eliminating the more objectionable aspects of Achilles' conduct, and by increasing the amount of moral commentary on the part of the author, the protagonists, and the minor characters. Emphasizing the distinctive attributes of magnanimity—the concern for honor and great actions, preoccupation with merits and deserts, contempt for pleasure and riches—they transform the Homeric into the chivalric ἦθος. They convert the *ferus* and *saevus* Pelides into a Renaissance nobleman.[10]

[9] *Elizabethan Critical Essays*, ed. G. Gregory Smith, 2 vols. (1904; reprint ed. London: Oxford University Press, 1971), 1:179.

[10] "Achilles and Renaissance Epic: Moral Criticism and Literary Tradition," in *Lebende Antike: Symposion Für Rudolf Sühnel* (Berlin: Erich Schmidt Verlag, 1967), p. 152.

It is precisely into a Renaissance nobleman that George Chapman attempts to convert the *ferus* and *saevus* Pelides in his Elizabethan translation of the *Iliad*. As I hope to show in the following section, at those moments in the poem when Homer depicts Achilles in a state of unbalanced emotion, Chapman presents the reader with a relatively blameless hero whose reason is firmly in control of his passions.

"A Fire Blown by a Wind": The Wrath of Achilles

The subject of the *Iliad* is the wrath of Achilles. But the poem is not, of course, merely a psychological study of a private character. The Homeric poems were composed in their final form in Asia Minor some time around the eighth century B.C. They were sung for a Hellenic society once firmly based in Mycenae on the Greek mainland, a society since dispersed and now relocated along the coast of Asia Minor. While the *Iliad* certainly is a heroic poem, Homer did not simply praise his heroes: he chose for his subject a not altogether exemplary episode—the wrath of Achilles—and insofar as the work is a critical analysis of a central hero of a civilization it is as well a study of the reasons for the decline of the Mycenean civilization (1550-1100 B.C.) that it depicts. Although he wrote long before our knowledge of Homeric history and philology had advanced to its present level of sophistication, René Le Bossu intuited clearly the important political dimension of Homer's epic; for in response to the Moderns' claim that the *Iliad* had no real subject, Le Bossu responded that Homer "has taken for the foundation of his Fable this great Truth; That a Misunderstanding between Princes is the Ruin of their own States."[11] That Pope accepted Le Bossu's view is suggested by the fact that the poet allowed it to remain in his revision

---

[11] Cited from Pope's "A General View of the Epic Poem, and of the *Iliad* and *Odyssey*. Extracted from *Bossu*," *TE*, 9:6. For the insight that the Homeric poems are, in part, analyses of the decline of Mycenaean civilization, I am indebted to Eric Voegelin, *Order and History*, Vol. II: *The World of the Polis* (1957; reprint ed. Baton Rouge: Louisiana State University Press, 1974), chap. three.

[8]

of Parnell's *Essay on Homer*, which was published along with the first volume of the *Iliad* translation. And Pope repeats Le Bossu's statement in his notes to Book III of the *Iliad*:

> The chief Moral of *Homer* was to dispose the ill Effects of Discord; the *Greeks* were to be shewn disunited. . . . The *Trojans* on the other hand were to be represented making all Advantages of the others Disagreement, which they could not do without a strict Union among themselves. *Hector* therefore who commanded them, must be endu'd with all such Qualifications as tended to the Preservation of it; as *Achilles* with such as promoted to the contrary.[12]

The wrath of Achilles, which Pope here acknowledges to be largely responsible for the discord in the Greek ranks, first breaks out in Book I. But it does not break out unprovoked: it erupts in response to Agamemnon's anger, which is in turn a response to the anger of Apollo. As the poem opens Homer says that Apollo is inflicting a plague upon the Greek camp specifically because Agamemnon has dishonored (ἠτίμησε, l. 94) Apollo's priest Chryses by taking his daughter Chryseis captive and not returning her. Chryses offers gifts as ransom for his daughter, but Agamemnon is not persuaded to acquiesce until the seer Calchas confirms that it is indeed Agamemnon's refusal to return Chryseis that has angered the god. The Greek chieftain does eventually acquiesce, but he demands in recompense not merely the ransom offered by the priest, but a recompense of a status equal to that which he is about to lose; for the prize (γέρας) he is about to lose he demands an equivalent prize. Achilles at this point angrily intercedes and tells Agamemnon that his demand that one of the Greeks give up his prize is unfair and that the king should wait to be duly recompensed until Troy is sacked and an equivalent prize once again becomes available.

Now Achilles' suggestion itself is entirely reasonable, but Homer does appear to question its propriety at this particular moment in the course of the war. The Greeks have been before Troy

12 *TE*, 7:191.

[9]

for nine years with no success and this frustration is felt acutely by Agamemnon, who is the Zeus-appointed leader of the Greek troops and for whose brother, Menelaus, the war is being fought, since it was from Menelaus that Helen was taken. Agamemnon is indeed the king, but Achilles, as all the Greeks know, is the greatest warrior. The seemingly endless siege of Troy may be engendering malaise among the Greek troops and hence eroding Agamemnon's prestige as commander-in-chief. The humiliation Agamemnon feels at being informed that it is he who is the cause of Apollo's anger, followed by the humiliation he suffers when he is told that he must give up a prize which is enjoyed by the other warriors, further erodes his status. And then to be upbraided by a man who is his political subordinate but whom all clearly regard as his superior in battle is too much for the king to bear.

That both Agamemnon and Achilles are at fault is suggested by Homer when he has Nestor, a figure whose judgment is reliable and clear-headed, characterize the situation as such. Nestor advises Agamemnon to put aside his anger (l. 282) and to refrain from taking Achilles' prize from him; and he tells Achilles not to challenge the king, since the superior *timē* ("honor" or "esteem") which Agamemnon enjoys is his by virtue of the kingship which Zeus has bestowed upon him. Both heroes reject Nestor's balanced advice and both, therefore, are culpable in Homer's view.

In Chapman's version of the scene the accent falls more heavily upon Agamemnon's share of the responsibility for the quarrel. Chapman's Achilles is represented as the exemplum of the rational man whose reason allows his passions to manifest themselves only after due provocation. When Agamemnon threatens to take Briseis, Achilles considers drawing his sword immediately and attacking the Greek leader. At this point Athena descends and persuades Achilles to stay his hand; since she herself and Hera, Athena says, care for both heroes equally, "hold back and obey us" (l. 214). Achilles responds:

[10]

χρὴ μὲν σφωΐτερόν γε, θεά, ἔπος εἰρύσσασθαι
καὶ μάλα περ θυμῷ κεχολωμένον ὣς γὰρ ἄμεινον·
ὅς κε θεοῖς ἐπιπείθηται, μάλα τ᾽ ἔκλυον αὐτοῦ.

(I ought to—and must—obey your commands, goddess,
Even though my breast seethes in anger. It is better that
     way,
Since the gods listen to those who obey them.)

[ll. 216-218]

Pope's translation of these lines is remarkably accurate:

'Tis just, O Goddess! I thy Dictates hear.
Hard as it is, my Vengeance I suppress:
Those who revere the Gods, the Gods will bless.

[ll. 288-290]

In Chapman's version of this exchange Athena says "Throw
reines on thy passions, and serve us" (l. 215). To which Achilles
replies:

                    . . . Though my heart
Burne in just anger, yet my soule must conquer
     th'angrie part
And yeeld you conquest. Who subdues his earthly part
     for heaven,
Heaven to his prayres subdues his wish.

[ll. 215-218]¹³

Two observations can be made of this passage that are relevant
to my argument. First, Chapman has presented a picture of Achilles
as a man who is acutely conscious of the problem of keeping the

¹³ All quotations from the *Iliad* in Greek are cited from *Tomi I et II, Iliadis
Libros I-XXIV Continentes*, ed. David B. Munro and Thomas W. Allen (1902;
reprint ed. Oxford: Oxford University Press, 1966). The literal translation from
the Greek is my own, as will be all such translations in this study. The translation
from Pope's *Iliad* is cited from the Twickenham edition, as will be all quotations
from Pope's poems. Quotations from Chapman's Homeric versions, as in this
instance, will be cited from Nicoll's edition.

[11]

passions under the control of the reason. This is surely implied in the statement of Homer's Achilles that "the gods listen to those who obey them," which Pope translates in the line "Those who revere the Gods, the Gods will bless," but Chapman, perhaps following the moralizing views of the Renaissance commentator whom Pope will later dub "the grave Spondanus,"[14] renders the insight wholly explicit. In so doing, the Elizabethan poet leaves the reader with the impression that Achilles already possesses the self-mastery which Homer suggests he has not won until the poem is concluded. And second, Chapman has his Achilles characterize his anger as "just" where the adjective is absent in the original.

The plague that besets the Greek camp as the *Iliad* opens comes, to be sure, as the direct result of the dishonor done by Agamemnon to Apollo's priest. But the plague must be taken as a general symbol for the spiritual disorder in the Greek camp, a disorder that is symptomatic not only of Agamemnon's impious intransigence, but of Achilles' arrogance as well. It appears that Chapman, however, wishes to restrict the significance of the plague to the "literal" level. When the heralds come to Achilles' tent to take Briseis from him upon Agamemnon's orders, Achilles warns them that he will no longer help to defend the Greek troops and says of Agamemnon's shortsightedness: "He, with a heart bent on destruction, makes sacrifice, but he is truly ignorant of the past and the future and what might best assure the safety of his Achaean warriors" (ll. 342-344). These lines are accurately transcribed by Pope, whose Achilles says:

> The raging Chief in frantick Passion lost,
> Blind to himself, and useless to his Host,

---

[14] Cited from Pope's *Observations* upon *Iliad* XI.188, TE, 8:43. In his *Observations* upon III.551 Pope refers to Spondanus as "the moral Expositor" (*TE* 7:217). The influence of Spondanus on Chapman's interpretation of this passage is suggested by Donald Smalley, "The Ethical Bias of Chapman's *Homer*," *Studies in Philology* 36 (1939):178, n. 52. For my analysis of the ways in which Chapman "rationalizes" Achilles' wrath I am indebted to Smalley's article as well as to Phyllis B. Bartlett, "The Heroes of Chapman's *Homer*," *The Review of English Studies* 17 (1941):257-280.

Unskill'd to judge the Future by the Past,
In Blood and Slaughter shall repent at last.
[ll. 446-449]

Chapman's version is a considerable amplification of the original;
his Achilles says:

But your king, in tempting mischiefe, raves,
Nor sees at once by present things the future—how
like waves
Ils follow ils, injustices, being never so secure
In present times, but after-plagues, even then, are seene
as sure.
Which yet he sees not and so sooths his present lust—
which, checkt,
Would checke plagues future, and he might, in
succouring right, protect
Such as fight for his right at fleete.
[ll. 341-347]

The plague with which the *Iliad* begins and to which Chapman's
Achilles refers twice in this passage—and it should be remarked
that Homer does not mention it here at all—is attributed by
Chapman to the anger of Agamemnon alone. It is almost as if
Chapman would have preferred to rewrite the opening lines of
the poem so that they would read "Sing, Goddess, of the wrath
of Agamemnon, that destructive wrath which brought so many
sorrows upon the Greeks."

Chapman's idealizing transformation of Achilles can be seen
most clearly in Book IX, where Homer's Achilles is at his least
ideal. Agamemnon now regrets his rash action in taking Briseis
from Achilles, and the Greek camp is in dire need of Achilles'
martial brilliance if they are to avert what is now virtually certain
destruction. As the priest Chryses had come to supplicate Aga-
memnon in the first book and offered "numberless gifts" (l. 12)
as ransom for his daughter, so now the embassy sent by Aga-
memnon offers Achilles compensation for the injury done to him.
The offer is as generous as it could possibly be: not only will

[13]

Briseis be returned with the assurance that she remain untouched, but in addition Agamemnon will give to him tripods, gold, cauldrons, twelve racehorses along with the prizes these horses have won, and seven beautiful women captured at Lesbos; and, along with other gifts, Agamemnon offers to him the hand of any one of his three daughters in Argos and the rule of seven cities situated near the sea (ll. 264-298). But Achilles rejects the offer even after his moral tutor, the aged Phoenix, tries to persuade him by reciting the tale of Meleager, who also at first refused to relinquish his wrath and then, when he finally did so, acted too late to receive precisely the kinds of gifts Achilles is now being presented with. Nor will Achilles be moved by Phoenix's reference to the spirits of prayer (the *litai*), the daughters of Zeus who come to soothe the resentment even of gods who have been offended by mortals, but who bring ruin (*atē*) upon those who will not be moved by their appeals.

To all of these entreaties Achilles is deaf. It had been the intention particularly of Phoenix to try, through his reference to the *litai* and to the exemplum of Meleager, to lead Achilles out of the closed circle of his obsessive anger by suggesting that he place his private grievance within a more general context of experience. That he does not respond suggests that he is still locked into his private world. He will not emerge until the slaughter of his fellow Greeks which rages around him is no longer an abstraction but is truly comprehended in its horror, and this does not occur until he experiences the death of Patroclus as a personal tragedy for which he feels largely responsible. But at this moment in the poem he is still locked into that private world and his anger at his mistreatment at the hands of Agamemnon still clouds his vision. After Odysseus has described to Achilles the many gifts that will be his if only he give up his wrath, after Phoenix patiently tries to persuade him that such a course is the only mature and sensible one to take, and after the blunt and straightforward Ajax expresses his exasperation with Achilles' intransigence by calling him "savage," "hard," "pitiless," and "implacable" (ll. 629, 630, 632, 636), Achilles is still unable to relinquish his anger and his temper flares up at the very mention

[14]

of Agamemnon's name. "I am in accord with everything you have said," Achilles replies to Ajax, "but my heart swells with anger whenever I recall what he has done, how rudely Atrides has treated me, as if I were some sort of worthless vagabond" (ll. 645-648). Pope's translation is accurate here:

> Well hast thou spoke; but at the Tyrant's Name,
> My Rage rekindles, and my Soul's on flame,
> 'Tis just Resentment and becomes the brave;
> Disgrac'd, dishonour'd, like the vilest Slave!
> [ll. 759-762]

Pope's Achilles, it is true, characterizes his "Resentment" at Agamemnon as "just," where this is merely implied in the original. But in his notes Pope leaves no doubt that he believes Achilles is acting in a pathological manner:

> We have here the true Picture of an angry Man, and nothing can be better imagin'd to heighten *Achilles*'s Wrath; he owns that Reason would induce him to a Reconciliation, but his Anger is too great to listen to Reason. He speaks with respect to them [i.e., to the assembly consisting of Odysseus, Phoenix, and Ajax], but upon mentioning *Agamemnon*, he flies into Rage: Anger is in nothing more like Madness, than that Madmen will talk sensibly enough upon any indifferent Matter; but upon the mention of the Subject that caused their Disorder, they fly out into their usual Extravagance.[15]

Or, as Pope remarks earlier in the book in a memorable description of Achilles' obsession with what the great warrior feels has been the intolerable treatment he received at the hands of Agamemnon:

> His Rage awaken'd by that Injury, is like a Fire blown by a Wind, that sinks and rises by fits, but keeps continually burning, and blazes but the more for those Intermissions.[16]

[15] *TE*, 7:471-472.
[16] Ibid., 7:452.

Here is how Chapman, in his greatly amplified version, renders
lines 645-648 of Homer's text:

> Out of thy heart I know thou speakst, and as thou
>   holdst me deare:
> But still, as often as I thinke how rudely I was usd
> And like a stranger for all rites fit for our good refused;
> My heart doth swell against the man that durst be so
>   profane
> To violate his sacred place—not for my private bane,
> But since wrackt vertue's generall lawes he shamelesse
>   did infringe,
> For whose sake I will loose the reines and give mine
>   anger swinge
> Without my wisedome's least impeach. He is a foole,
>   and base,
> That pitties vice-plagu'd minds, when paine,
>   not love of right, gives place.
>
> [ll. 611-619]

In Homer and in Pope, Achilles is portrayed here as so consumed
by private hatred that it clouds his public conscience. Chapman,
however, whose interpretation of this passage appears to have
been once again influenced by "the grave Spondanus,"[17] has his
Achilles expressly state, to the contrary, that it is not "for my
private bane" that he refuses to come to terms with Agamemnon;
he wishes, rather, by refraining from battle to give Agamemnon
a useful and eminently deserved lesson in the public art of king-
ship, since Agamemnon has violated his "sacred place" as king
by transgressing "wrackt vertue's generall lawes," laws that were
"fit" for the general "good." Achilles' rational faculty is repre-
sented by Chapman as in secure control of his passions; since
Agamemnon has violated his divinely-appointed position as king
and made a mockery of the meaning of true virtue, Achilles makes

---

[17] As Smalley notes ("The Ethical Bias of Chapman's *Homer*," p. 182), it was
Spondanus, in his *Homer: Quae extant omnia . . . cum Latina ver-
sione . . . Perpetuis . . . in Iliada simul et Odysseam J. Spondani . . . commentariis*
(1583), who "comments on Achilles' zeal for the public good."

[16]

a conscious and very deliberate decision to "loose the reines and give mine anger swinge / Without my wisedome's least impeach." In the same spirit of self-mastery with which Chapman's Achilles vents his just anger in Book IX, so he decides to contain it again in the scene of reconciliation in Book XIX. Our quarrel has only enhanced the position of the Trojans, Homer's Achilles tells Agamemnon, and we should now regard it as a thing of the past, "since necessity bids us to restrain our anger. Therefore I now declare an end to my wrath; it is not right to be so obstinately angry for ever" (ll. 66-68). Pope once again is succinct and reasonably accurate. Our quarrel, his Achilles says to Agamemnon,

> . . . no more the Subject of Debate,
> Is past, forgotten, and resign'd to Fate:
> Why should (alas) a mortal Man, as I,
> Burn with a Fury that can never die?
> Here then my Anger ends.
>
> [ll. 67-71]

The quarrel with Agamemnon Chapman's Achilles refers to as "Past things yet past our aide" (l. 58). He continues:

> Fit griefe for what wrath rulde in them must make
>   th'amends repaid
> With that necessitie of love that now forbids our ire—
> Which I with free affects obey. Tis for the senseless fire
> Still to be burning, having stuffe, but men
>   must curbe rage still,
> Being fram'd with voluntarie powres, as well to checke
>   the will
> As gives it raines.
>
> [ll. 59-64]

In the ninth book Chapman's Achilles had declared that he would "loose the reines" (l. 617) of his anger against Agamemnon and he now says that, since he possesses "voluntarie powres," he will "checke the will." It is interesting that Chapman has his Achilles introduce the image of a "senseless fire" in order to contrast the indomitability of its natural "rage" with the anger of a man,

[17]

who should possess the "voluntarie powres" which can control such anger. It will be recalled that Pope, whose representation of Achilles' passionate nature is truer to Homer's than is Chapman's, compares Achilles' wrath to "a Fire blown by a Wind, that sinks and rises by fits, but keeps continually burning, and blazes but the more for those Intermissions." Where Chapman remarks upon the qualitative difference between the anger of Achilles and a "senseless fire," Pope points out their equivalence.

CHAPTER TWO

The Passionate Design:
Book XXIV

Painting the Passions

How can we account for the shift in attitude, from the time of
Chapman to the time of Pope, in the depiction of Achilles' char-
acter? What were the factors, apart from his own extraordinary
intuitions about Homer, which enabled Pope to see his way past
the moralistic reading of Achilles' character which he inherited
from the Renaissance? Part of the answer lies, of course, in the
waning of Renaissance epic with its distinctive emphasis upon
the exemplary nature of the central hero. In the early eighteenth
century the tradition was no longer as alive as it was in the
sixteenth, when, at the peak of the English expression of Ren-
aissance nationalism, an Edmund Spenser could write a *Faerie
Queene* with King Arthur as its central hero or a Sir Philip Sidney
could refer to epic as "the most accomplished kinde of Poetry"
since the "image" of the epic hero "inflameth the mind with
desire to be worthy."[1] Alexander Pope's projected epic, for ex-
ample, which featured the exemplary central character Brutus,
the legendary founder of Britain, was aborted after line eight of
the prologue. And then there was the reassertion, derived ulti-
mately from Aristotle's *Poetics* and the revival of interest in that
work, of the crucial distinction between the "moral" and the

---

[1] *Eliz. Crit. Essays*, ed. Smith, 1:179.

[19]

"poetical" treatment of character. "The *Manners* of the Epic Poem ought to be *poetically good*," Le Bossu writes, "but it is not necessary they be always *morally* so."[2] So André Dacier, in his *La Poëtique d'Aristote avec des Remarques* (1692), reminds his readers that " 'tis not a Moral, but a Poetical Goodness"[3] which the poet should aim for in the representation of character. The notion is expressed again and again in the neoclassical period. In the preface to his *Aeneis*, for example, Dryden states that "the critics have concluded that it is not necessary the manners of the hero should be virtuous. They are poetically good, if they are of a piece."[4]

But also significant in explaining the shift of attitude toward the representation of Achilles' character is the increased interest, since the middle of the seventeenth century, in the analysis of the "passions" themselves, considered not so much as "perturbations" of the soul but rather as morally neutral phenomena. This process, which can be seen, in part, as a development of medieval and Renaissance voluntarism,[5] is already fully worked

[2] "A General View of the Epic Poem and of the *Iliad* and *Odyssey*. Extracted from Bossu," *TE*, 9:20

[3] *Aristotle's Art of Poetry. Translated from the Original Greek, according to Mr. Goulston's Edition, Together with Mr. D'Acier's Notes Translated from the French* (London, 1705) , p. 243. Cf. *Spectator* 548 (Nov. 28, 1712): "Achilles is placed in the greatest point of Glory and Success, though his Character is Morally Vicious, and only Poetically Good" (*The Spectator*, ed. Donald F. Bond, 5 vols. [Oxford: Clarendon Press, 1965], 4:464).

[4] "Dedication of the Aeneis" (1697), *Essays of John Dryden*, selected and edited by W. P. Ker, 2 vols. (Oxford: Clarendon Press, 1926), 2:159.

[5] In the course of the seventeenth century, writers of tragedy, for instance, tended to represent the fall of a good but not perfect man less as the consequence of a free choice than as the consequence of a sudden or irresistible breaking out of passion. The "voluntarist" interpretation of moral transgression, that is, gradually replaced the "intellectualist" view. The intellectualist view of the Aristotelian-Thomistic tradition stressed the capacity of man's *intellectus* to know the good; the will—the *voluntas*—could act only if the reason had presented the will with an apparent good. In the voluntarist interpretation, the will could act independently of the reason, thus rendering the rational faculty helpless. For an excellent discussion of the distinctions between these two traditions and of their relevance to the analysis of scenes of moral choice in *Othello*, *Macbeth*, and *Hamlet*, see the chapter entitled "Reason Panders Will" in J. V. Cunningham's

out in Descartes' *Traité des passions de l'âme* (1646). The relevance of Descartes' analyses for artistic representation is made abundantly clear by Charles Le Brun in his *Expression des passions* (first published in 1698) and Le Brun's treatise, in turn, was reprinted, retranslated, and used extensively throughout the eighteenth century. The "common drawing-book" of Le Brun,[6] as William Hogarth was to call it, greatly influenced, for example, *An Essay on the Theory of Painting* (1715) written by Pope's friend Jonathan Richardson.

This contemporary interest in the artistic depiction of the passions is what to a large degree enabled Pope to represent, often with greater fidelity to the original than had Chapman, the character of Achilles, whose "prevailing Passion," according to Pope, was "Anger."[7] So interested was Pope in the depiction of the passions that he included as part of the Poetical Index which he appended to the final volume of the *Iliad* a section entitled "*Descriptions of the* INTERNAL PASSIONS, *or of their visible* EFFECTS."[8] Among the internal passions which Pope says are depicted in those passages which I discussed in the previous chapter are the "Anger" and "Resentment" of Achilles in Book I and the same character's "Hardness of Heart" in Book IX.

Pope's view of Achilles' character may not, however, appear to be novel among translators of the *Iliad*, for Chapman, in the dedicatory preface (1614) to his *Odysses*, says of Homer:

Woe or Wonder: The Emotional Effect of Shakespearean Tragedy (Denver: University of Denver Press, 1951). The willed action which precipitates the catastrophe in Shakespeare's tragedies from *Julius Caesar* (1599) on—with the possible exception of *Hamlet* (1601)—is represented in the intellectualist tradition; cf. Virgil Whitaker, "Philosophy and Romance in Shakespeare's 'Problem' Comedies," in *The Seventeenth Century: Studies in the History of English Thought and Literature*, by R. F. Jones and others (1951; reprint ed. Stanford: Stanford University Press, 1969). On the rise of voluntarism in the seventeenth century and its impact upon the drama, see S. Blaine Ewing, *Burtonian Melancholy in the Plays of John Ford* (Princeton: Princeton University Press, 1940), and G. F. Sensabaugh, *The Tragic Muse of John Ford* (Stanford: Stanford University Press, 1944).

[6] *The Analysis of Beauty* (London, 1753), p. 127.

[7] *TE*, 8:415.

[8] Ibid., 8:602-603.

the first word of his *Iliads* is μῆνιν, wrath; the first word of
his *Odysses*, ἄνδρα, Man—contracting in either word his each
worke's Proposition. In one, Predominant Perturbation; in the
other, over-ruling Wisdome. . . .⁹

The "Proposition" or subject of the *Iliad*, then, is, according to
Chapman, "Predominant Perturbation." What does Chapman
mean by "Predominant Perturbation" and is there any distinction
to be drawn between a "Predominant Perturbation" and a "pre-
vailing Passion"?

The term "perturbation" appears prominently in Chapman's
poem, *Euthymiae Raptus; or The Teares of Peace* (1609). This
poem is particularly relevant to an understanding of what Chap-
man may mean by "Predominant Perturbation" in the *Odysses*
preface, for *The Teares of Peace* begins with a vision of Homer,
and it is Homer who eventually leads the poet to "true Peace."
"True Peace" is the patroness of peace with God, and peace with
God is, in turn, the goal of "Learning." And Learning is

> To haue skill to throwe
> Reignes on your bodies powres, that nothing knowe;
> And fill the soules powers, so with act, and art,
> That she can curbe the bodies angrie part;
> All perturbations; all affects that stray
> From their one obiect; which is to obay
> Her Soueraigne Empire; as her selfe should force
> Their functions onely, to serue her discourse;
> And, that; to beat the streight path of one ende
> Which is, to make her substance still contend,
> To be Gods Image. . . .
>
> [ll. 504-514]¹⁰

Here we have a thoroughly conventional Renaissance definition
of the soul, although the usual tripartite division is reduced to
two: the rational, sensitive, and vegetable have been abbreviated

⁹ *Chapman's Homer*, ed. Nicoll, 2:4.
¹⁰ *The Poems of George Chapman*, ed. Phyllis Brooks Bartlett (New York:
Oxford University Press, 1941), p. 184. All quotations from Chapman's original
poems are cited from this edition.

[22]

into the rational and the sensitive. Learning consists in developing the ability "to throwe / Reignes on your bodies powres, that nothing knowe." The sensitive soul, that is, has no intellective powers; it can "nothing knowe." The rational soul, in order to realize its potentiality as "Gods Image," which is reason, must learn to restrain "all perturbations" and "all affects." A "perturbation," then, is that disturbance of the soul, which, like both the "bodies angrie part" and the "affects" or emotions, must be restrained if governance by the rational soul is to prevail.

The word "perturbation" appears three other times in *The Teares of Peace* and each time the word refers to a disturbance in the soul that prevents the due subordination of the sensitive to the rational part. The "Soule" is not God's "true Image" (l. 375), Peace tells the poet, until it is

> . . . imprest
> By Learning and impulsion; that inuest
> Man with Gods forme in liuing Holinesse,
> By cutting from his Body the excesse
> Of Humors, perturbations and Affects;
> Which Nature (without Art) no more eiects,
> Then, without tooles, a naked Artizan
> Can, in rude stone, cut th'Image of a man.
> [ll. 377-384]

Those who are not learned but are nevertheless truly wise, the "Interlocutor" goes on to say, often

> Rule perturbations, live more humanely
> Then men held lernd. . . .
> [ll. 385-386]

And Peace later laments that, while "Learned men" may develop complex arts which can explore external nature, these arts may contribute nothing toward improving man's inward nature, since they "touch not"

> . . . at his perturbations;
> Nor giue them Rule, and temper to obay

[23]

DESIGN

Imperiall Reason; in whose Soueraigne sway,
Learning is wholly vs'd, and dignified. . . .

[ll. 747-750]

A more precise definition of what Chapman may mean by "perturbation" in the *Odysses* preface can, however, be gleaned from the word's appearance in a work written by Chapman just one year before. In *The Revenge of Bussy D'Ambois* (1613), Clermont D'Ambois lectures the Marquesse Renel upon the high spiritual price that he believes must be paid for holding a powerful position in the state:

If you would Consull be (sayes one) of Rome,
You must be watching, starting out of sleepes;
Every way whisking; gloryfying Plebeians;
Kissing Patricians hands, rot at their dores;
Speake and doe basely; every day bestow
Gifts and observance upon one or other:
And what's th'event of all? Twelve rods before thee;
Three or foure times sit for the whole tribunall;
Exhibite Circean games; make publike feasts;
And for these idle outward things (sayes he)
Would'st thou lay on such cost, toile, spend thy spirits?
And to be voide of perturbation,
For constancie, sleepe when thou would'st have sleepe,
Wake when thou would'st wake, fear nought, vexe for
    nought,
No paines wilt thou bestow? no cost? no thought?

(III.iv.127-141)[11]

The price to be paid for the acquisition of such "idle outward things" (l. 136) is "perturbation" (l. 138).

This entire speech is a translation of a passage from the *Discourses* of Epictetus, Book IV, Chapter 10. It is a translation not from the original Greek, however; it is rather a rendering, as

[11] *Bussy D'Ambois and The Revenge of Bussy D'Ambois*, ed. Frederick S. Boas (Boston and London: D. C. Heath and Co., 1905), pp. 238-239.

[24]

F. L. Schoell has conjectured,[12] of the Latin translation of Hieronymous Wolfius (originally published in 1563 and reprinted in 1595). Here is the section of Wolfius' version upon which Chapman appears to have based Clermont's speech:

> Si consulatum expetis, vigilandum tibi est, circumcursandum, manus deosculandae, ad alienas fores computrescendum, multa dicenda, multa facienda illiberalia, munera mittenda multis, nonnullis strenulae quotidianae. Et quis *eventus* est? Duodecim fasciculi virgarum: ter quaterve pro tribunali sedere; circenses ludos exhibere, epulum publice praebere. Demonstret mihi aliquis, quid praeter haec sit? Ergo pro *vacuitate perturbationum*, pro *constantia*, pro eo ut dormiens dormias, vigilans vigiles, nihil timeas, nulla angaris: nihil impendere vis, nihil laboris capessere?[13]

The verbal similarities between Chapman's English and Wolfius' Latin ("And what's th'event of all?" [l. 133] appears to be modeled upon Wolfius' "Et quis *eventus* est?"; "And to be voide of perturbation / For constancie" corresponds to Wolfius' "Ergo pro *vacuitate perturbationum*, pro *constantia*") suggest that Chapman was in fact translating Wolfius. Wolfius' choice of the phrase *pro vacuitate perturbationum* as a translation of the Greek ὑπὲρ ἀπαθείας further suggests that Wolfius wanted to render the Greek words of the Stoic Epictetus[14] with Latin terms that would carry strong Stoic connotations, connotations that Chapman in turn preserves by rendering the Latin *perturbatio* as "perturbation." And in the Stoic philosophers writing in Latin, *perturbatio* means precisely what I have suggested the term means in Chapman's *Teares of Peace*: a disturbance in the soul that prevents the due subordination of its irrational to its rational part.

In the *De Officiis*, for example, a work that follows closely

---

[12] *Études sur L'Humanisme Continental en Angleterre à la Fin de la Renaissance* (Paris: Librairie Ancienne Honoré Champion, 1926), pp. 122-123.

[13] Ibid.

[14] *Epictète: Entretiens, Livre IV* (Paris: Association Guillaume Budé, 1965), p. 80.

the *Peri Kathēkontos* of the Stoic Panaetius of Rhodes and a work that Chapman almost certainly knew well,[15] Cicero writes to his son Marcus, who is now studying philosophy in Athens, that "we must keep ourselves free from every disturbing emotion (*omni . . . animi perturbatione*), but also from excessive pain and pleasure, and from anger (*iracundia*), so that we may enjoy that calm of soul (*tranquilitas animi*) and freedom from care which bring both moral stability (*constantiam*) and dignity of character (1.20.69)."[16] In the *De Finibus* Cicero, in the person of M. Cato, defines perturbations (*perturbationes animorum*) as those disturbances of the soul "which harass and embitter the life of the foolish (*insipientum*)." The word *perturbatio*, Cicero continues, appears, by its very sound, to denote something vicious (*vitiosa*). Nor are *perturbationes* "excited by any natural influence" (*vi aliqua naturali moventur, De Fin.* 3.10.35).[17] Since, in Stoic doctrine, to live naturally is to live reasonably, Cicero is saying here that the man whose soul is beset with perturbations cannot live the life of reason. In the *Tusculan Disputations* Cicero says that the Stoic Zeno defines *perturbatio* as "an agitation of the soul alien from right reason and contrary to nature" (4.6).[18] Later in the same work Cicero reiterates this definition: *perturbationes* are "troubled and agitated movements of the soul alien from reason and bitterly hostile to peace of mind and the peaceful life" (4.15.34).[19] In the *De Natura Deorum* Cicero, speculating upon the question of whether or not the gods exist, says that, should men no longer believe in the gods, piety, reverence, and religion will disappear and thus life will be in constant turmoil and confusion (*perturbatio vitae et magna confusio*, 1.2.4).[20]

[15] See Janet Spens, "Chapman's Ethical Thought," *Essays and Studies* 11 (1925): especially pp. 149ff.

[16] Trans. Walter Miller, LCL (Cambridge, Mass. and London: Harvard University Press and William Heinemann, 1951).

[17] Trans. H. Rackham, LCL (London and New York: William Heinemann and the Macmillan Co., 1914).

[18] Trans. J. E. King, LCL (London and New York: William Heinemann and G. P. Putnam's Sons, 1927).

[19] Ibid.

[20] Trans. H. Rackham, LCL (1933; reprint ed. Cambridge, Mass. and London: Harvard University Press and William Heinemann, 1967).

This definition of "perturbation" as a disturbance in the soul that prevents the due subordination of its irrational to its rational part is then transmitted to the Middle Ages and to the Renaissance.

But is there any distinction to be drawn between "perturbations" and "passions"? In the Renaissance these terms seem at times to be interchangeable. In 1576 Thomas Rogers divided his *Philosophical Discourse, Entitulated, The Anatomie of the minde* into two parts: the first dealt with "Perturbations (and discourseth of that parte of the minde of man which is voide of reson)," the second part with "Morall vertues (so called because it is of that parte of the minde which is endued with reson)."[21] "The Passions," Lily B. Campbell has written, "were variously spoken of during the Renaissance as perturbations, affections, and passions." But, Campbell continues, when perturbations and affections "were spoken of as passions, it was obviously because they were regarded as opposed to actions, for in actions man acted upon external things: in passions man was acted upon by external things."[22] And there is, consequently, a distinction to be drawn between the ethical connotations of "passions" and "perturbations." In Stoic philosophy the man whose soul is in a state of perturbation is held strictly responsible for his defective spiritual condition. In Boethius' *De Consolatione Philosophiae*, for example, when Lady Philosophy first encounters the dejected protagonist she chides him for his spiritual turmoil (*de . . . mentis perturbatione conquesta est*).[23] The term "passion" has more ethically neutral connotations,[24] for while a man will be held

---

[21] Cited by Lily B. Campbell, *Shakespeare's Tragic Heroes: Slaves of Passion* (1930; reprint ed. New York: Barnes and Noble, Inc., 1968), p. 69.

[22] Ibid.

[23] I. pr. ii. 51, cited from the LCL edition (1918; reprint ed. Cambridge and London: Harvard University Press and William Heinemann, 1936).

[24] Erich Auerbach discusses the ethically neutral connotations of the Latin *passio* in contrast to the pejorative connotations of *perturbatio* in the excursus entitled "*Gloria Passionis*" in *Literary Language and its Public in Late Latin Antiquity and in the Middle Ages*, trans. Ralph Manheim (New York: Bollingen Foundation, 1965), pp. 67-81. Auerbach cites St. Augustine's objection, in *De Nuptiis et Concupiscentia* (2.33.55), to the translation of ἐν πάθει ἐπιθυμίας in 1. Thess. 4:5 as *in passione concupiscentiae* ("by the lust of concupiscence");

[27]

responsible for his spiritual "perturbations," he may be exempt from moral responsibility if he has committed an error while in the throes of a violent and irresistible "passion." For, as St. Thomas says (*ST*Ia2ae. 77,7), if the cause of a particular error "is in no way voluntary, but only a natural phenomenon such as sickness or the like, and the resultant emotional state completely inhibits deliberate decision, then whatever actions follow are not only involuntary but also completely sinless."[25]

What I have referred to as the ethically more neutral connotations of the term "passions" corresponds, in fact, to Chapman's usage in *The Teares of Peace*. When the poet comes upon Peace, who is grieving for man's sorry spiritual condition, he asks, in lines 177-178, "If this were true Peace I found out, / That felt such passion?" The poet asks Peace why she is afflicted, and she defends her open display of grief by answering:

> Homer tould me that there are
> Passions, in which corruption hath no share;
> There is a ioy of soule; and why not then
> A griefe of soule, that is no skathe to men?
> For both are Passions, though not such as raigne
> In blood, and humor, that engender paine.
> . . . .
> Griefe, that dischargeth Conscience, is delight. . . .
> [ll. 184-189; 195]

"Ioy" and "griefe" are "passions"; and such "passions," unlike the perturbations mentioned in lines 381, 385, and 747 of *The Teares of Peace* and in *The Revenge of Bussy D'Ambois* III.iv.138, "hath no share" in the "corruption" of the soul.

Now Pope, despite Dr. Johnson's objections to his theory of the ruling passion, did not overtly subscribe to a deterministic view of human behavior. It would be inappropriate in the present

---

for, Augustine says, " 'passion in the Latin tongue, especially in ecclesiastical usage, is not generally understood as having a censorious meaning (*passio in lingua latina, maxime usu loquendi ecclesiastico, non ad vituperationem consuevit intellegi*),' " *Lit. Lang. and its Public*, p. 68.

[25] *Summa Theologiae*, ed. Fearon, p. 183.

context to address the problem in great detail, but let it suffice to say that the poet was relieved to have Warburton absolve the *Essay on Man* (completed in 1734) of the charge of fatalism leveled at the poem by Professor Crousaz; that Pope restated his belief in the freedom of the will to Spence in 1744; and that as early as 1725, when the first volume of the *Odyssey* was published, his views on the subject were made as clearly as possible. In Book I of the *Odyssey* Zeus laments the fact that men are constantly blaming the gods for the misfortunes which they bring upon themselves:

> Perverse Mankind! whose Wills created free,
> Charge all their woes on absolute Decree;
> All to the dooming gods their ills translate,
> And Follies are miscall'd the crimes of Fate.
>   [ll.41-44, Pope's translation]

Pope in his commentary expresses his approval of this observation and he applauds Homer for recognizing that it is "the folly of man, and not the decree of Heaven" that "is the cause of human calamity."[26] But Pope did indeed share the contemporary interest in depicting the "passions"—a term which I have suggested had more ethically neutral connotations than "perturbations"—and this interest enabled him to represent, with less distortion and with greater ethical immunity than had Chapman, the rise and abatement of Achilles' wrath. For the very fact that "perturbations" were considered in Chapman's time as unqualifiedly unnatural disturbances in the soul led the Elizabethan translator, writing in the tradition of Renaissance epic with its demand for a perfect hero, to depict Achilles as a man more often than not in control of his "Predominant Perturbation."

The interest in the depiction of the passions is evident everywhere in the neoclassical period. In epic and tragic theory the neoclassical emphasis upon the writer's obligation to represent the passions seems at times even to take primacy over the Aristotelian notion that it is plot (*mythos*) and not character (*ēthos*)

---

[26] *TE*, 9:31.

that is the soul of tragedy (*Poetics* 1450a39). Sir William Davenant, for example, writes in his "Preface to *Gondibert*" (1650) that "wise Poets think it more worthwhile to seek out truth in the Passions than to record the truth of Actions."[27] In Dryden's *Essay of Dramatic Poesy* (1668) Lisideius offers the following definition of the drama, a definition which is assented to by the other participants of the dialogue: "A play," Lisideius says,

> ought to be a just and lively image of human nature, representing its passions and humours, and the changes of fortune to which it is subject, for the delight and instruction of mankind.[28]

The drama, according to this definition, is not primarily an imitation of an action. It is, rather, a representation of the "passions and humours" of human nature; the only reference to plot is implied in the phrase "changes of fortune" and such changes appear to be of importance only insofar that they will help render the depiction of the "passions and humours" more "just and lively."

Strikingly similar to the definition of tragedy offered by Lisideius is Pope's own, as we may infer it from some remarks he makes in his *Essay on Homer's Battles*:

> It is worth taking Notice . . . what Use *Homer* every where makes of each little Accident or Circumstance that can naturally happen in a Battel, thereby to cast a Variety over his Action; as well as of every Turn of Mind or Emotion a Hero can possibly feel, such as Resentment, Revenge, Concern, Confusion, &c. The former of these makes his Work resemble a large History-Piece, where even the less important Figures and Actions have yet some convenient Place or Corner to be shewn

[27] Cited from *Critical Essays of the Seventeenth Century*, ed. Joel E. Spingarn, 3 vols. (1908; reprint ed. London: Oxford University Press, 1957), 2:3. I owe this observation about Davenant and the following observation about Lisideius' definition of drama to Dean T. Mace, "Dryden's Dialogue on Drama," *Journal of the Warburg and Courtauld Institutes* 25 (1962):87-112.

[28] *Of Dramatic Poesy and Other Critical Essays*, ed. George Watson, 2 vols. (London and New York: Everyman's Library, 1962), 1:268.

in; and the latter gives it all the Advantages of Tragedy in those various turns of Passion that animate the Speeches of his Heroes, and render his whole Poem the most *Dramatick* of any Epick whatsoever.[29]

What especially distinguishes tragedy, according to Pope, are "those various Turns of Passion that animate the Speeches of ... Heroes." Such "Turns of Passion"—and not, necessarily, the structure of events which constitute the plot—render a poem "*Dramatick.*"

And so Dryden, in the *Heads of an Answer to Rymer* (1677), approvingly quotes the following remarks which he translates from Rapin's *Réflexions* (I.xxvi.):

'Tis not the admirable intrigue, the surprising events, the extraordinary incidents that make the beauty of a tragedy; 'tis the discourses when they are so natural and passionate.[30]

This statement strongly suggests that the Aristotelian notion of "tragic wonder" (τὸ θαυμαστόν), which was, for Aristotle, primarily an effect achieved through the unexpected incident in the plot (*Poetics* 1452a; cf. Rapin's "admirable intrigue," "surprising events," "extraordinary incidents") is, by the late seventeenth century, often subordinated to the representation of the "passions" themselves.[31] A similar suspicion about the primacy of

[29] *TE*, 7:255.

[30] *Of Dramatic Poesy*, ed. Watson, 1:220.

[31] Neoclassical treatises often stressed the importance of the emotional effect of "admiration," which was to be evoked in the audience by the representation of the passions of the hero. The writers of these treatises at times appear to believe that it was only in their own period that "admiration" at last took its rightful place beside "fear" and "pity" as one of the three uniquely tragic emotions. Boileau, for example, in a letter to Charles Perrault (1700), remarks that Corneille "n'a point songé, comme les poètes de l'ancienne tragédie, à émouvoir la pitié et la terreur, mais à exciter dans l'âme des spectateurs, par la sublimité des pensées et par la beauté des sentiments, une certaine admiration, dont plusieurs personnes, et les jeunes gens surtout, s'accommodent souvent beaucoup mieux que des véritables passions tragiques" ("Corneille was not at all concerned, as were the ancient tragedians, with evoking pity and terror, but he rather wished to stir up in the souls of the audience, through the sublimity of his thoughts and

[31]

plot is expressed by Dryden earlier in the *Heads of an Answer to Rymer* when he writes that although "Aristotle places the fable [i.e., the μῦθος, or plot] first" in importance, "the fable is not the greatest masterpiece of a tragedy."[32]

The neoclassical unities of time, place, and action may in fact be seen not so much as a rigidly rationalistic scheme but rather as an attempt to placate the demand for verisimilitude so that the stage can be cleared for those highly emotional speeches, such as Racine's "tirades," which will give full range to the

---

the beauty of his sentiments, a certain effect of admiration which many people—and the young especially—often find more pleasing than the traditional tragic emotions"; the French is cited from *Eliz. Crit. Essays*, ed. Smith, 1:393). As the passage from the *Poetics* (1452a) alluded to in the text demonstrates, however, Aristotle himself considered "admiration" (τὸ θαυμαστόν; in Latin, *admiratio*) to be as essential to the tragic effect as "pity" and "fear." "Admiration" is regarded as a novel effect of tragedy by Boileau because the term has lost its primary association with the Aristotelian notion that τὸ θαυμαστόν is produced, most importantly, by the unexpected—but, once understood, causally significant—incidents in the plot. It is to the neoclassical notion of "admiration" René Bray, for instance, alludes in *La Formation de la Doctrine Classique en France* (Paris: Hachette, 1927): "Corneille est de tous celui qui se libère le plus complètement de la théorie traditionelle des passions tragiques, en joignant ou en substituant au pathétique de la terreur et de la pitié le pathétique de l'admiration," p. 319 ("Corneille is the one who most completely frees himself from the traditional theory of the tragic emotions when he joins to, or even substitutes for, the emotions of fear and pity the emotion of admiration"). Hence J. V. Cunningham is correct when he argues against the view that the tragic effect of "admiration" was first introduced into literary theory by Minturno in the sixteenth century (see Cunningham's dissertation, "Tragic Effect and Tragic Process in Some Plays of Shakespeare and their Background in the Literary and Ethical Theory of Classical Antiquity and the Middle Ages," Stanford University, 1945, esp. pp. 138-231). Cunningham points out that modern historians of Renaissance literary theory did not sufficiently realize, until the publication of Marvin T. Herrick's article "Some Neglected Sources of *Admiratio*" (*Modern Language Notes* 62 [1947]:222-226), that the term was essential to Aristotle's definition of tragedy.

[32] *Of Dramatic Poesy*, ed. Watson, 1:211. Of the six parts of tragedy—plot (μῦθος), character (ἦθη), diction (λέξις), thought (διάνοια), spectacle (ὄψις), and song (μελοποιία)—"plot," Aristotle says, "is the first principle, and, as it were, the soul of tragedy" (ἀρχὴ μὲν οὖν καὶ οἷον ψυχὴ ὁ μῦθος τῆς τραγῳδίας, *Poetics* 1450a39).

representation of the passions. While adherence to the principle of the unity of action, for example, might imply an overriding concern with preserving verisimilitude, the defense of the unity of action, as Dean T. Mace suggests, may rather be attributable to the fact that "careful painting of the movements of the soul cannot be done in the midst of a swiftly moving and changing action which allows neither the considerable time or ample space required for 'pathetic' discourses."[33] It is for this reason that the Abbé d'Aubignac, in his *La Pratique du Théâtre* (1657), recommends that the dramatist depict as few incidents on the stage as possible, and that he should especially eliminate those incidents that are not sufficiently "pathetic." For the Abbé, the historical accuracy of the events narrated in the plot is to be violated only if the plot contains too few pathetic incidents; if this is the case, then the poet is free to create such incidents, as did Corneille in his *Horace*, when he invented the character Sabine "pour introduire dans son théâtre toutes les passions d'une femme."[34] It is for this same reason that Dryden in *All for Love*, for example, embellishes upon not only his Shakespearean original but upon historical fact as well by inventing the scene in which Octavia comes to Alexandria to compete with Cleopatra for Antony's allegiance.

FROM INEXORABLE RESENTMENT TO PERFECT TRANQUILITY

It was largely this contemporary interest in the representation of the passions that allowed Pope to make artistic sense of the two final books of the *Iliad* and thus to counter the opinion, held by Dryden and others, that "the funerals of Patroclus and the redemption of Hector's body [are] not (properly speaking) a part of the main action."[35] Dryden's comment, cited from *A Parallel Betwixt Painting and Poetry* (1697), is made in the tradition of

[33] "Dryden's Dialogue on Drama," p. 108.
[34] "In order to introduce into the theater all the emotions of a woman," François Hédelin, Abbé d'Aubignac, *La Pratique du Théâtre* (Paris, 1657), p. 133.
[35] *Of Dramatic Poesy*, ed. Watson, 2:206.

DESIGN

the Moderns with their preference of Virgil to Homer. The "action" of the *Iliad*, Dryden says, truly concludes with the slaying of Hector, since Homer knew that now "Troy was as good as already taken." The ending of the *Aeneid* is superior to that of the *Iliad* because, according to Dryden, Virgil "concludes with the death of Turnus; for after that difficulty was removed Aeneas might marry, and establish the Trojans when he pleased."³⁶ As the *Aeneid* ends with the victory of the central hero over his antagonist, so, the argument runs, should the *Iliad* have ended. Dryden is here repeating the criticisms of the conclusion of the *Iliad* made by that paragon of the Moderns, the Abbé, in the fourth dialogue of Charles Perrault's famous *Paralèlle des Anciens et des Modernes* (1688-1696); the *Iliad* has no clearly defined single subject and no moral intention, the Abbé says, because the poem is in reality a collection of diverse songs, "un amas de plusieurs chansons cousuës ensemble." If Homer's aim was to praise the Greeks, why, the Abbé asks, did he not end the poem with the sacking of Troy? And if the subject of the poem is truly "the valor and the wrath of Achilles, as some would claim, it ought to end with the death of Hector, just as Virgil concluded with the death of Turnus."³⁷

The critical document that could, to a large degree, provide Pope with an explanation of the function of the final two books of the *Iliad* was the *Traité du poëme épique* (1675) by René Le Bossu: "Bossu's admirable Treatise of the Epic Poem," Pope writes in the *Iliad* preface, will give the reader "the justest Notion of his [i.e., Homer's] Design and Conduct."³⁸ So taken was Pope by the authority of Le Bossu that he appended to the first volume of his *Odyssey* (1725) a summary of that critic's treatise which he entitled "A General View of the Epic Poem and of the *Iliad* and *Odyssey*. Extracted from Bossu." Le Bossu, following Aristotle in the *Poetics* (1451a16), is well aware that "the Unity of the Epic Action . . . does not consist in the Unity of the Heroe";

---

³⁶ Ibid., 2:207.
³⁷ *Parallèle des Anciens et des Modernes*, ed. H. R. Gauss and M. Imdahl (Munich: Eidos, 1964), pp. 292, 295.
³⁸ *TE*, 7:23.

[34]

but as one who shared the contemporary interest in the representation of the passions, he surely stresses the importance of character (*ēthos*) more emphatically than does Aristotle. For Le Bossu the representation of character becomes, in fact, that which distinguishes one epic from another. "The *Passions* of Tragedy," Le Bossu writes, "are different from those of the Epic Poem. In the former, *Terror* and *Pity* have the chief place; the Passion that seems most peculiar to Epic Poetry, is *Admiration*," by which Le Bossu means the "fabulous" or "wonderful," what Renaissance critics referred to as "*meraviglia*." "Besides this *Admiration*, which in general distinguishes the Epic Poem from the Dramatic," Le Bossu continues,

> each Epic Poem has likewise some *peculiar Passion*, which distinguishes it in particular from other Epic Poems, and constitutes a kind of singular and individual difference between these Poems of the same Species. These singular Passions correspond to the *Character* of the *Hero*. *Anger* and *Terror* reign throughout the *Iliad*, because Achilles is angry, and the most terrible of all Men. The *Aeneid* has all the *soft* and *tender Passions*, because that is the Character of *Aeneas*. The Prudence, Wisdom, and Constancy of *Ulysses* do not allow him either of these Extremes, therefore the Poet does not permit one of them to be predominant in the *Odyssey*.

What follows makes this an interesting gloss upon Longinus' famous comparison between the *Iliad* and *Odyssey*. In the *Odyssey*, Le Bossu continues, Homer

> confines himself to *Admiration* only, which he carries to an higher pitch than in the *Iliads*: And 'tis upon this account that he introduces a great many more Machines in the *Odyssey* into the Body of the Action, than are to be seen in the Actions of the other two Poems.[39]

---

[39] *TE*, 9:20. The quotations from the Greek of Longinus which follow are cited from "*Longinus*" on the Sublime, ed. D. A. Russell (Oxford: Clarendon Press, 1964).

Longinus in the *Peri Hypsous* (9.11-15) expresses his preference for the *Iliad* over the *Odyssey* and the chief reason he gives is that Homer, he believes, composed the consistently sublime *Iliad* at the height of his powers, while the more relaxed and digressive *Odyssey* was the product of Homer's old age. The *Odyssey* is far less passionate than it is "fabulous" (μυθικόν) and in it Homer wanders "in the incredible regions of romance" (ἐν τοῖς μυθώδεσσι καὶ ἀπίστοις). The Greek word μυθικόν can be rendered as "the fabulous," "the wonderful," that which, in other words, will evoke "admiration"—in the Renaissance sense of *"meraviglia"*—in the audience. Aristotle had observed in the *Poetics* that "the element of the wonderful (τὸ θαυμαστόν) is required in tragedy" and in the epic it has, he says, even wider scope, because the person who is acting is not visibly before us (1460a), and therefore, he implies, not subject to the scrutiny of the eye. In Renaissance and Augustan defenses of the heroic poem this passage from the *Poetics* becomes of immense importance, for it is specifically the emotion of "admiration" which these critics believed it was the chief intention of the epic to evoke. Hence Le Bossu says that "the Passion that seems most peculiar to Epic Poetry, is *Admiration*." For Le Bossu the reason that in the *Odyssey* Homer "confines himself" to the task of evoking *"Admiration* only" is attributable not to the character of the author, as Longinus had suggested, but rather to the character of the central hero: Odysseus is neither angry, like Achilles, nor "soft and tender," like Aeneas; because he is so evenly tempered a character, his personal characteristics are not sufficiently extreme so as to infuse the epic with a distinctive flavor, and therefore the poem must derive its tone from the "Admiration" which is the distinctive emotion evoked by the epic poem in general.

But the character of Achilles is indeed extreme. And so the action of the *Iliad* is, according to Le Bossu, the poet's recording of the passionate anger of Achilles. In discussing the action of an epic poem in general, Le Bossu, following Aristotle (*Poetics* 1459a17), says that it "ought to have a *Beginning*, a *Middle*, and an *End*." He then goes on to discuss the action of the *Iliad* specifically:

[36]

Homer's design in the *Iliads* is to relate the Anger and Re-
venge of *Achilles*. The Beginning of this Action is the Change
of *Achilles* from a calm to a passionate temper. The Middle
is the Effects of his Passion, and all the illustrious Deaths it is
the Cause of. The End of this same Action is the Return of
Achilles to his Calmness of temper again. . . . We see him as
calm at the End of the Poem, during the Funeral of *Hector*,
as he was at the Beginning of the Poem, whilst the Plague
raged among the *Grecians*. The End is just, since the Calmness
of temper *Achilles* enjoy'd, is only an Effect of the Revenge
which ought to have preceded: And after this no Body expects
any more of his Anger. Thus has *Homer* been very exact in
the Beginning, Middle, and End of the Action he made choice
of for the Subject of his *Iliads*.[40]

With this analysis Pope was in complete agreement as his notes
to Books XXIII and XXIV and his translation of these books
attest. In his opening note to Book XXIII, for example, Pope
responds to those who object to the final two books as super-
fluous. "This, and the following Book, which contain the De-
scription of the Funeral of *Patroclus*, and other Matters relating
to *Hector*, are," Pope concedes, "undoubtedly superadded to the
grand Catastrophe of the Poem; for the Story is compleatly fin-
ish'd with the Death of that Hero in the 22ᵈ Book. Many judi-
cious Criticks," Pope continues,

> have been of opinion that *Homer* is blameable for protracting
> it. *Virgil* closes the whole Scene of Action with the Death of
> *Turnus*, and leaves the rest to be imagin'd by the Mind of the
> Reader: He does not draw the Picture at full Length, but
> delineates it so far, that we cannot fail of imagining the whole
> Draught. There is however one thing to be said in favour of
> *Homer* which may perhaps justify him in his Method, that
> what he undertook to paint was the *Anger* of Achilles: And
> as that Anger does not die with *Hector*, but persecutes his very
> remains, so the Poet still keeps up his Subject; nay it seems to

[40] *TE*, 9:14-15.

require that he should carry down the Relation of that Resentment, which is the Foundation of his Poem, till it is fully satisfy'd: And as this survives *Hector*, and gives the Poet an Opportunity of still shewing many sad Effects of *Achilles'* Anger, the two following Books may be thought not to be Excrescencies, but essential to the Poem.[41]

Each epic poem is distinguished by a *"peculiar Passion,"* Le Bossu wrote, which corresponds to "the *Character* of the Hero. *Anger* and *Terror* reign throughout the *Iliad*, because *Achilles* is angry." And since the wrath of Achilles is not yet at an end at the close of Book XXII, neither has the *Iliad* reached its proper end.

Pope faced a problem, however, in depicting the abatement of the passion of anger in Achilles, and the problem was this: how was he to reconcile the classical principle of the conservation of character with the conclusion of the poem, in which the previously unyielding Achilles—the Achilles whose very implacability establishes the tone of the entire poem—uncharacteristically yields with compassion to Priam's request for Hector's body? For the principle of consistency or conservation of character had a long history in classical and neoclassical criticism. It was stated, perhaps most influentially, by Horace in the *Ars Poetica*:

> Aut famam sequere aut sibi convenientia finge.
> scriptor honoratum si forte reponis Achillem,
> impiger, iracundus, inexorabilis, acer,
> iura neget sibi nata, nihil non arroget armis.
> sit Medea ferox invictaque, flebilis Ino,
> perfidus Ixion, Io vaga, tristis Orestes.
> si quid inexpertum scaenae committis et audes
> personam formare novam, servetur ad imum,
> qualis ab incepto processerit, et sibi constet.
> [ll. 119-127]

(Either follow tradition or invent what is self-consistent. If, when you write, you happen to bring back to the stage the

[41] *TE*, 8:485-486.

[38]

honoring of Achilles, let him be impatient, passionate, ruthless, fierce; let him claim that laws are not for him, let him ever make appeal to the sword. Let Medea be fierce and unyielding, Ino tearful, Ixion treacherous, Io a wanderer, Orestes sorrowful. If it is an untried theme you entrust to the stage, and if you boldly fashion a fresh character, have it kept to the end even as it came forth at the first, and have it self-consistent.)[42]

This well-known passage posed a severe problem for the Augustan translator of *Iliad* XXIV, for Horace recommends that, should the poet choose to depict a nontraditional character, such a depiction must be "kept to the end even as it came forth at the first"; and Horace selects, as his leading example of this very principle of consistency of character, Achilles himself, who must be presented on the stage, Horace says, as *impiger, iracundus, inexorabilis, acer*.

Pope phrases the problem most eloquently in his opening comments upon Priam's moving speech to Achilles in Book XXIV:

> The Curiosity of the Reader must needs be awaken'd to know how *Achilles* would behave to this unfortunate King; it requires all the Art of the Poet to sustain the violent Character of *Achilles*, and yet at the same time to soften him into Compassion.[43]

Such a feat requires all the Art of the Translator as well and Pope makes a great effort to "sustain the violent Character of Achilles." He does so in three related ways. First, he explicitly refers to Achilles' anger, both in his notes and in the text of the translation itself, where no mention of it is made in the original. At the very beginning of Book XXIV, for example, Pope defends

---

[42] *Satires, Epistles, and Ars Poetica*, trans. H. Rushton Fairclough, LCL (1926; reprint ed. Cambridge, Mass. and London: Harvard University Press and William Heinemann, 1970), pp. 460-461. I have slightly altered Fairclough's translation. John S. Coolidge, in "Fielding and the 'Conservation of Character' " (*Modern Philology* 57 [1960]:245-259), discusses the problems posed by this doctrine for Fielding—who had in *Tom Jones*, for example, rigorously adhered to it—when he came to write *Amelia*.

[43] *TE*, 8:561.

Homer against Plato's criticism, in *Republic* III.388a, of the scene in which Achilles expresses his grief over Patroclus' death. Criticism against such graphic expressions of grief, Pope writes,

> will vanish if we remember that all the Passions of *Achilles* are in the extreme; his Nature is violent and it would have been an Outrage to his general Character to have represented him as mourning moderately for his Friend.[44]

When Hermes, in the guise of the courier Argeiphontes, urges Priam later in Book XXIV to go to Achilles and to request that Achilles return the body of Hector, he says in Pope's translation:

> Adjure him by his Father's silver Hairs,
> His Son, his Mother! urge him to bestow
> Whatever Pity that stern Heart can know.
> [ll. 571-573]

There is no mention of Achilles' "stern Heart" in the original. Homer's Argeiphontes says:

> καί μιν ὑπὲρ πατρὸς καὶ μητέρος ἠϋκόμοιο
> λίσσεο καὶ τέκεος, ἵνα οἱ σὺν θυμὸν ὀρίνῃς
>
> ([and] entreat him in the name of his father,
>   the name of his mother of the lovely hair,
> and his child, and so move the heart within him.)
> [ll. 466-467]

Pope, however, has translated the Greek word θυμός (l. 467)—which means "spirit," "heart," or "soul"—as "stern Heart" in order to sustain his portrayal of Achilles' angry character. Priam, in Homer, speaks to Achilles of his (Priam's) son, Hector, "whom you recently killed as he fought in defense of his country" (τὸν σὺ πρῴην κτεῖνας ἀμυνόμενον περὶ πάτρης, l. 500). Chapman's Priam, correspondingly, describes Hector as "he . . . by thee / (Late fighting for his countrey) slaine" (ll. 442-444). But Pope, once again, emphasizes Achilles' angry nature. Of Hector, "his Country's last Defense" (l. 619), Pope's Priam says to Achilles, "Him too thy Rage has slaine" (l. 622). Homer's Priam says to

---

[44] Ibid., 8:535.

Achilles that, in order to secure Hector's body, "I bring gifts beyond number" (φέρω δ' ἀπερείσι' ἄποινα, l. 502). Chapman translates this literally with the phrase "Infinite is that I offer you" (l. 445). In Pope's version, however, Priam says, "Large Gifts, proportion'd to thy Wrath, I bear" (l. 624). Achilles, in Homer, describes himself as the one who has "killed so many of your noble sons" (ὅς τοι πολέας τε καὶ ἐσθλοὺς / υἱέας ἐξενάριξα, ll. 520-521); Chapman's Achilles correspondingly describes himself as one who "hath slaine so many a worthy sonne" (l. 465). In Pope's version Achilles becomes "The Man whose Fury has destroy'd thy Race" (l. 656). Priam, in Pope's translation, tells Achilles that, once he has accepted the ransom for Hector's body, "Safe may'st thou sail, and turn thy Wrath from *Troy*" (l. 702). There is no mention of "Wrath" either in Homer ("you may go back to your native land," σὺ δὲ... ἔλθοις / σὴν ἐς πατρίδα γαῖαν, ll. 556-557) or in Chapman ("Accept what I have brought, / And turne to Phthia," ll. 500-501). One final example: Achilles, in Pope's version, suggests that the old king should be prevented from seeing his son's corpse as it is being placed on Priam's chariot

> . . . lest th'unhappy Sire
> Provok'd to Passion, once more rouze to Ire
> The stern *Pelides*; . . .
>
> [ll. 732-734]

There is no mention of the "Ire" of "stern *Pelides*" in the original; Homer says that, if Priam is provoked to anger,

> 'Αχιλῆϊ δ' ὀρινθείη φίλον ἦτορ,
> καί ἑ κατακτείνειε, . . .
>
> (Achilles' own heart might be stirred,
> And so he might kill him, . . .)
>
> [ll. 585-586]

Pope has here once again attributed to a Greek word possessing a generalized meaning—ἦτορ, "heart," l. 585—the more specialized connotations of the anger he believes to be characteristic of Achilles' "violent Nature."

Second, in order to make the scene of reconciliation plausible with respect to what he perceives to be Achilles' violent and implacable character, Pope stresses both in the text and in his notes that it is only through divine intervention that Achilles is able to assent to Priam's request. At the opening of Book XXIV Zeus expresses his dissatisfaction with Achilles' treatment of Hector's body and he asks Thetis to tell Achilles to accept Priam's offer of ransom. It is, surely, a difficult matter to judge to what degree Homer intended his gods to be viewed as projections of human feelings and motivations or, conversely, as the determinants of those feelings and motivations. I should recall here Richmond Lattimore's balanced statement, made in the introduction to his translation, that there is "one thing the gods-as-persons of Homer do not do: they do not change human nature. They manipulate Achilleus, Aineias, Paris, but they do not make them what they are. The choices are human; and in the end, despite all divine interferences, the Iliad is a story of people."[45] In Pope's version of *Iliad* XXIV, however, the accent falls more heavily upon the divine promptings than upon the will of Achilles, for in his commentary Pope writes:

> The poem is now almost at the Conclusion, and *Achilles* is to pass from a State of an almost inexorable Resentment to a State of perfect Tranquility; such a Change could not be brought about by human Means: *Achilles* is too stubborn to obey any thing less than a God: This is evident from his rejecting the Persuasion of the whole *Grecian* Army to return to the Battle: So that it appears that this Machinery was necessary, and consequently a Beauty to the Poem.
>
> If the Poet had conducted these Incidents merely by human Means, or suppos'd *Achilles* to restore the Body of *Hector* entirely out of Compassion, the Draught had been unnatural,

---

[45] *The Iliad of Homer* (1951; reprint ed. Chicago and London: University of Chicago Press, 1971), p. 48. Cf. the remarks of D. S. Margoliouth, *The Homer of Aristotle* (Oxford: Basil Blackwell, 1923), p. 127: "In most cases wherein the gods are introduced [in Homer], they effect nothing which would not have taken place without their intervention."

because unlike *Achilles*: Such a Violence of Temper was not to be pacify'd by ordinary Methods.[46]

And later in the book, after Achilles has listened patiently to Priam's request, Pope comments as follows:

> We are now come almost to the end of the Poem, and consequently to the end of the Anger of *Achilles*: And *Homer* has describ'd the Abatement of it with excellent Judgment. We may here observe how necessary the Conduct of *Homer* was, in sending *Thetis* to prepare her Son to use *Priam* with civility: It would have ill suited with the violent Temper of *Achilles* to have used *Priam* with Tenderness without such Preadmonition; nay, the unexpected Sight of his Enemy might probably have carry'd him into Violence and Rage: But *Homer* has avoided these Absurdities; for *Achilles* being already prepared for a Reconciliation, the Misery of this venerable Prince melts him into Compassion.[47]

Finally, just after he has placed Hector's body upon Priam's chariot, Achilles asks the ghost of Patroclus not to be angry with him for having accepted the ransom. Achilles, in Pope's version, says:

> O Friend! forgive me that I thus fulfill
> (Restoring *Hector*) Heav'ns unquestion'd Will.
> 　　　　　　　　　　　[ll. 742-743]

There is no mention of "Heav'ns unquestion'd Will" in the original:

μή μοι, Πάτροκλε, σκυδαινέμεν, αἴ κε πύθηαι
εἰν Ἄϊδός περ ἐὼν ὅτι Ἕκτορα δῖον ἔλυσα
πατρὶ φίλῳ, ἐπεὶ οὔ μοι ἀεικέα δῶκεν ἄποινα.

(Do not be angry with me, Patroclus, if you learn,
　though you are in the house of Hades, that I gave back
　brilliant Hector

---

[46] *TE*, 8:541.
[47] Ibid., 8:563.

[43]

DESIGN

to his dear father, for the ransom he gave me was not
unseemly.)

[ll. 592-594]

Third, Pope makes Priam even more pathetic, has him draw
even more attention to the personal suffering he has experienced
than does Homer; thus, when Achilles does eventually assent to
Priam's request, Pope thereby creates the impression in the reader
that Achilles' display of compassion is more a momentary soft-
ening than a true deviation from his otherwise stubborn and
intractable nature. Here is Priam's great speech in the original:

μνῆσαι πατρὸς σοῖο, θεοῖς ἐπιείκελ' Ἀχιλλεῦ,
τηλίκου ὥς περ ἐγών, ὀλοῷ ἐπὶ γήραος οὐδῷ·
καὶ μέν που κεῖνον περιναιέται ἀμφὶς ἐόντες
τείρουσ', ουδέ τίς ἐστιν ἀρὴν καὶ λοιγὸν ἀμῦναι.
ἀλλ' ἤτοι κεῖνός γε σέθεν ζώοντος ἀκούων
χαίρει τ' ἐν θυμῷ, ἐπί τ' ἔλπεται ἤματα πάντα
ὄψεσθαι φίλον υἱὸν ἀπὸ Τροίηθεν ἰόντα·
αὐτὰρ ἐγὼ πανάποτμος, ἐπεὶ τέκον υἷας ἀρίστους
Τροίῃ ἐν εὐρείῃ, τῶν δ' οὔ τινά φημι λελεῖφθαι.
πεντήκοντά μοι ἦσαν, ὅτ' ἤλυθον υἷες Ἀχαιῶν·
ἐννεακαίδεκα μέν μοι ἰῆς ἐκ νηδύος ἦσαν,
τοὺς δ' ἄλλους μοι ἔτικτον ἐνὶ μεγάροισι γυναῖκες.
τῶν μὲν πολλῶν θοῦρος Ἄρης ὑπὸ γούνατ' ἔλυσεν·
ὃς δέ μοι οἶος ἔην, εἴρυτο δὲ ἄστυ καὶ αὐτούς,
τὸν σὺ πρῴην κτεῖνας ἀμυνόμενον περὶ πάτρης,
Ἕκτορα· τοῦ νῦν εἵνεχ' ἱκάνω νῆας Ἀχαιῶν
λυσόμενος παρὰ σεῖο, φέρω δ' ἀπερείσι' ἄποινα.
ἀλλ' αἰδεῖο θεούς, Ἀχιλεῦ, αὐτόν τ' ἐλέησον,
μνησάμενος σοῦ πατρός· ἐγὼ δ' ἐλεεινότερός περ,
ἔτλην δ' οἶ' οὔ πώ τις ἐπιχθόνιος βροτὸς ἄλλος,
ἀνδρὸς παιδοφόνοιο ποτὶ στόμα χεῖρ' ὀρέγεσθαι.

(Remember your father, you-who-are-like-the-gods-
Achilles,
for he is as old as I am and is on the sorrowful threshold
of old age;

[44]

and those who dwell around him
afflict him, nor is there anyone to defend him against
  war and destruction.
Yet surely he, when he hears that you are still living,
rejoices and therefore hopes, all his life long,
that he will see his dear son return from Troy.
But my lot has been hapless, for I have had the noblest
  sons
in Troy, and not one of them remains alive.
I had fifty when the sons of the Achaeans came here.
Nineteen were born from the womb of a single mother
and other women bore the rest in my palace.
Violent Ares broke the strength in the knees of many of
  them;
but one survived and he protected his city and his
  people,
and this one you recently killed as he defended his
  country,
Hector; for whose sake I come now to the ships of the
  Achaeans
offering ransom to you, and the ransom I bring is
  limitless.
Honor the gods, then, Achilles, and take pity upon me,
remembering your father; for I am even more to be
  pitied,
for I have brought myself to do what no other mortal on
  earth has done:
I place my lips on the hands of the man who has slain
  my children.)

                    [ll. 486-506]

And here is Pope's version:

> Ah think, thou favour'd of the Pow'rs Divine!
> Think of thy Father's Age, and pity mine!
> In me, that Father's rev'rend Image trace,
> Those silver Hairs, that venerable Face;
> His trembling Limbs, his helpless Person, see!
> In all my Equal, but in Misery!

Yet now perhaps, some Turn of human Fate
Expells him helpless from his peaceful State;
Think from some pow'rful Foe thou see'st him fly,
And beg Protection with a feeble Cry,
Yet still one Comfort in his Soul may rise;
He hears his Son still lives to glad his Eyes;
And hearing still may hope, a better Day
May send him thee to chase that Foe away.
No comfort to my Griefs, no Hopes remain,
The best, the bravest of my Sons are slain!
Yet what a Race? e'er *Greece* to *Ilion* came,
The Pledge of many a lov'd, and loving Dame;
Nineteen one Mother bore—Dead, all are dead!
How oft, alas! has wretched *Priam* bled?
Still One was left, their Loss to recompense;
His Father's Hope, his Country's last Defence.
Him too thy Rage has slain! Beneath thy Steel
Unhappy, in his Country's Cause he fell!
　　For him, thro' hostile Camps I bent my way,
For him thus prostrate at thy Feet I lay;
Large Gifts, proportion'd to thy Wrath, I bear;
Oh hear the Wretched, and the Gods revere!
　　Think of thy Father, and this Face behold!
See him in me, as helpless and as old!
Tho' not so wretched: There he yields to me,
The First of Men in sov'reign Misery.
Thus forc'd to kneel, thus grov'ling to embrace
The Scourge and Ruin of my Realm and Race;
Suppliant my Childrens Murd'rer to implore,
And kiss those Hands yet reeking with their Gore!
[ll. 598-633]

Priam, in the original, begins his speech by stating simply:

Remember your father, you-who-are-like-the-gods-
　　Achilles,
for he is as old as I am and is on the sorrowful threshold
　　of old age; ...
[ll. 486-487]

And Chapman, in this instance, is just as plain:

[46]

> See in me, O godlike Thetis' sonne,
> Thy aged father.
>
> [ll. 432-433]

Pope's Priam, however, in order to melt Achilles into compassion, draws a much more detailed and pathetic picture of Achilles' father:

> Ah, think, thou favour'd of the Pow'rs Divine!
> Think of thy Father's Age, and pity mine!
> In me, that Father's rev'rend Image trace,
> Those silver Hairs, that venerable Face;
> His trembling Limbs, his helpless Person, see!
> In all my Equal, but in Misery!
>
> [ll. 598-603]

And Pope's Priam draws attention to his private suffering where no mention of this is made in the original. All of his children, Priam complains, are

> . . . Dead, all are dead!
> How oft, alas! has wretched *Priam* bled?
> [ll. 616-617]

Similarly, where Homer's Priam says simply that it is for Hector's sake that "I come now to the ships of the Achaeans offering ransom to you" (ll. 501-502), Pope's Priam draws attention both to the personal danger to which he has exposed himself ("For him [i.e., Hector], thro' hostile Camps I bent my way," l. 622) and to the personal humiliation he has had to undergo ("For him thus prostrate at thy Feet I lay," l. 623). Pope has Priam emphasize this note of personal humiliation again at the conclusion of his speech:

> Think of thy Father, and this Face behold!
> See him in me, as helpless and as old!
> Tho' not so wretched: There he yields to me,
> The First of Men in sov'reign Misery.
> Thus forc'd to kneel, thus grov'ling to embrace
> The Scourge and Ruin of my Realm and Race;
> Suppliant my Childrens Murd'rer to implore,

[47]

And kiss those Hands yet reeking with their Gore!
[ll. 626-633]

Chapman's version of these lines is much more spare and therefore closer to the original (ll. 503-506 of the Homeric text):

Pitie an old man like thy sire—different in onely this,
That I am wretcheder, and beare that weight of miseries
That never man did, my curst lips enforc't to kisse that
    hand
That slue my children.

[ll. 448-451]

And Congreve's Priam speaks, as simply as does Homer's, of how he has come to "kiss those hands which have my children slain."[48]

In coming to terms with the scene of reconciliation between Achilles and Priam, then, Pope was faced with the problem of how "to sustain the violent Character of *Achilles*, and yet at the same time soften him into Compassion." He does this 1) by making explicit references to Achilles' anger both in the text and in his notes; 2) by stating that Achilles returns Hector's body largely because the gods have demanded that he do so; 3) by having Priam draw excessive attention to his private suffering and thereby suggesting that Achilles' act of compassion is a momentary deviation from his otherwise unyielding character.

Not only does Pope effectively address the problem of how to sustain Achilles' distinctive character while, at the same time, showing him to be compassionate toward Priam, but he simultaneously seizes upon the opportunity to present Achilles in Book XXIV as, at last, a hero worthy of being a protagonist in a Renaissance epic. As E. R. Curtius has suggested, Isadore of Seville transmits to the Middle Ages and to the Renaissance the definition of the hero as one who combines the qualities of *sapientia et fortitudo*. In his book of etymologies Isadore defines

---

[48] Congreve translated passages from Book XXIV, which were printed by Tonson in *Examen Poeticum* (1693). This line from Congreve's translation is cited from *TE*, 7:cxli.

the epic in the following way: "It is called heroic song because it tells the deeds of brave men. For hero is the name given to men who by their wisdom and courage (*sapientia et fortitudo*) are worthy of heaven" (*Et.* I,39,9).[49] In the *Aeneid* it was the warrior Turnus, referred to by Virgil as "*alius Achilles*" (*Aen.* VI.89), who represented for the Latin poet the predominantly Achillean virtue of *fortitudo* separated from *sapientia*. In Aeneas, however, the two virtues are combined, for it is Aeneas whom Virgil refers to as *pietate insignis et armis* ("remarkable both for his piety and for his martial prowess," *Aen.* VI.403).

But these were the virtues of the ideal Homeric hero as well. Toward the beginning of the *Odyssey* Athena, in trying to urge Telemachus to assume some responsibility for the sorry state of affairs on the island of Ithaca since the departure of Odysseus, describes Odysseus to his son as the kind of hero whom he, Telemachus, should now try to emulate: Odysseus, she tells him, is a man who is proficient in both word and deed (ἔργον τε ἔπος τε, II.272). The hero of the *Iliad*, however, is more accomplished as a doer of deeds than as a speaker of words, as he himself admits in his speech in Book XVIII in which he renounces his wrath and decides to return to the fighting. While it is true, he tells his mother Thetis, that no other Greek can match him as a warrior (ἐν πολέμῳ, 1.106), it is also true that there are others who are more gifted at speaking wisely and well (ἀγορῇ, 1. 106). By the time we reach Book XXIV, however, Homer shows us that Achilles does indeed possess the ability to speak wisely and well and Pope underscores this in his translation and in his notes. In the opening lines of his speech to Priam in which he describes the two urns—the one the source of evil, the other of good—from which Zeus distributes the fortunes of men, Achilles says:

> Alas! what Weight of Anguish hast thou known?
> Unhappy Prince! thus guardless and alone

[49] Cited from *European Literature and the Latin Middle Ages*, trans. Willard R. Trask (1953; reprint ed. New York and Evanston: Harper & Row, 1963), p. 175.

Alas! what Weight of Anguish hast thou known?
Unhappy Prince! thus guardless and alone
To pass thro' Foes, and thus undaunted face
The Man whose Fury has destroy'd thy Race?
Heav'n sure has arm'd thee with a Heart of Steel,
A Strength proportion'd to the Woes you feel.
Rise then: Let Reason mitigate our Care:
To mourn, avails not: Man is born to bear.

[ll. 653-660]

"Let Reason mitigate our Care," Pope's Achilles says. There is no mention of the word "Reason" in the original; what Homer's Achilles says is "let us allow our grief to remain hidden in our hearts" (ll. 522-523). Pope includes the word in order to stress that Homer depicts Achilles here as, at last, fully rational—even if he is by nature stern and unyielding—and therefore as, at last, a complete hero, as the translator says in his notes:

> There is not a more beautiful Passage in the whole *Ilias* than this before us: *Homer* to shew that *Achilles* was not a mere Soldier, here draws him as a Person of excellent Sense and sound reason: *Plato* himself (who condemns this Passage) could not speak more like a true Philosopher: And it was a piece of great Judgment thus to describe him; for the Reader would have retain'd but a very indifferent Opinion of the Hero of a Poem, that had no Qualification but mere Strength: It also shews the Art of the Poet thus to defer this part of his Character till the very Conclusion of the Poem: By these means he fixes an Idea of his Greatness upon our Minds, and makes his Hero go off the Stage with Applause.[50]

And so after Achilles returns the body to Priam and when the old king gazes in wonder at Achilles' "godlike Aspect and majestic Size" (Pope's translation, l. 799), Pope says of Achilles that Homer

[50] *TE*, 8:564.

now commends him for his more amiable Qualities: He softens the terrible Idea we have conceiv'd of him, as a Warrior, with several Virtues of Humanity; and the angry, vindictive Soldier is become calm and compassionate. In this place he makes his very Enemy admire his Personage, and be astonish'd at his manly Beauty. So that tho' Courage be his most distinguishing Character, yet *Achilles* is admirable both for the Endowments of Mind and Body.[51]

To the virtue of *fortitudo* Homer, Pope suggests, in the twenty-fourth book adds that of *sapientia*; Achilles goes off the stage with applause because he has become, at last, an ideal hero—by both Homeric and Renaissance standards—worthy of imitation.

[51] Ibid., 8:570.

PART II: LANGUAGE

CHAPTER THREE

Elevation, Decorum, and Liveliness

ELEVATION AND DECORUM

Samuel Johnson's reverence for Pope's *Iliad* is well known. In the *Life of Pope* he refers to the "English *Iliad*" as "certainly the noblest version of poetry which the world has ever seen" and he asserts that "its publication must be considered as one of the greatest events in the annals of learning." It is, he says, "a poetical wonder," "a performance which no age or nation can pretend to equal."[1] The lavishing of unqualified praise, however, is not characteristic of Johnson's judicious mind. Toward the conclusion of the *Life of Pope* (*The Lives of the English Poets* was completed in 1781) he expresses some reservations about Pope's translation. "Each of the first six lines of the *Iliad*," Johnson writes, "might lose two syllables with very little diminution of the meaning."[2] Johnson is here repeating the critical remarks he made over twenty years earlier in an *Idler* paper dated October 6, 1759. In trying to define and to defend what he means by the term "easy" poetry Johnson says:

> Where any artifice appears in the construction of the verse, that verse is no longer easy. . . . The first lines of Pope's *Iliad*

[1] *Lives of the Poets*, ed. Hill, 3:119, 236.
[2] Ibid., 3:250.

[55]

afford examples of many licenses which the easy writer must decline.

Achilles' *wrath*, to Greece the *direful spring*
Of woes unnumber'd, *heav'nly* Goddess sing,
The wrath which *hurl'd* to Pluto's *gloomy reign*
The souls of *mighty* chiefs untimely slain.

In the first couplet the language is distorted by inversions, clogged with superfluities, and clouded by a harsh metaphor; and in the second there are two words used in an uncommon sense, and two epithets inserted only to lengthen the line; all these practices may in a long work be pardoned, but they always produce some degree of obscurity and ruggedness.[3]

How just are Johnson's criticisms? Would they, in all probability, have been made in Pope's time, or do they represent a newer, a more modern view of what is a "natural" style, a view more in line with Coleridge's critique, in his *Biographia Literaria*, of Pope's translation of the famous night-piece at the end of *Iliad* VIII? There Coleridge contrasted "the almost faultless position and choice of words, in Pope's *original* compositions, particularly in his satires and moral essays" with "his translation of Homer, which, I do not stand alone in regarding as the main source of our pseudo-poetic diction."[4]

To the question of the justness of Johnson's criticisms I shall return, but in order to address the question it is necessary first of all to try to discover what Pope was aiming for in the opening lines of the *Iliad*. "A perfect Judge," Pope wrote, "will *read* each Work of Wit / With the same Spirit that its Author *writ*."[5] Is Johnson in this *Idler* paper showing himself to be something less than a "perfect Judge"? Is it likely that Pope, as he began to unfold to the literary world his long-awaited translation of our most ancient heroic poem, wanted to make Homer sound "easy"?

[3] *The Yale Edition of the Works of Samuel Johnson*, ed. W. J. Bate et al., 9 vols. (New Haven and London: Yale University Press, 1958-1971), 2:239-40.

[4] *Biographia Literaria*, ed. J. Shawcross, 2 vols. (Oxford: Clarendon Press, 1907), 1:26. The first edition of the work was published in 1817.

[5] *An Essay on Criticism*, ll. 233-234, cited from TE, 1:266.

Johnson, as we know, for example, from his famous response to *Lycidas*, was notoriously impatient with such traditional notions as the relevance of generic expectations to the proper apprehension of a work's meaning;[6] could it be that he is here betraying what would become the modern disregard for the ancient principle of *decorum*?

For what the modern reader must first of all recover if he is to listen with a sympathetic ear to Pope's Homer is precisely this ancient principle of decorum. From the beginning of the Western literary tradition through at least the middle of the eighteenth century, writers and critics scrupulously observed the principle that there should be a decorous—that is, a "fitting," an "appropriate"—relationship between subject matter and style: ordinary, mundane subjects should be treated in an appropriately ordinary, mundane style; elevated and important subjects in an appropriately impassioned and weighty style.

Nor is this conception of decorum an arbitrarily formalistic criterion; it derives from an ancient epistemological principle concerning the inverse relation between the importance of objects of knowledge and their capacity to be known or apprehended by the senses.[7] I will touch upon this subject in a later section,

[6] On Johnson's lack of true sympathy for generic criticism, see, for example, W. R. Keast, "The Theoretical Foundations of Johnson's Criticism," in *Critics and Criticism*, ed. R. S. Crane (Chicago and London: University of Chicago Press, 1952), particularly p. 407; see also William K. Wimsatt, Jr. and Cleanth Brooks, *Literary Criticism: A Short History* (New York: Alfred A. Knopf, 1957), p. 325; as well as Jean H. Hagstrum, *Samuel Johnson's Literary Criticism* (1952; reprint ed. Chicago and London: University of Chicago Press, 1967), pp. 31-37.

[7] For my awareness of the significance and pervasiveness of the ancient epistemological principle that there is an inverse relation between the degree of accuracy which can be expected in any representation, on the one hand, and the degree of elevation or the importance of the subject matter, on the other, I am greatly indebted to Wesley Trimpi's unpublished paper, "Knowledge and Representation: The Origins of Renaissance Neoclassicism," read at Dominican College, San Rafael, California, Nov. 10, 1973. The substance of this paper is contained in Trimpi's book, forthcoming from the Princeton University Press, on the origins and continuity of literary theory. The same author discusses the relevance of this principle to a difficult and longstanding problem in classical philology in his remarkable essays, "The Meaning of Horace's *Ut Pictura Poesis*,"

but let it suffice for the moment to quote two representative remarks from treatises of Aristotle, remarks that may well appear, at first glance, to have a rather remote relation to problems of literary style. The first is from the treatise *On the Parts of the Animals*:

> Of things constituted by nature some are ungenerated, imperishable, and eternal, while others are subject to generation and decay. The former are excellent beyond compare and divine, but less accessible to knowledge. The evidence that might throw light on them, and on the problems which we long to solve respecting them, is furnished but scantily by sensation; whereas respecting perishable plants and animals we have abundant information, living as we do in their midst. . . . The scanty conceptions to which we can attain of celestial things give us, from their excellence, more pleasure than all our knowledge of the world in which we live.[8]
>
> [1.5, 644b23-645a27]

The second is from his treatise *On the Soul*:

> We regard all knowledge as beautiful or valuable, but one kind more so than another, either in virtue of its accuracy (κατ' ἀκρίβειαν), or because it relates to higher and more wonderful things (θαυμασιωτέρων).[9]
>
> [1.1, 402a1-5]

There are two criteria for judging the value of knowledge: it is valuable either by virtue of its exactitude or because its objects

---

Journal of the Warburg and Courtauld Institutes 36 (1973): 1-34 and "Horace's 'Ut Pictura Poesis': The Argument for Stylistic Decorum," *Traditio* 34 (1978): 29-73. The two passages from Aristotle which I shall quote in the text were discussed by Trimpi in the paper he delivered at Dominican College. Among other passages that are implicit defenses of the principle mentioned above, see Plato's *Critias* 106-107, Aristotle's *Nichomachean Ethics* 1.3, 1094b13-28 and 1.7, 1098a21-23.

[8] Trans. W. Ogle, *The Basic Works of Aristotle*, ed. R. McKeon (New York: Random House, 1941), p. 656.

[9] Trans. W. S. Hett, LCL (1936; reprint ed. Cambridge, Mass. and London: Harvard University Press and William Heinemann, 1964), p. 9.

possess, in the translation of J. A. Smith, "a higher dignity and greater wonderfulness."[10] That which cannot be known or rendered with exactitude and experienced by the senses—that which is, in other words, *not familiar*—will inspire wonder.[11]

This principle becomes the epistemological basis of the ancient characters or levels of style and their corresponding literary genres. The high style is appropriate to the genres of tragedy and epic; it is elevated above the concerns of the everyday and it attempts to evoke, through both the grandeur of its language and of its subject matter, the emotion of wonder. It is a style that wants to draw attention to itself. The low or plain style— the style appropriate to genres such as comedy, the epigram, the epistle, and Horatian satire—is more familiar. It is a poetic style that wants to go unnoticed, so unnoticed, in fact, that it can be mistaken for prose. As Horace says of his own plain style in the fourth *sermo* of his first book: "I write lines that bear a closer resemblance to prose (*sermoni propriora*, l. 42) than to poetry." Alexander Pope paraphrases this stylistic objective when, in one of his imitations of Horace's satires (II.i), he tells William Fortescue that, since the style of his satires is so familiar, his friend is equally free to "term" him either "Verse-man or Prose-man" (l. 64).[12]

The style of Horatian satire, then, is familiar. In its attempt to imitate the rhythms and syntax of conversational prose, such a style might well be described as "easy," that quality which Johnson remarked was not sufficiently present in the opening lines of Pope's *Iliad*. But what Pope was aiming for in translating Homer was a style that was the reverse of the familiar or the easy, for he was translating an epic, which was for the Renais-

---

[10] *Basic Works of Aristotle*, ed. McKeon, p. 535.

[11] On wonder as an effect of poetic diction, see Aristotle's *Rhetoric* 3.2.1404b8- 15, Longinus' *Peri Hypsous*, Demetrius' *Peri Hermēneias* ("On Style") 59-60, 282-283, Quintilian's *Institutio Oratoria* 8.3.2-6. These passages are cited in chapter four of J. V. Cunningham, *Woe or Wonder*. For a history of wonder as a literary-critical term, the reader should consult this chapter of Cunningham's excellent book.

[12] *TE*, 4:11.

sance-Augustan audience, as it had been for the ancient, the most elevated of literary genres. And this was no ordinary epic; it was the oldest, most venerable poem in the world. In order to convey that sense of distance and the accompanying sense of wonder, Pope drew upon the traditional means—described by Aristotle in the *Poetics* and established in English by Milton in *Paradise Lost*—for achieving an elevated, impassioned style.

In chapter XXII of the *Poetics* Aristotle describes the best style as that which is clear (σαφῆ) without being mean (ταπεινήν). The clearest style would use only current or proper words; but such a style would never rise above the mean or lowly (ταπεινήν). If a diction is to be lofty (σεμνή) and rise above the everyday, it must employ unusual words (τοῖς ξεινικοῖς κεχρημένη). Such an elevated diction, Aristotle goes on to say, will be 1) composed of rare or unusual words; it will be 2) metaphorical; and it will 3) make use of words or phrases that are unusually lengthened. Aristotle then finds fault with a particular critic who "ridiculed the tragedians for using phrases which no one would employ in ordinary speech: for example, δωμάτων ἄπο instead of ἄπο δωμάτων . . . and the like. It is precisely because such phrases are not part of the current idiom that they give distinction to the style. This, however, he failed to see."[13]

This traditional method for achieving an impassioned, elevated style had met with serious opposition from at least the period of the 1590s when Donne and particularly Jonson, reacting in part against the more florid extravagances of their Petrarchan ancestors, wrote English poems employing the classical plain style.[14] This movement toward simplicity of diction—or at least, in the case of Donne, toward a greater directness of speech—then received authoritative sanction from the attitudes toward style advocated by the Royal Society. All "Ornaments of speak-

[13] Trans. Butcher, pp. 86 and 87.

[14] Those who are perplexed to hear the style of Donne's poems identified with the classical plain style should read J. V. Cunningham's essay "Lyric Style in the 1590's," in *The Collected Essays of J. V. Cunningham* (Chicago: Swallow Press, 1976), pp. 311-324. Donne's poems written in the classical plain style are his epigrams, elegies, satires, and verse letters rather than the *Songs and Sonnets*.

ing," Thomas Sprat writes in a well-known passage, "are in open defiance against *Reason*: professing, not to hold much correspondence with that; but with its Slaves, *the Passions*." Men should now write, he recommends, "with a native easiness; bringing all things as near to Mathematical plainness, as they can."[15]

But the method for achieving a suitably elevated style, as described by Aristotle, was by no means forgotten in the early eighteenth century. It was Joseph Addison, Pope wrote in the preface to his translation of the *Iliad*, "who first determin'd me to undertake this Task."[16] By the time the first volume of Pope's *Iliad* was published in 1715, it appears Addison had determined Thomas Tickell as well to undertake the very same task and, as in part a consequence of this development, Pope and Addison had begun to drift apart. But the two men were on excellent terms in 1712 and on January 26 of that year Addison, in one of his eighteen papers on *Paradise Lost*, discussed a subject of great relevance to Pope's future undertaking, and that subject was the style appropriate to a heroic poem. "The Language of an heroic Poem," Addison writes in *Spectator* 285, "should be both Perspicuous and Sublime."[17] Addison gives no specific advice as to how "perspicuity" is to be achieved, but he describes with complete clarity how the epic poet can achieve an elevated style by means of three devices discussed by Aristotle in *Poetics* XXII. These three devices, each of which Addison illustrates with examples from *Paradise Lost*, are 1) the use of bold metaphors; 2) the use of "Idioms of other Tongues," which includes "placing the Adjective after the Substantive, with several other foreign Modes of Speech"; and 3) "the length'ning of a Phrase by the Addition of Words, which may either be inserted or omitted."[18] All three of these devices may be found in the opening lines of

[15] *History of the Royal Society*, 2nd ed. (London, 1702), pp. 111-113. The first edition appeared in 1667.

[16] *TE*, 7:23.

[17] *Spectator*, ed. Bond, 3:10. The relevance of this *Spectator* paper to the formulation of Pope's stylistic intentions in his *Iliad* was first brought to my awareness by Richard C. Gustafson's Ph.D. dissertation, "The Perspicuous and the Sublime: A Historical Study of the Language of Pope's *Iliad*," University of Kansas, 1960.

[18] *Spectator*, ed. Bond, 3:12-13.

[61]

Pope's *Iliad*: 1) "the direful Spring / Of Woes unnumber'd" is a bold metaphor; 2) "Woes unnumber'd" is a Latinate idiom in which the adjective is placed after the substantive and "to Greece the direful Spring" is a "Transposition of Words"; 3) "heav'nly Goddess," "Pluto's gloomy Reign," and "mighty Chiefs" are all examples of "the length'ning of a Phrase by the Addition of Words, which may either be inserted or omitted."

In *Idler* 77 Johnson objects to each one of these phrases. In two instances his criticism may be justified. "The direful Spring / Of Woes unnumber'd" is indeed a harsh metaphor, and one that is not present in the original Greek; and Pope's choice of the word "Reign" in line three is, perhaps, somewhat forced, although Dryden uses it in a similar sense in his *Aeneis* and Johnson himself accepted this usage of the word in his *Dictionary of the English Language*.[19] But every detail, including these two, of Johnson's criticism of the opening lines of Pope's *Iliad* may be viewed, in broader terms, as a critique of the traditional means of achieving an elevated style as formulated by Aristotle in the *Poetics*. It is a critique of the principle of decorum itself insofar that Johnson—apart from his suggestion that such alleged blemishes "may in a long work be pardoned"[20]—does not here consider the relevance of generic expectations to Pope's stylistic choices.

LIVELINESS VERSUS ELEVATION

θρῴσκωσιν κύαμοι μελανόχροες ἢ ἐρέβινθοι
(the black-skinned beans and chickpeas bounce high into the air)

[Homer's *Iliad*, XIII.589]

---

[19] *Aen.* 1.52, 178, 738; III.326; IV.451; V.1035; VI.129. The use of the word "reign" as a synonym for "realm" has a long pedigree in English poetry; in his dictionary Johnson lists "kingdom" and "dominions" as synonyms of "reign" and then cites two examples, one from Prior and the other from the third line of Pope's *Iliad*.

[20] Johnson is here virtually paraphrasing Horace's liberal remarks about Homer in the *Ars Poetica*. "When a work is long" (*operi longo*, l. 360), Horace suggests, and if the poet is as consistently great as is Homer, we can easily excuse occasional and perhaps inevitable lapses of judgment.

Light leaps the golden grain, resulting from the
ground
[Pope's *Iliad*, XIII.742]

As I will suggest in the fifth chapter, the influence of Longinus
can explain to a large degree why Pope, as the quotations cited
above suggest, tends to generalize—or to elevate—Homer's more
particularized diction. Yet some of the more periphrastic at-
tempts at generalization can be explained, without necessarily
having to allude to Longinus, as an inheritance of what I would
like to call the ancient antagonism between elevation and veri-
similitude, an antagonism that becomes especially acute in the
Augustan period. As William K. Wimsatt and Cleanth Brooks
have noted, the high, middle, and low styles "appear by the mid-
eighteenth century to have been simplified into the polar concepts
of the lofty and the low."[21] The process was well under way at
the beginning of the century, however, and it posed a problem
for the translator of Homer, the author who was long recognized
as possessing the rare capacity for spanning all three levels of

---

[21] Wimsatt and Brooks, *Literary Criticism*, p. 342. Eric Auerbach, both in
Mimesis and in the essay "*Sermo Humilis*" in *Literary Language and its Public
in Late Latin Antiquity and the Middle Ages*, suggests that this antagonism
between elevation and verisimilitude is characteristic of all classicizing periods.
Auerbach argues that in the Middle Ages and in the nineteenth century, however,
when the classical levels of style do not exert so strong an influence, the "sublime"
and the "realistic" may be found in the same work, as they are, for example, in
Dante's *Commedia* and in the novels of Balzac. In commenting upon Longinus'
comparison between the *Iliad* and *Odyssey* in *Peri Hypsous* 9. 11-15, D. A.
Russell says that the association, made by both Aristotle (*Poetics* 1459b14) and
Longinus, of the *Iliad* with the "pathetic" and the *Odyssey* with the "ethical,"
is fundamentally a distinction between the kind of work which is intensely
elevated and the kind of work which is realistic and hence milder in tone ("*Lon-
ginus*" *On the Sublime*, ed. with an introduction and commentary by D. A.
Russell [Oxford: Clarendon Press, 1964], p. 99). Cf. also Quintilian's distinction
(*Inst. Orat.* 6.2) between the quality of πάθος depicted in tragedy and of ἦθος
in comedy. The later seventeenth-century notion, discussed in chapter two of
this book, that the higher genres such as tragedy and epic should imitate the
"passions" themselves may be viewed as an extreme development of the ancient
antagonism between the "pathetic" and the "ethical." It would become more
and more difficult, in the course of the seventeenth and eighteenth centuries, to
combine the two within the same literary work.

style. Aristotle, for example, praised Homer for his ability to represent the kind of "familiar" (οἰκεῖα) subject matter which was beyond the range of the more precious and frigid poet Choerilus (*Topics* 157a14-16). Dionysius of Halicarnassus, one of the ancient critics upon whom Pope relied most heavily, in his essay *On the Style of Demosthenes* describes the two major literary styles as the "graceful" (ἡ γλαφυρά) and the "austere" (τὸ σεμνόν). But there is a third kind of style, Dionysius continues, "which is a mixture obtained by selecting the best qualities of the other two. . . . The standard of excellence in this style was set by Homer, and there is no style that could be said to combine the other two qualities of charm and dignity more effectively."[22]

With Dionysius' evaluation of Homer's style Pope was in complete agreement. It was indeed the striking of this middle ground that, according to Pope himself, proved most difficult for the Homeric translator. "Nothing that belongs to *Homer* seems to have been more commonly mistaken," Pope writes in the *Iliad* preface, "than the just Pitch of his Style." Pope continues:

> Some of his Translators having swell'd into Fustian in a proud Confidence of the *Sublime*; others sunk into Flatness in a cold and timorous Notion of *Simplicity*. Methinks I see these different Followers of *Homer*, some sweating and straining after him by violent Leaps and Bounds, (the certain Signs of false Mettle) others slowly and servilely creeping in his Train, while the Poet himself is all the time proceeding with an unaffected and equal Majesty before them."[23]

[22] Dionysius describes the graceful style in section 38, the austere style in section 39, and the mixture of the two in sections 40 and 41. The translation is that of Stephen Usher, *Dionysius of Halicarnassus: The Critical Essays in Two Volumes*, LCL (Cambridge, Mass. and London: Harvard University Press and William Heinemann, 1974), 1:399.

[23] *TE*, 7:18. Cf. Pope's early estimate of Homer's style, which he makes in a letter to Ralph Bridges dated April 5, 1708: "The great Beauty of Homer's Language, as I take it," Pope writes, "consists in that noble simplicity, which runs through all his works; (and yet his diction, contrary to what one would imagine consistent with simplicity, is at the same time very Copious)," *The*

Elevation must, on the one hand, not be transformed into fustian; and for this reason the translator should avoid using that "painted and poetical diction,"[24] as Pope says in the *Odyssey* postscript, so indulged in by contemporary writers of tragedy. And, on the other hand, simplicity and naturalness must not be dismissed as meanness and vulgarity. Hence Pope, again in the *Odyssey* postscript, defends the style of the *Odyssey* against the charge, made by Longinus, that because the poem is less elevated than the *Iliad* it is therefore inferior. "The *Odyssey* is not always cloth'd in the majesty of verse proper to Tragedy," Pope concedes, "but sometimes . . . descends into the plainer Narrative, and sometimes even to that familiar dialogue essential to Comedy. However, where it cannot support a sublimity, it always preserves a dignity, or at least a propriety."[25] And then, in words which appear to paraphrase Dionysius' description of Homer's style, Pope writes:

Indeed the true reason that so few Poets have imitated *Homer* in these lower parts, has been the extreme difficulty of preserving that mixture of Ease and Dignity essential to them. For it is as hard for an Epic Poem to stoop with success, as for a Prince to descend to be familiar, without diminution to his greatness.[26]

The great task for Pope, then, was to achieve a style that could, when it was necessary, stoop with success and thus manage to maintain a perfect mixture of ease and dignity. An associated problem was to write in a manner that was both "lively" or verisimilar as well as elevated, for these qualities were often seen as being mutually exclusive. This stylistic problem may be seen to derive from the ancient epistemological principle, discussed earlier, that there is an inverse relation between the excellence

Correspondence of Alexander Pope, ed. George Sherburn, 5 vols. (Oxford: Clarendon Press, 1956), 1:44.

[24] *TE*, 10:388. It is ironic that Pope, who was to be castigated by Wordsworth and Coleridge for the conspicuousness of his "poetic diction," preceded these writers in his use of the term in a derogatory sense.

[25] Ibid., 10:386.

[26] Ibid., 10:389.

of an object and the degree of exactness with which the object can be known. As those objects which can be known with exactness will tend to be less important than those which are less apprehensible to the senses, so those objects of artistic representation that can be rendered with a great degree of verisimilar accuracy will tend to be those that are less important, less elevated. This antagonism between verisimilitude and elevation is central, for example, to Dryden's problematic *Essay of Dramatic Poesy*, of which Samuel Johnson remarked, "it will not be easy to find, in all the opulence of our language, a treatise so artfully variegated with successive representations of opposite probabilities."[27] There Lisideius argues for his preferring the French drama to the English because it is the more elevated. And his opponent Neander concedes the point: " 'Tis true," he says, that "those beauties of French poesy are such as will raise perfection higher where it is." But English drama is the more "lively"—that is, the more lifelike—imitation of nature because its beauties, Neander argues, are those not "of a statue, but of a man."[28]

Pope alludes to the problem often in the notes that accompany his *Iliad*. While Homer, for example, writes in a manner that is more "lively" than does Virgil, Pope suggests, the Latin poet is the more consistently elevated. There are more speeches in the *Iliad* than there are in the *Aeneid*, Pope observes at one point, and these "many continued Conversations . . . a little resembling

[27] *Life of Dryden, Lives of the English Poets*, ed. Hill, 1:198.

[28] *Of Dramatic Poesy and Other Critical Essays*, ed. Watson, 1:56. It is Neander, who had praised the liveliness of English drama, rather than Lisideius, who had praised the elevation of French drama, who goes on to argue in favor of the use of rhyme rather than of blank verse in serious plays since blank verse, Neander says, "is acknowledged to be too low for a poem" (*Of Dramatic Poesy*, 1:87). That Neander—whose position is often taken to be that of Dryden himself—argues first in favor of liveliness and then in favor of elevation suggests that Dryden wished to resist the ancient antagonism between liveliness and elevation and to find a *via media* between them. Robert D. Hume, following the lead of Dean T. Mace ("Dryden's Dialogue on Drama"), suggests that the whole of the *Essay of Dramatic Poesy* may be viewed as "a struggle between literal and ideal representation" (*Dryden's Criticism* [Ithaca and London: Cornell University Press, 1970], p. 195).

[66]

common Chit-chat" render the Greek poem "more natural and animated, but less grave and majestic."[29] And in comparing the funeral games in the *Iliad* and the *Aeneid* Pope says that "there is in general more Variety of natural Incidents, and a more lively Picture of natural Passions, in the Games and Persons of *Homer*" while there is "a greater Pomp of Verse in those of Virgil."[30] In Virgil's description of the sea race in particular, Pope comments, there is "more Poetry and Majesty" while in Homer's chariot race there is "more Nature, and lively Incidents"; but it must be admitted, he says, that "in Virgil the description is nobler, it has something more ostentatiously grand, and seems a Spectacle more worthy the Presence of Princes and of great Persons."[31]

Joseph Spence's *Essay on Mr. Pope's Odyssey* (first published 1726/1727) is a series of five dialogues between Philypsus (literally, "lover of elevation") and Antiphaus ("opponent of [stylistic] glitter"). Philypsus, Spence writes,

> was so possest with the Pleasure which he felt from fine Thoughts and warm Expressions, that He did not take a full Satisfaction in low Beauty, and simple Representations of Nature; the other, on the contrary, had such an aversion to Glitterings and Elevation, that he was distasted at any the least appearance of either.[32]

It is the opinion of Antiphaus that Pope in his translation of the *Odyssey* too often sacrificed liveliness in order to achieve a great degree of elevation. As an illustration of an extreme case of this tendency in general rather than in Pope's work in particular, Antiphaus makes reference to a history painting which both men

---

[29] *TE*, 8:122.

[30] Ibid., 8:531.

[31] Ibid., 8:532.

[32] Cited from *An Essay on Mr. Pope's Odyssey in Five Dialogues*, 2nd ed. (London, 1737), p. 2. Cf. the following passage, in which the word "artificial," it is worth noting, already possesses connotations which would become common in the nineteenth century: "If *Philypsus* wou'd sometimes condemn a point as low and mean, tho' in reality proper enough, and naturally express'd; *Antiphaus*, in his turn, might happen now and then to blame a Passage which requir'd a good degree of Ornament, as being too glaring and artificial" (Ibid., p. 3).

[67]

have recently viewed together. "I never saw anything more truly ridiculous," he tells Philypsus,

> Than the Piece we were looking at the other Day, in your Picture-Gallery—Good Heaven! The Duke of *Marlborough* in the heat of an Engagement, with a full-bottom'd Wig, very carefully spread over his Shoulders![33]

What strikes Antiphaus as ridiculous is the disproportion between the elevated representation of the Duke "with a full-bottom'd Wig, very carefully spread over his Shoulders" and the rough-and-tumble actuality—the liveliness or verisimilitude—of the representation of the battle in which he is taking part.

Just as "the many continued Conversations . . . a little resembling common Chit-chat" give to the *Iliad* a "natural and animated" air, so do other verisimilar and everyday details. "Representations of common, or even domestic things," Pope writes in the *Odyssey* postscript, "are frequently found to make the liveliest impression on the reader."[34] It was apparently easier for Pope to translate in a manner that was "grave and majestic," however, than in one that was "natural and animated." "Let it be remember'd," the poet says in the same postscript,

> that the same Genius that soar'd the highest, and from whom the greatest models of the *Sublime* are derived, was also he who stoop'd the lowest, and gave to the simple Narrative its utmost perfection. Which of these was the harder task to *Homer* himself, I cannot pretend to determine; but to his Translator I can affirm (however unequal all his imitations must be) that of the latter has been much the more difficult.[35]

The great difficulty of writing well in a plain and unaffected style which Pope alludes to here was memorably stated by Cicero who says in the *Orator* (xxiii.77) that "plainness of style seems easy to imitate at first thought, but when attempted nothing is more

[33] Ibid., p. 22.
[34] TE, 10:387.
[35] Ibid., 10:389.

difficult."[36] A major stylistic problem for the Augustan translator or writer of epic—perhaps *the* major stylistic problem—was, then, to learn to stoop with success. This was a problem not only for Pope, but also for his collaborators in the translation of the *Odyssey*. When he began to translate Book XX of the *Odyssey*, for example, Elijah Fenton came across the following simile:

ὡς δὲ κύων ἀμαλῇσι περὶ σκυλάκεσσι βεβῶσα
ἄνδρ' ἀγνοιήσασ' ὑλάει μέμονέν τε μάχεσθαι,
ὥς ῥα τοῦ ἔνδον ὑλάκτει ἀγαιομένου κακὰ ἔργα·

(Just as a bitch, standing guard over her helpless puppies,
when she sees a stranger, growls and is eager to fight in their defense,
so his [Odysseus'] heart growled within him as he viewed, with indignant scorn, these evil actions.)[37]
[ll. 14-17]

The prospect of having to translate this relatively homely simile, as well as other correspondingly humble details, with the appropriate degree of Augustan dignity elicited the following frustrated reaction from Fenton:

> How I shall get over the bitch and her puppies, the roasting of the black puddings, as Brault translated it, and the cowheel that was thrown at Ulysses' head, I know not.[38]

It is this same problem of how to stoop with success that Pope faces when he comes to translate the scenes of domestic conflict

[36] Trans. G. L. Hendrickson and H. M. Hubbell, LCL (1939; reprint ed. Cambridge, Mass. and London: Harvard University Press and William Heinemann, 1971), p. 363.
[37] The Greek is cited from *The Odyssey of Homer*, ed. W. B. Stanford, 2 vols. (London: Macmillan, 1947).
[38] *The Correspondence of Alexander Pope*, ed. Sherburn, 2:233. James Sutherland cites this passage and discusses the problems it posed for the Augustan translator in *A Preface to Eighteenth Century Poetry* (Oxford: Clarendon Press, 1948), pp. 88ff.

on Olympus from the *Iliad*. Pope's Jove is generally a more august figure than Homer's Zeus, closer in many ways to Milton's God than to Homer's more wayward deity. Pope "improved the theology of Homer,"[39] Gibbon believed, and one reason the English poet did this was, no doubt, that he did not want to invite a typically "Modern" scorn for Homer's allegedly primitive view of the divine. Certainly Dryden, Pope felt, carried the burlesque tone too far.[40] But part of the issue may be stylistic. Where Homer, for example, in his representation of Olympus will often descend to the domestic level, Pope attempts to maintain the level of his translation at a higher pitch. In Book I, for example, after Achilles has withdrawn from the battle, he asks his goddess-mother Thetis to appeal to Zeus and to ask him to take vengeance upon the Greeks who had so dishonored him. When Thetis does beg this of Zeus, his immediate response is:

ἦ δὴ λοίγια ἔργ' ὅ τέ μ' ἐχθοδοπῆσαι ἐφήσεις
Ἥρῃ, ὅτ' ἄν μ' ἐρέθῃσιν ὀνειδείοις ἐπέεσσιν·
ἡ δὲ καὶ αὔτως μ' αἰεὶ ἐν ἀθανάτοισι θεοῖσι
νεικεῖ, καί τέ μέ φησι μάχῃ Τρώεσσιν ἀρήγειν.

(It will be catastrophic indeed if you incite hostilities
between Hera and myself, so that she will provoke me
    with words of reproach.
For even as things stand she constantly quarrels with me
    in front of the other immortals
and she accuses me of helping the Trojans in battle.)
                                                    [ll. 518-521]

Here is Pope's translation:

[39] *The History of the Decline and Fall of the Roman Empire*, ed. J. B. Bury, 7 vols. (London and New York: Methuen and Co., Macmillan and Co., 1896), 1: 29, n. 4.

[40] See, for example, Pope's remarks on Dryden's description of Hephaestus at the end of Book I. "Mr. *Dryden*," Pope writes, "has treated *Vulcan* a little barbarously. He makes his Character perfectly comical, he is the Jest of the Board, and the Gods are very merry upon the Imperfections of his Figure" (*TE*, 7:124).

[70]

> What hast thou ask'd? Ah why should *Jove* engage
> In foreign Contests, and domestic Rage,
> The Gods Complaints, and *Juno*'s fierce Alarms,
> While I, too partial, aid the *Trojan* Arms?
>
> > [ll. 672-675]

Pope entirely leaves out Zeus' remark about how Hera continually nags at him because she feels he is favoring the Trojans. This homely touch creates a specific and not very elevated image of how Hera treats the father of gods and men. Pope chooses therefore to translate the details into more dignified generalities such as "domestic Rage" and "*Juno*'s fierce Alarms."

It is interesting to observe that the note of domestic conflict is more clearly sounded in the translations of two of Pope's most important predecessors, George Chapman and John Dryden. Here is the translation of Chapman (Chapman's complete translation was published in 1611):

> Works of death thou urgest. O, at this
> Juno will storme and all my powers inflame with
> > contumelies.
> Ever she wrangles, charging me in eare of all the Gods
> That I am partiall still that I adde the displeasing oddes
> Of my aide to the Ilians.
>
> > [ll. 500-504]

And here is Dryden (1700):

> Know'st thou what Clamors will disturb my Reign,
> What my stun'd Ears from *Juno* must sustain?
> In Council she gives Licence to her Tongue,
> Loquacious, Brawling, ever in the wrong.
> And now she will my partial Pow'r upbraid,
> If alienate from *Greece*, I give the *Trojans* Aid.[41]
>
> > [ll. 697-702]

---

[41] Dryden included his translation of the first book of the *Iliad* in his *Fables Ancient and Modern; Translated into Verse, from Homer, Ovid, Boccace and Chaucer: with Original Poems* (1700). The lines are cited from *The Poems of John Dryden*, ed. James Kinsley, 4 vols. (Oxford: Clarendon Press, 1958), 4:1601.

Chapman presents Hera as a wife who "Ever . . . wrangles, charg-ing . . . in eare of all the Gods" that her husband is "partiall" to the Trojans. And Dryden who, one must admit, certainly somewhat overdoes it here, has his Jupiter characterize his nag-ging wife as "Loquacious" and "Brawling," and as one who gives "Licence to her Tongue."

I do not mean these remarks to be a criticism of Pope's height-ening of Homer's domestic scenes, for the eighteenth-century renderings are completely successful in their own august manner. And surely the translator himself was well aware of the dangers involved in excessive elevation. As Pope makes abundantly clear in his *Peri Bathous*, there is something undeniably ludicrous in transforming the phrase "shut the door" into "The Wooden Guardian of our Privacy / Quick on its Axle turn"[42] in order to satisfy the demands of epic decorum. Yet it was perhaps the increasingly rigorous contemporary demand that an epic be writ-ten in so consistently elevated a diction—which, with only the greatest difficulty, could stoop with success—that caused Pope to abandon his own original epic, the *Brutus*. Pope apparently felt that many of the lines he did compose were more bombastic than truly elevated, for he chose some of these lines as examples of false elevation in his *Peri Bathous*. One might speculate further and suggest that this stylistic dilemma will account, in part, for the obsolescence of epic and the rise in the importance of heroic verse satire in the Augustan period. It was not so much that the "heroic impulse"—a vaguely defined concept, in any case—was spent, or even that the sad spectacle of contemporary society especially invited bitter satiric commentary more than it deserved the lofty praise of the epic muse. If one could not, as a writer of epic, sustain elevation without yielding to bombast, and es-pecially if one could not descend to the familiar without dimi-nution to the greatness of epic, it was at least entirely possible to exploit the comic possibilities of *in*decorum. Hence the writer of heroic satire, in order to make his critical point, could exploit

[42] *Poetry and Prose of Alexander Pope*, ed. Aubrey Williams (Boston: Hough-ton Mifflin, 1969), p. 426.

[72]

the disproportion between this very elevation of diction and the moral poverty of the subject matter such a style is meant—comically—to represent. As Pope himself remarks in the *Odyssey* postscript: "the use of the grand style on little subjects, is not only ludicrous, but a sort of transgression against the rules of proportion and mechanics: 'Tis using a vast force to lift a *feather*."[43]

[43] *TE*, 10:387.

CHAPTER FOUR

"Homer makes us Hearers, and *Virgil* leaves us Readers": Pope and the Ancient Distinction between the Oral and the Written Styles

THE SKIAGRAPHIC STYLE

I focused my discussion of poetic diction around the figure of Samuel Johnson for two related reasons: first, because he is such a great defender of Pope's translation, the remarks he makes that are critical should therefore be scrutinized with care; and second, he straddles two critical traditions, the classical-Augustan-Renaissance and the modern. In his critical objections to works written in the earlier tradition he is often curiously modern[1] and we

---

[1] Consider, for example, Johnson's critique of *Lycidas*, in which he applies the incipiently Romantic doctrine of "sincerity" to a poem written in the tradition of the pastoral elegy. One should also point out Johnson's preference for Richardson over Fielding; that preference is, in part, the result of the critic's leaning toward what would come to be known as "realism" and his lack of responsiveness to literature that establishes much of its meaning through traditional Christian allegory and symbolism. For enlightening discussions of the relationship of Fielding's *Tom Jones* to the traditional symbolism of western narrative literature, see chapters five and six ("Fielding: The Argument of Design," "Fielding: The Definition of Wisdom") in Martin C. Battestin's *The Providence of Wit: Aspects of Form in Augustan Literature and the Arts* (Oxford: Clarendon Press, 1974), pp. 141-192, and Henry Knight Miller, *Henry Fielding's* Tom Jones *and the Romance Tradition*, English Literary Studies Monograph Series, no. 6 (Toronto: University

can see in his attitudes the outlines of positions that will be more fully elaborated by critics of succeeding generations. His remarks on the opening lines of Pope's *Iliad*, for example, anticipate both Wordsworth's and Coleridge's objections to the "poetic diction" which they felt marred not only Pope's translation but, through its extraordinary prestige, was responsible for corrupting contemporary poetic style as well.

Judging from his remarks in *Idler* 77, it would appear that Johnson was unqualifiedly opposed to poetic ornamentation. Yet precisely the opposite is true of his central defense of Pope's translation, part of which reads as follows:

> It has been objected by some, who wish to be number'd among the sons of learning, that Pope's version of Homer is not Homerical; that it exhibits no resemblance to the original and characteristick manner of the Father of Poetry, as it wants his awful simplicity, his artless grandeur, his unaffected majesty. . . . To a thousand cavils one answer is sufficient; the purpose of a writer is to be read, and the criticism which would destroy the power of pleasing must be blown aside. Pope wrote for his own age and his own nation: he knew that it was necessary to colour the images and point the sentiments of his author; he therefore made him graceful, but lost him some of his sublimity.[2]

Where Johnson had some twenty years earlier criticized the opening lines of Pope's *Iliad* for what he perceived to be their overly elaborate style, he is here condoning these very same practices. Johnson's argument, on the surface, is common-sensical and pragmatic: the elegant style of Pope's Homer was what the age demanded; a less polished style, a style as simple and unaffected as Homer's, would go unread in an age that expected a high degree of literary polish.

---

of Victoria, 1976). For Johnson's relationship to the perceptual standards of criticism to be developed by Wordsworth and Coleridge, see William Edinger's admirably subtle and detailed *Samuel Johnson and Poetic Style* (Chicago and London: University of Chicago Press, 1977).

[2] *Life of Pope, Lives of the Poets*, ed. Hill, 3:238, 240.

This is surely part of the truth. Pope certainly wanted his translation to be read and appreciated by the polite and sophisticated audience of his day, and he and his friends went to great lengths to recruit many of them as subscribers for the projected volumes of the English *Iliad*. But Johnson's remarks may well lead the modern reader to conclude that Pope as a translator was not receptive to Homer's "awful simplicity, his artless grandeur, his unaffected majesty," which is untrue. As early as 1708 Pope expressed his feeling for these qualities. "The great Beauty of Homer's Language," Pope wrote in a letter to Ralph Bridges, "consists in that noble simplicity, which runs through all his works."[3] And in the *Iliad* preface Pope speaks of the "pure and noble Simplicity" which "is nowhere in such Perfection as in the *Scripture* and our Author."[4] In his notes Pope describes Homer's style as analogous to the style of "those free Painters who (one would think) had only made here and there a few very significant strokes, that give Form and Spirit to all the Piece"; "*little Exactnesses* are what we should not look for in *Homer*."[5] This description of Homer's style is strikingly reminiscent of Aristotle's description of the direct and simple oral style of deliberative oratory to which he compares the style of Homeric epic.

In *Rhetoric* III.12 Aristotle distinguishes between the relative degrees of accuracy or of finish one should expect from the oral and the written styles of oratory:

> It should be observed that each kind of rhetoric has its own appropriate style. The style of written prose is not that of spoken oratory, nor are those of political and forensic speaking the same. . . . The written style is the more finished, the spoken better admits of dramatic delivery.

Aristotle then goes on to remark that while "constant repetitions of words and phrases are very properly condemned in written speeches," in speeches designed for an audience of listeners rather than of readers such repetitions will have a powerfully dramatic effect if delivered with an appropriate amount of histrionic flair.

[3] *Correspondence*, ed. Sherburn, 1:44.
[4] *TE*, 7:18.
[5] Ibid., 7:272, 191.

And then as an example of the effective use of the sort of repetition characteristic of the oral style, Aristotle quotes Homer's lines about Nereus from the "Catalogue of the Ships" in Book II of the *Iliad*:

> Nireus from Syme [led three balanced vessels],
> Nireus son of Aglaia [and of the king Charopos],
> Nireus, the most beautiful man [who came to Ilion].

An asyndetic statement such as this, Aristotle suggests, while appropriate to the oral style of delivery, would appear awkward or crude in a written composition. Aristotle then goes on to distinguish between the different degrees of literary finish to be expected from those styles which can be said to belong to spoken oratory:

> Now the style of oratory addressed to public assemblies is really just like a rough sketch or outline (σκιαγραφία). The bigger the throng, the more distant is the point of view: so that, in the one and the other, high finish in detail is better away. The forensic style is the more highly finished; still more so is the style of language addressed to a single judge, with whom there is very little room for rhetorical artifices, since he can take the whole thing in better, and judge of what is to the point and what is not; the struggle is less intense and so the judgement is undisturbed. This is why the same speakers do not distinguish themselves in all these branches at once; high finish is wanted least where dramatic delivery is wanted most, and here the speaker must have a good voice, and above all, a strong one. It is ceremonial oratory (ἡ ἐπιδεικτικὴ λέξις) that is most literary, for it is meant to be read; and next to it forensic oratory.[6]

In this passage, therefore, Aristotle compares the style of oratory addressed to public assemblies—with which the style of Homer

---

[6] Aristotle, *Rhetoric*, trans. W. R. Roberts, and *Poetics*, trans. I. Bywater (New York: The Modern Library, 1954), pp. 196-199. I am indebted to Wesley Trimpi's essay "The Meaning of Horace's *Ut Pictura Poesis*" for bringing to my awareness Aristotle's distinction between the oral and the written styles.

has just been associated—to a "rough sketch or outline" (*skiagraphia*). E. M. Cope, in his excellent commentary on the *Rhetoric*, defines *skiagraphia* as "a painting in outline and *chiaroscuro*, or light and shade, without colour, and intended to produce its effect only *at a distance*—herein lies the analogy to public speaking—consequently rough and unfinished, because *from the distance* all niceties and refinements in style and finish would be entirely thrown away."[7] More finished than this "skiagraphic" political style (δημηγορική) is the forensic (δικανή), and more finished still is the style of language addressed to a single judge. But the most refined of all rhetorical styles is the "epideictic," for it is meant to be read.

Aristotle's distinction between the bold and direct oral style and the more intricate written style has great relevance for understanding Pope's strategy in translating Homer. His version has been criticized, from its first appearance, for its allegedly excessive polish. "A pretty poem," Richard Bentley said in the famous remark, "but you must not call it Homer."[8] And even Pope's most forceful and eloquent defender, Samuel Johnson, feels he must excuse the polish of Pope's translation and he does so by resorting to the following argument. "In all nations," Johnson writes in the *Life of Pope*, "the first writers are simple, and . . . every age improves in elegance." Virgil embellished Homer because by Virgil's time "the demand for elegance so much increased, that mere nature would be endured no longer."[9] Pope sympathized with this view, and although he agreed with Mme. Dacier in preferring "the simplicity of the ancient world to the luxury of ours,"[10] he knew that many of Homer's words and phrases, if translated too literally, would simply offend the elegant taste of his contemporary audience. This demand exercised his ability for inventing more or less elaborate periphrases; so Homer's "little boy" (πάϊς, *Il.* XV.362) becomes a "sportive

[7] *The Rhetoric of Aristotle with a Commentary by Edward Meredith Cope*, ed. J. E. Sandys, 3 vols. (Cambridge: Cambridge University Press, 1877), 3:152.
[8] Cited from *Lives of the Poets*, ed. Hill, 3:213n.
[9] Ibid., 3:239.
[10] *TE*, 10:394.

Wanton" (XV.418), a "bold horsefly" (μυίης θάρσος, XVII.570) becomes a "vengeful Hornet" (XVII.642). Pope translated in this way, he says, "because a Translator owes so much to the Taste of the Age in which he lives."[11] But Aristotle's distinction between the "skiagraphic" oral style and the more refined and meticulous written style suggests that there may be a less specialized and therefore more persuasive explanation for many of Pope's embellishments of Homer's style. For while in the "skiagraphic" style of spoken oratory—to which Aristotle compares the style of Homer—high finish is superfluous and uncalled for, the utmost of literary polish is indeed *required* in written compositions—such as Pope's *Iliad*—because here the reader is given the opportunity to scrutinize the text at leisure.

ANCIENTS VERSUS MODERNS

But the question must be asked: was Pope aware of the Aristotelian distinction? And, if he was, why did he not invoke it in order to defend Homer against the charge of stylistic roughness and inexactness brought against him by Moderns such as Charles Perrault? For if the Homeric poems were designed above all to be heard rather than read, it becomes clear, in the light of Aristotle's distinction, why in oral presentation minute stylistic refinements would be superfluous. And why did Pope not defend his own style of translation for the related reason that, in written compositions, a high degree of finish is required?

As Marvin T. Herrick has observed, "by 1620 there was no excuse for any educated Englishman's not knowing the *Rhetoric*."[12] Pope had access to the text both in the original Greek and in the adaptation by Thomas Hobbes, *A Brief of the Art of Rhetoric*, "containing all that Aristotle hath written in his three books on that subject" (1681). Book III, chapter xi of Hobbes's adaptation deals with "the Difference between the Stile to be

[11] *TE*, 8:64.
[12] "The Early History of Aristotle's *Rhetoric* in England," *Philological Quarterly* 5 (1926):257.

used in Writing, and the Stile to be used in Pleading."[13] Pope in fact alludes to the *Rhetoric* once in the *Iliad* preface and three times in the notes he published along with his version of the *Odyssey*, but it must be admitted that in none of these instances does he specifically mention Aristotle's distinction. Even when Pope comes to translate the lines about Nireus, he recalls with reverence the remarks made by Demetrius (in his *Peri Hermē-neias*, or *On Style*) on this passage, but he does not mention the *Rhetoric*, the entire third book of which was a major source of the *Peri Hermēneias* and a work that Demetrius himself cites several times.

It is conceivable, however, that even if Pope was aware of Aristotle's distinction, he might not have wanted to draw too much attention to it because of its possibly primitivistic implications. Pope certainly knew that the Homeric poems had at some point been sung, for in *An Essay on the Life, Writings, and Learning of Homer*—which Pope himself revised—Thomas Parnell says that the *Iliad* and the *Odyssey*, although each was originally a unified whole, were brought from Asia to Greece "in several separate Pieces" which were called "Rhapsodies; from whence they who sung them had the Title of *Rhapsodists*."[14] In his *Essay on Homer's Battles* Pope comments that Homer repeats, more often than do his successors in the writing of epic, identical verses that describe the manner in which warriors are killed. The orally delivered nature of Homer's verse is implied in Pope's suggestion that Homer's audience "delighted in those reiterated Verses" and that such verses "have a certain antiquated Harmony not unlike the Burthen of a Song, which the Ear is willing to suffer, and as it were rests upon."[15] But to stress too

---

[13] *Aristotle's Treatise on Rhetoric Literally Translated with Hobbes' Analysis, Examination Questions and an Appendix Containing the Greek Definitions*, ed. Theodore Buckley (London: George Bell and Sons, 1890), p. 37. Hobbes does not mention Homer in his adaptation, in *A Brief of Rhetoric* III. xi, of Aristotle's distinction between the oral and the written styles, so that even if Pope had read Hobbes, he might not necessarily have associated the oral style with Homer.

[14] *TE*, 7:57.

[15] Ibid., 7:254.

often the orally-delivered—which was perhaps to imply the or-ally-*composed*—nature of the Homeric poems was to play di-rectly into the hands of the enemy, that is, of the Moderns. For in the later seventeenth and in the eighteenth century the con-ception of Homer as a singer or a group of singers was often associated with the theory that the poems were in reality a col-lection of disconnected and primitive songs that were eventually grouped arbitrarily under the names "Iliad" and "Odyssey." So, for example, the Abbé—who in Perrault's *Parallèle des Anciens et des Modernes* (1688-1696) represents the position of the Mod-erns—suggests that neither of the Homeric poems is a unified whole; both quite probably represent, he says, "Rhapsodies, which mean, in Greek, a collection [or "heap"] of various songs sewn loosely together."[16] In 1713 Henry Felton, questioning the au-thorship of the Homeric epics, writes, "I have argued hitherto for *Virgil*, and it will be no Wonder, that his poem should be more correct in the Rules of Writing, if that strange Opinion prevaileth, that *Homer* writ without any View or Design at all, that his poems are loose, independent Pieces tacked together, and were originally only so many *Songs* or *Ballads* upon the *Gods* and *Heroes*, and the *Siege of Troy*."[17]

Pope inherited and believed deeply in the classical and Ren-aissance view of Homer as expressed by Anthony Collins in his *Discourse of Free Thinking* (1713). In the *Iliad*, Collins writes, Homer displays a "Universal Knowledge of things" and the poem was designed "for Eternity, to please and instruct Mankind."[18] In his *Remarks Upon a Late Discourse of Freethinking*, a work published just two years before the appearance of the first volume of Pope's *Iliad*, Richard Bentley condescendingly responded to the views of Collins:

[16] "Rapsodies, qui signifie en Grec, un amas de plusieurs chansons cousuës ensemble"; the French is cited from the edition of H. R. Jauss and M. Imdahl (Munich: R. Baldwin, 1964), p. 292.

[17] Cited from *A Dissertation on Reading the Classics and Forming a Just Style*, 5th ed. (London, 1753), p. 19.

[18] *A Discourse of Free-Thinking Occasioned by the Rise and Growth of a Sect call'd Free-Thinkers* (London, 1713), p. 9.

[81]

Take my word for it, poor Homer, in those circumstances and early times, had never such aspiring thoughts. He wrote a sequel of Songs and Rhapsodies, to be sung by himself for small earnings and good cheer, at Festivals and other days of Merriment; the *Ilias* he made for the Men, the *Odysseis* for the other Sex. These loose Songs were not collected together in the form of an Epic Poem, till Pisistratus' time about 500 years later.[19]

One wonders, in the light of this complacent observation, about some of the possible implications of Bentley's notorious remark on Pope's *Iliad*. Could it be that one mustn't call it Homer because, in part, Pope's assumption about the unity of the poem—an assumption which breathes through the formal and elegantly turned lines and is evident everywhere in the preface and in the notes—was inimical to the profound historical insight of the great scholar? It is at any rate certainly understandable why Pope, in view of the primitivistic and derogatory connotations of the orally-delivered nature of the poems as expressed by Bentley, would not want to invoke in Homer's defense Aristotle's description of the oral style in *Rhetoric* III.12. Nor does Samuel Johnson in his defense of Pope's *Iliad* in the *Life of Pope* anywhere suggest that Virgil's or Pope's refinement upon the "mere nature" to be found in Homer can be explained in terms of the transformation into a written medium of poems that were originally designed for the ear rather than for the eye. It may well be that Johnson's hesitation to associate the Homeric poems with oral recitation is the direct result of his opposition to any theory which would suggest that the poems were not unified. Boswell, for example, reports that Johnson, in response to a remark that "Homer was made up of detached fragments," "denied this; observing, that you could not put a book of the Iliad out of its place; and he believed the same might be said of the Odyssey."[20]

Johnson's hesitation is understandable, for in the eighteenth century Homer was as controversial an author as the translator

[19] *Remarks upon a late Discourse of free-thinking* (London, 1713), p. 18.
[20] *The Journal of a Tour to the Hebrides* (London and Toronto: J. M. Dent & Sons, 1909), p. 128.

[82]

himself. The Greek poet was coming to be seen as either a natural genius who paid little attention to the confining rules of art, or as a crude primitive whose works possessed neither unity nor the intention to instruct. Even so coolly rational a voice as that of Joseph Addison could, in *Spectator* 160 (September 3, 1711), compare the genius of Homer to "a rich soil in a happy Climate, that produced a whole Wilderness of noble Plants rising in a thousand beautiful Landskips without any certain Order or Regularity." Addison contrasts this kind of genius to that characteristic of Plato, Aristotle, Cicero, Milton, and Francis Bacon. "This second Class of great Geniuses" he compares to "the same rich Soil under the same happy Climate, that has been laid out in Walks and Parterres, and cut into Shape and Beauty by the Skill of the Gardener."[21]

How very sensitive the issue of the quality of Homer's genius was in the early eighteenth century can be seen from Pope's quarrel with Mme. Dacier over the French scholar's angry objections to what she believed Pope had written in the *Iliad* preface. In that preface Pope used the very same garden metaphor as had Addison in order to describe Homer's style. "Our Author's Work," Pope says,

> is a Wild Paradise, where if we cannot see all the Beauties so distinctly as in an order'd Garden, it is only because the Number of them is infinitely greater. 'Tis like a copious Nursery which contains the Seeds and first Productions of every Kind, out of which those who follow'd him have but selected some particular Plants, each according to his Fancy, to cultivate and beautify. If some things are too luxuriant, it is owing to the Richness of the Soil; and if others are not arriv'd to Perfection or Maturity, it is only because they are over-run and opprest by those of a stronger Nature.[22]

Since Mme. Dacier, as she herself admits, knew no English, she never in fact read either Pope's translation or his preface. She should have welcomed Pope as a comrade in arms against the

[21] *Spectator*, ed. Bond, 2:129.
[22] *TE*, 7:3.

anti-Homeric slurs of the Moderns. But instead she reacted impulsively and defensively, not to what Pope had in fact written, but to what she *thought* he had written, in the *Iliad* preface. Pope's comparison of the *Iliad* to a "wild Paradise," which is cited above, is paraphrased as follows in Mme. Dacier's *Reflexions sur la première partie de la préface de M. Pope* (1719):

> Selon Mr. Pope, le poeme d'Homere est un amas confus de beautez, qui n'ont ni ordre ni symmetrie. Un plant, ou l'on ne trouve que des semences, & rien de parfait ni de formé.[23]

> (According to Mr. Pope, Homer's poem is a chaotic heap of beauties, which possesses neither order nor symmetry. A plant, where one finds only seeds, and nothing perfect or fully grown.)

Pope, Mme. Dacier wrongfully asserts, believes that the *Iliad* is an "amas confus de beautez." The word "amas" recalls Perrault's description of the Homeric poems as "a collection [amas] of various songs sewn loosely together." That Mme. Dacier would jump to the conclusion that Pope, simply because he compares the *Iliad* to a "wild Paradise" as opposed to an "order'd Garden," has joined the ranks of the Moderns suggests how volatile an issue was Homer's alleged primitivism in the famous war between the Ancients and the Moderns. In fact, when taken in the context of English statements about gardens in the early eighteenth century, Pope's remarks may be seen as advocating not wildness itself, but a very contrived and "artificial Rudeness,"[24] as Addison put it, which was seen as a healthy alternative to the more rigidly geometric French garden such as that at Versailles. The metaphor was useful to Pope in the context of his defense of Homer in the *Iliad* preface because he felt it would help to counter the charges of the Moderns, from Scaliger through Perrault, who championed Virgil because of the Latin poet's allegedly more meticulous style; if Homer's genius was less meticulous, Pope's metaphor suggests, it was also more abundant and

---

[23] Mme. Dacier published her remarks at the end of vol. III of her translation of the *Iliad*, second edition, unpaginated. This passage is cited from *TE*, 10:449.
[24] *Spectator* 414 (June 25, 1712), cited from Bond, 3:551.

fruitful. These, then, are some of the reasons why Pope may have been reluctant to defend Homer's alleged inexactness on the grounds that such a quality is only to be expected in poems that are designed to be heard rather than read. But regardless of whether Pope was aware of Aristotle's description of the relative degrees of literary finish to be expected from the oral and the written styles, his awareness of the *principle* of the distinction is implied in his perceptive remark that *"Homer* makes us Hearers, and *Virgil* leaves us Readers"[25]; and it is evident everywhere in the translation itself.

VIRGIL, POPE, AND THE HOMERIC EPITHET

In attempting to adapt Homer's "skiagraphic" style to a written medium, Pope as a translator faced many of the same problems as had Virgil in the Roman poet's attempt to simulate, in a written medium, Homer's oral style. One of the chief problems Virgil faced in rejuvenating Homeric epic was how to retain the skiagraphic effect of Homer's style while writing a poem that he knew would be read with the closest attention to detail. The skiagraphic effect Virgil achieved, in part, through his choice of the stately dactylic hexameter of Homer. He had also to face the problem of what could be done with Homer's formulaic phrases and recurring epithets, epithets which at times have little relevance to the narrative context in which they appear. Such an "inexact" quality of style, when heard at a large public gathering—that is, when experienced "at a distance"—might well go unnoticed. But when *read*, that is, when experienced by both the ear *and* the eye, they might well appear awkward and crude. The Homeric phrase ὑγρὰ κέλευθα ("watery path"), for example, is intended to be experienced "at a distance"; it might well not have been perceived as a metaphor by the Homeric audience but rather, as Milman Parry suggests, as a phrase synonymous with "the sea."[26] Once the phrase becomes written,

---

[25] *TE,* 7:8.

[26] "Were ὑγρὰ κέλευθα found once in Greek epic," Parry writes, "we might perhaps give the phrase all its force, but by the time one has read the *Iliad* and

however, it is subject to close scrutiny, and, after repeated readings, it may come to appear colorless and mechanical, unless it is either varied or subtly qualified by the narrative context.

Virgil, then, in attempting to transform Homer's oral style into a written style that would be subject to the scrutiny of the eye, will often turn the Homeric epithet into a descriptive adjective. Virgil's reference to Dido as *infelix Dido*, for example, would have appeared at first, to the Roman reader whose expectations with regard to epic had been shaped by his experience with

---

Odyssey one has met the phrase four more times" ("The Traditional Metaphor in Homer," *The Making of Homeric Verse*, ed. A. Parry [London: Oxford University Press, 1971], p. 371). The notion that the eye demands greater clarity and exactness than does the ear is ancient (see Trimpi, "The Meaning of Horace's *Ut Pictura Poesis*," pp. 21-25). It is a notion which is, in fact, a basis for Aristotle's distinction between the relative degrees of accuracy or refinement to be expected from the oral and the written styles: the written style is the most refined of rhetorical styles because it is subject to the scrutiny of the eye. It is for this reason that Aristotle says in *Poetics* XXIV that the "astonishing" (τὸ θαυμαστόν) can be more easily incorporated into epic than into tragedy, since in epic "we cannot actually see the person who is performing the action. Because the incidents in the pursuit of Hector would show themselves to be absurd if they were put on the stage—the Achaeans standing there, not pursuing him, and (Achilles) signaling to them to stand back—whereas in the epic we do not notice this" (*Aristotle's Poetics: The Argument*, trans. G. F. Else [Cambridge: Harvard University Press, 1967], p. 622). Horace recalls this observation in the *Ars Poetica* when he suggests that, in the drama, astonishing events should be narrated rather than acted, since "less vividly is the mind stirred by what finds entrance through the ears than by what is brought before the trusty eyes, and what the spectator can see for himself. . . . You will not bring upon the stage what should be performed behind the scenes, and you will keep much from our eyes, which an actor's ready tongue will narrate anon in our presence; so that Medea is not to butcher her boys before the people, nor impious Atreus cook human flesh upon the stage, nor Procne be turned into a bird, Cadmus into a snake. Whatever you thus show me, I discredit and abhor" (ll. 180-188, *Satires, Epistles, and Ars Poetica*, trans. Fairclough). Dio Chrysostom, in his *Twelfth, or Olympic Discourse*, has an imaginary Phidias similarly argue that while it was easy for Homer to describe the astonishing acts performed by Zeus, in the art of sculpture such a depiction would be "absolutely impossible" since the viewer could examine the work of art "with his eyes from close at hand and in full view," and the eyes "are harder to convince and demand greater clearness" than do the ears (*Discourses*, trans. J. W. Cohoon, 5 vols., LCL [London and Cambridge, Mass.: William Heinemann and Harvard University Press, 1939], 2:83). I am indebted to Trimpi's article for these references.

Homer, to be no more specific than the typical Homeric epithet. Virgil describes Dido as *infelix* throughout Books I and IV.[27] She is referred to as *infelix* at the conclusion of the first book; the love-sick queen is begging Aeneas, who has just arrived in Carthage, to tell her about the famous events surrounding the fall of Troy:

> nec non et vario noctem sermone trahebat
> infelix Dido longumque bibebat amorem,
> multa super Priamo rogitans, super Hectore multa;
> nunc quibus Aurorae venisset filius armis,
> nunc quales Diomedis equi, nunc quantus Achilles.

(Unhappy Dido, too, with varied talk prolonged the night and drank deep draughts of love, asking much of Priam, of Hector much; now of the armor wherein the son of Aurora came; now of the wondrous steeds of Diomedes; now of giant Achilles.)

[ll. 748-752]

At the beginning of the fourth book Dido is described by Virgil as *infelix*:

> uritur infelix Dido totaque vagatur
> urbe furens, . . .

(Unhappy Dido burns, and all through the city wanders in a frenzy, . . .)

[ll. 68-69]

Virgil's reader would soon have to come to see that in both these instances the "epithet" *infelix* is far from superfluous; as a descriptive adjective *infelix* has great psychological power, for Dido is *infelix* specifically because she is about to be betrayed in love and will as a result soon take her own life.

And so it is with many of Virgil's imitations of Homer's repetitions. In the first four books of the *Aeneid* Virgil portrays the

---

[27] Aside from the instances in *Aeneid* I.749 and IV.68 cited below, Virgil refers to Dido as *infelix* in *Aeneid* I.712 and IV.450 and 529.

LANGUAGE

recently founded, now flourishing city of Carthage as an ex-
emplum for the exiled Trojans. As the Phoenicians had endured
hardships before founding Carthage, so must Aeneas and his
men steel themselves against temptation, obey the dictates of
fate, and go on to Italy in order to found Rome. One of the
devices Virgil uses in order to suggest this analogy between the
founding of Carthage and the imminent founding of Rome is
verbal repetition, but verbal repetition subtly qualified—unlike
many of Homer's—by narrative context. Both the Trojans and
the Phoenicians, for example, are described in *Aeneid* I as *iactati*,
harassed by forces beyond their control. Aeneas is *multum . . .
et terris iactatus et alto* ("much buffeted on sea and land," l. 3);
the Phoenicians, before founding Carthage, had been *iactati un-
dis et turbine* ("tossed by waves and whirlwind," l. 442). Virgil
first mentions Carthage with the following phrase: *urbs antiqua
fuit* ("there was an ancient city," *Aeneid* I.12); the almost iden-
tical phrase, appearing in precisely the same position in the line,
is used by Virgil in Aeneas' description of the fall of Troy: *urbs
antiqua ruit* ("the ancient city falls," *Aeneid* II.363).[28]

Like Virgil, Pope is clearly aware of the skiagraphic effect of
Homer's style. In the *Iliad* preface he says that Homer's "Expres-
sion is like the colouring of some great Masters, which discovers
itself to be laid on boldly, and executed with rapidity." In his
commentary upon the simile in Book V of the *Iliad* in which
Homer compares the fury of Diomedes' onslaught against the
Trojans to a tumultuous river, Pope advises the reader that he
should not expect the development of a Homeric simile to cor-
respond in every detail to the original point of comparison:

> We must not expect from *Homer* those minute resemblances
> in every Branch of a Comparison, which are the pride of mod-
> ern Similes. If that which one may call the main Action of it,

[28] The Latin is cited from *P. Virgilii Maronis Opera*, ed. F. A. Hirtzel (1900;
reprint ed. Oxford: Clarendon Press, 1966). The translation is adapted from that
of H. Rushton Fairclough, *Virgil: Eclogues, Georgics, Aeneid I-VI*, LCL (1916;
reprint ed. Cambridge, Mass. and London: Harvard University Press and William
Heinemann, 1965).

or the principal Point of Likeness, be preserv'd; he affects, as to the rest, rather to present the Mind with a great Image, than to fix it down to an exact one. He is sure to make a fine Picture in the whole, without drudging on the under Parts: like those free Painters who (one would think) had only made here and there a few very significant Strokes, that give Form and Spirit to all the Piece.[29]

And to take just one more example out of many, in his commentary on Book III.47ff. Pope defends Homer against what Scaliger had perceived as a redundancy in one of Homer's general descriptions: "It must be observ'd in general," Pope writes, "that *little Exactnesses* are what we should not look for in *Homer*; the Genius of his Age was too incorrect, and his own too fiery to regard them."[30]

On the question of how to render Homer's recurring epithets, Pope's response is analogous to Virgil's. "Upon the whole," Pope writes in the *Iliad* preface,

> it will be necessary to avoid that perpetual Repetition of the same Epithets which we find in *Homer*, and which, tho' it might be accommodated to the Ear of those Times, is by no means so to ours: But one may wait for Opportunities of placing them, where they derive an additional Beauty from the Occasions on which they are employed; and in doing this properly, a Translator may at once shew his Fancy and his Judgment.[31]

At the end of the first book Pope puts his theory into practice. Homer is describing the scene on Olympus when Hephaestus tries to avert a potentially dangerous domestic squabble between Zeus and Hera. Hephaestus makes a brief speech to Hera pleading with her to obey the commands of the awesome father of gods and men and he then passes around a bowl of nectar—the "Reconciler Bowl," as Dryden put it in his translation of the

[29] *TE*, 7:272.
[30] Ibid., 7:191.
[31] Ibid., 7:20.

arms (θεὰ λευκώλενος), smiled at him," Homer says, "and, smiling, she accepted the cup from her son's hands" (ll. 595-596). Here is Pope's translation of these lines:

> He [Vulcan] said, and to her Hands the Goblet heav'd,
> Which, with a Smile, the white-arm'd Queen receiv'd.
>
> [ll. 766-777]

And here is how the poet explains his retaining the epithet in this particular context:

> The Epithet λευκώλενος, or *white-arm'd*, is used by *Homer* several times before in this Book. This was the first Passage where it could be introduced with any Ease or Grace, because the Action she is here describ'd in, of extending her Arm to the Cup, gives it an occasion of displaying its Beauties, and in a manner demands the Epithet.[32]

By omitting this particular epithet as well as others in contexts in which their inclusion would appear superfluous or awkward, Pope was opening himself up to the charge that he was inappropriately modernizing Homer. But Pope was not the first great Homerophile to be so accused.

It is worth observing that Virgil's early detractors speak of his style in terms that are strikingly similar to the ways in which the style of Pope's Homer will be criticized. Suetonius, for example, writes in his *Life of Virgil* (44) that a certain Marcus Vipsanius called Virgil "the inventor of a new kind of affected language" (*novae cacozeliae reportorem*);[33] Quintilian defines *cacozelia* as "perverse affectation" (*Inst. Orat.* VIII.56-57), a charge that would frequently be leveled at the style of Pope's *Iliad*. Aulus Gellius, comparing in his *Attic Nights* Virgil's adaptation of a Homeric line with the original, says "that of Homer seems to be simpler and more natural, that of Virgil more modern (νεωτερικώτερος)" (XIII.xxvii.3). Later in the same work Gellius recalls Favorinus' disapproval of Virgil's adaptation of some lines

---

[32] Ibid., 7:124.

[33] *Suetonius*, trans. J. C. Rolfe, 2 vols., LCL (Cambridge, Mass. and London: Harvard University Press and William Heinemann, 1914), 1:480-481.

of Pindar which describe the eruption of Mt. Etna. "Where Pindar has more closely followed the truth and has given us a realistic description of what actually happened there, and what he saw with his own eyes," Gellius says, "Virgil labors to find grand and sonorous words" (*in strepitu sonituque verborum conquirando laborat*, XVII.x.11-12).[34] And Macrobius, after comparing with their originals Virgil's translations of particular lines from Homer, observes that the Greek poet "has expressed the whole action in a few words" whereas Virgil "has used a number of clauses to say the same thing" (*Saturnalia* 5.3.1-2).[35]

ANTIQUATED WORDS AND HOMER'S REPETITIONS

Although similar criticisms were to be made of Pope's Homer—and, since the translator knew the works of the ancient writers mentioned above, he could well have anticipated such criticisms—it must be stressed that Pope realized that too much elegant variation would make his translation appear inappropriately modern. In order, therefore, to preserve what he felt was the poem's antique simplicity, Pope adhered to the two following stylistic principles: first, he would make use of old words, and second, he would try to translate as accurately as possible, even if this meant preserving certain "archaic" qualities of style that might seem alien to contemporary English.

"Perhaps the Mixture of some *Graecisms* and old Words after the manner of *Milton*, if done without too much Affectation," Pope writes in the *Iliad* preface, "might not have an ill Effect in a Version of this particular Work, which most of any other seems to require a venerable *Antique* Cast."[36] This was a strategy that

[34] *The Attic Nights of Aulus Gellius*, trans. J. C. Rolfe, 3 vols., LCL (Cambridge, Mass. and London: Harvard University Press and William Heinemann, 1927), 2:504-505 and 3:242-243.

[35] *Macrobius: The Saturnalia*, trans. with intro. and notes by Percival Vaughan Davies (New York and London: Columbia University Press, 1969), p. 290. For the preceding citations from Macrobius, Aulus Gellius, and Suetonius I am indebted to Wesley Trimpi, "Horace's 'Ut Pictura Poesis,' " p. 31 n. 3.

[36] *TE*, 7:19.

Pope followed when he began to translate Homer, and he reaffirmed it when the task was finally completed. For in the postscript (1726) to his *Odyssey* Pope writes:

> A just and moderate mixture of old words may have an effect like the working old Abbey stones into a building, which I have sometimes seen to give a kind of venerable air. . . . In reading a style judiciously antiquated, one finds a pleasure not unlike that of travelling on an old *Roman* way.[37]

In his use of a diction that is at times "judiciously antiquated," Pope is placing himself in a long tradition of classical and neoclassical stylistic criticism. His remarks in the *Iliad* preface may well be an echo of Addison's comments, in *Spectator* 285 (June 26, 1712), upon Milton's style in *Paradise Lost*. Milton, Addison writes, "had infused a great many *Latinisms*, as well as *Hebraisms*, into the Language of his Poem" and he has also revived "old Words," a device "which . . . makes his Poem appear the more venerable, and gives it a greater Air of Antiquity."[38] To achieve this illusion of venerability, Pope frequently makes use of words and phrases, themselves often consciously antiquated, culled from the epic diction bequeathed to him by Spenser, Milton, and Dryden, his famous predecessors in the writing of English epic.

But Pope wanted to avoid using archaisms to an extreme. It was this extreme that he attacked two years before he wrote the *Iliad* preface. On June 10, 1713, Pope contributed a satirical paper to the *Guardian* (No. 78) entitled "A Receipt to Make An Epick Poem." After recommending the sort of "Fable," the "Manners," the "Descriptions," and the "Machines" suitable to an epic poem, Pope goes on to discuss the "Language" or "Diction":

> *Here it will do well to be an Imitator of* Milton, *for you'll find it easier to imitate him in this than any thing else.* Hebraisms and Graecisms *are to be found in him, without the*

[37] Ibid., 10:390.
[38] *Spectator*, ed. Bond, 3:12-13.

[92]

trouble of Learning the Languages. I knew a Painter, who (like our Poet) had no Genius, make his Dawbings be thought Originals *by setting them in the* Smoak: *You may in the same manner give the venerable Air of Antiquity to your Piece, by darkening it up and down with* Old English. *With this you may be easily furnished upon any Occasion, by the Dictionary commonly Printed at the end of* Chaucer.[39]

Such an "ostentatious display of simplicity," in the words of Sir Joshua Reynolds (*Eighth Discourse*), was inimical to the stylistic tradition of Ben Jonson and John Dryden to which Pope was heir.[40]

[39] *The Prose Works of Alexander Pope*, ed. Norman Ault (Oxford: Basil Blackwell, 1936), 1:120.

[40] Ben Jonson disapproved of a consciously antiquated diction, for in the *Discoveries* (published in 1640) he writes that "*Spenser*, in affecting the Ancients, writ no Language" (*The Works of Ben Jonson*, ed. C. H. Herford and Percy and Evelyn Simpson, 11 vols. [Oxford: Clarendon Press, 1925-1952], 8:618). Dryden was skeptical about Milton's reviving of old words. In the preface to *Sylvae* (1685) Dryden writes that "Milton's *Paradise Lost* is admirable; but am I therefore bound to maintain that there are no flats amongst his elevations? . . . Cannot I admire the height of his invention, and the strength of his expression, without defending his antiquated words, and the perpetual harshness of their sound?" (*Of Dramatic Poesy and Other Critical Essays*, ed. Watson, 2:32). In his preface to *Don Sebastian* (1690) Dryden discusses the style of this particular play and defends his limited use of antiquated words by contrasting his own example with that of Milton: "here and there some old words are sprinkled which, for their significance and sound, deserved not to be antiquated; such as we find in Sallust among the Roman authors, and in Milton's *Paradise* amongst ours; though perhaps the latter, instead of sprinkling, has dealt them with too free a hand, even sometimes to the obscuring of his sense" (2:46). In *A Discourse Concerning Satire* (1693) Dryden is less critical of Milton's practice (2:150), but in his "Postscript to the Reader" which he appended to his *Aeneis* (1697) Dryden appears to have returned to his earlier position, for he criticizes those who are "for raking in Chaucer (our English Ennius) for antiquated words, which are never to be revived, but when sound and significancy is wanting in the present language" (2:259). And in his final critical preface (1700) Dryden defends his modernization of Chaucer's language, in the tales he translated in *Fables Ancient and Modern*, against those who think he "ought not to have translated Chaucer into English" because "there is a certain veneration due to his old language; and that it is little less than profanation and sacrilege to alter it. . . . When an ancient word, for its sound and significancy, deserves to be revived, I have that reasonable

[93]

In writing in a style that was occasionally antiquated, but antiquated in a "judicious" manner, Pope, then, was reiterating many of the most enduring principles of neoclassical stylistic criticism. And he was also following the *via media* recommended by that most reasonable of classical critics, Quintilian. Since "there is a special dignity conferred by antiquity," Quintilian says, "old words . . . give our style a venerable and majestic air: this is a form of ornament of which Virgil has made unique use. . . . But we must not over-do it, and such words must not be dragged out from the deepest darkness of the past" (*ex ultimis tenebris repetenda*, *Inst. Orat.* VIII.iii.24-25).[41] This is an excellent summary of Pope's strategy in translating Homer: in his own poetic tradition he will reach back as far as Spenser and borrow from him words and phrases in order to simulate "the Simplicity of the old Father of Poetry."[42] And so, for example, for the Homeric phrase "of whirling Xanthos" (ξάνθου δινήεντος, *Iliad* XIV.434), Pope writes "where gentle *Xanthos* rolls his easy Tyde" (*Iliad* XIV.507); here Pope's translation echoes the first line—"in ev'ry Town, where *Thamis* rolls his Tyde"[43]—from his own Spenserian imitation, "The Alley." But

---

veneration for antiquity to restore it. All beyond this is superstition" (2:287-288). In his *Eighth Discourse* (1778), Sir Joshua Reynolds, in discussing Poussin's abhorrence of "that affectation and that want of simplicity, which he observed in his countrymen," suggests that the great French painter may at times have fallen into "the contrary extreme." Reynolds writes that "when simplicity, instead of being a corrector, seems to set up for herself; that is, when an artist seems to value himself solely upon this quality; such an ostentatious display of simplicity becomes then as disagreeable and nauseous as any other kind of affectation" (*Discourses on Art*, ed. Robert R. Wark [London: Collier Books, 1969], p. 134). Samuel Johnson recalls Ben Jonson's criticism of Spenser's style when, in the *Life of Milton*, he writes that Milton "had formed his style by a perverse and pedantick principle. He was desirous to use English words with a foreign idiom. . . . Of him, at last, may be said what Jonson says of Spenser, that he wrote no language" (*Lives of the English Poets*, 1:190-191).

[41] *The Institutio Oratoria of Quintilian*, trans. H. E. Butler, 4 vols., LCL (1921-1922; reprint ed. London and Cambridge: William Heinemann and Harvard University Press, 1953), 3:224-225.

[42] *TE*, 8:255.

[43] *TE*, 6 (*Minor Poems*):43.

[94]

as far as reviving the diction of Chaucer is concerned, Pope did not deviate from the position he took in *Guardian* 78; this he would no doubt have regarded, following Quintilian, as dragging words and phrases "from the deepest darkness of the past."

Just as Pope wished to take a *via media* with regard to the revival of antiquated words, so he wished to pursue this same path with regard to his retaining the peculiarities of Homer's style. Pope was in fact more interested in the potentialities of a literal translation of Homer than has commonly been supposed, for in the *Iliad* preface he asserts that a "rash Paraphrase" may

> lose the Spirit of an Ancient, by deviating into the modern Manners of Expression. If there be sometimes a *Darkness*, there is often a *Light* in Antiquity, which nothing better preserves than a Version almost literal.[44]

Insufficient literalness is in fact a major complaint Pope levels against his three most important English predecessors in the field of Homeric translation. Chapman's Homer is more a "loose and rambling . . . Paraphrase" than a true translation.[45] Hobbes offers "a correct Explanation of the Sense in general, but for Particulars and Circumstances he continually lopps them, and often omits the most beautiful"; Hobbes's version is wrongly esteemed "a close translation."[46] For Dryden's efforts at translating the first book of the *Iliad* and "The Last Parting of Hector and Andromache" Pope has only the highest praise, but his praise is subject to the following qualification: Dryden, according to Pope, has not "in some Places truly interpreted the Sense, or preserved the Antiquities."[47] When Pope comes to translate the scene between Hector and Andromache in Book VI, he writes in his commentary:

> Mr *Dryden* has formerly translated this admirable Episode, and with so much Success, as to leave me at least no hopes of

[44] Ibid., 7:17.
[45] Ibid., 7:21.
[46] Ibid., 7:21-22.
[47] Ibid., 7:22.

improving or equalling it. The utmost I can pretend is to have avoided a few modern Phrases and Deviations from the Original, which have escaped that great Man.[48]

It is interesting to observe in contrast that Dryden—who, as a Homeric translator, can be described as a Modern in comparison with Pope—felt he had translated the Hector and Andromache episode "perhaps too literally."[49]

With regard to the question of whether or not a translator should retain Homer's repetitions, therefore, Pope writes:

> I hope it is not impossible to have such a Regard to these, as neither to lose so known a Mark of the Author on the one hand, nor to offend the Reader too much on the other . . . ; but it is a Question whether a profess'd Translator be authoriz'd to omit any.[50]

He elaborates his position further when, in his commentary upon *Iliad* XIX.197ff., he quotes with approval the following remarks from Boivin's *Apologie d'Homère et Bouclier d'Achille* (1715):

> That useless Nicety . . . of avoiding every Repetition which the Delicacy of later Times has introduced, was not known to the first Ages of Antiquity: The Books of *Moses* abound with them. Far from condemning their frequent Use in the most ancient of Poets, we should look upon them as the certain Character of the Age in which he liv'd: They spoke so in his Time, and to have spoken otherwise had been a Fault. And indeed nothing is in itself so contrary to the true Sublime, as that painful and frivolous Exactness, with which we avoid to make use of a proper Word because it was us'd before.
>
> It was from two Principles equally true, that among several People, and in several Ages, two Practices entirely different took their Rise. *Moses, Homer,* and the Writers of the first

---

[48] Ibid., 7:349.

[49] Preface to *Examen Poeticum: Being the Third Part of Miscellany Poems* (1693), cited from *Of Dramatic Poesy and Other Critical Essays,* ed. Watson, 2:166.

[50] *TE,* 7:20.

Times, had found that Repetitions of the same Words recall'd the Ideas of Things, imprinted them much more strongly, and render'd the Discourse more intelligible. Upon this Principle, the Custom of repeating Words, Phrases, and even entire Speeches, insensibly establish'd itself both in Prose and Poetry, especially in Narrations.

The Writers who succeeded them observ'd, even from *Homer* himself, that the greatest Beauty of Style consisted in Variety. This they made their Principle: They therefore avoided Repetitions of Words, and still more of whole Sentences; they endeavour'd to vary their Transitions; and found out new Turns and Manners of expressing the same Things.

Either of these Practices is good, but the Excess of either is vicious: We should neither on the one hand, thro' a Love of Simplicity and Clearness, continually repeat the same Words, Phrases, or Discourses; nor on the other, for the Pleasure of Variety, fall into a childish Affectation of expressing every thing twenty different Ways, tho' it be never so natural and common.

Nothing so much cools the Warmth of a Piece or puts out the Fire of Poetry, as that perpetual Care to vary incessantly even in the smallest Circumstances. In this, as in many other Points, *Homer* has despis'd the ungrateful Labour of too scrupulous a Nicety.[51]

There are, it is true, primitivistic connotations to Boivin's opposing the simplicity of "the first Ages of Antiquity" to the "delicacy of later Times"; the French critic does not describe this opposition in the more neutral terms of Aristotle's distinction between the simpler and more direct oral style and the more meticulous written style. But those who charge the style of Pope's *Iliad* with excessive prettiness should nevertheless read this passage with care, for it strongly suggests that the translator was well aware of the dangers of such modern affectation. Nor was Pope the only Augustan figure who held such views. Boivin's description of the style of "the Writers of the first Times" was

[51] Ibid., 8:379-380.

LANGUAGE

to be echoed in a work by Pope's great friend and chief aid in helping him to find subscribers for the *Iliad* translation. In *Gulliver's Travels* Jonathan Swift suggests that one measure of the superior spiritual strength of the Houyhnhnms is the simplicity and directness of their language, which is contrasted, it is implied, to the more decadent fastidiousness of the language of Gulliver. "It put me to the Pains of many Circumlocutions," Gulliver says of the problems he experienced in trying to communicate with the Houyhnhnms, "to give my Master a right Idea of what I spoke; for their Language doth not abound in Variety of Words, because their Wants and Passions are fewer than among us."[52] For both Swift and Pope, an inappropriate degree of fussiness in the use of language implies spiritual decay.

So that while Pope does employ the modern principle of variety in rendering Homer's repetitions of words, phrases, and speeches, he also attempts to affect the style of "the first Ages of Antiquity" by preserving such repetitions wherever they may not "offend the Reader too much." At one point in his notes, for example, Pope feels compelled to excuse his literal translation of a compound epithet. "Perhaps this Line is translated too close to the Letter," he writes, "and the Epithets might have been omitted. But there are some Traits and Particularities of this Nature, which methinks preserve to the Reader the Air of *Homer*."[53] In accordance with this principle Pope will at times even retain Homer's identically repeated set speeches. And he will often translate literally many of Homer's formulaic phrases. Pope's "liquid Road" (*Iliad* I.409), for example, is a literal translation of Homer's formulaic ὑγρὰ κέλευθα (*Iliad* I.312); and in his *Odyssey* Pope translates this same Homeric phrase (*Odyssey* IV.842, IX.252), with a similar degree of literalness, as "the wat'ry plain" (*Odyssey* IV.1099) and "the wat'ry way" (*Odyssey* IX.300). So Pope literally translates the Homeric formulaic phrase "starry sky" (οὐρανῷ ἀστερόεντι, *Iliad* IV.44; οὐρανοῦ ἀστερόεν-

[52] Cited from Part IV, Chapter IV, *Gulliver's Travels*, 1726, ed. Herbert Davis with an intro. by Harold Williams (1941; reprint ed. Oxford: Basil Blackwell, 1965), p. 242.
[53] *TE*, 7:195.

[98]

τος, *Iliad* V.769, VIII.46, XIX.130) as "starry Skies" (*Iliad* IV.66), "starry Poles" (*Iliad* V.959), "starry Sky" (*Iliad* VIII.56), and "starry Heav'n" (*Iliad* XIX.130). Where Pope does not render Homer's stock phrases literally, he will often substitute for a given Homeric phrase a corresponding phrase either of his own invention or culled from the contemporary epic diction bequeathed to him chiefly by Spenser, Milton, and Dryden. Characteristic of this second method is the phrase "the Vault of Stars" (*Iliad* VI.134) which Pope uses to translate the previously discussed formulaic οὐρανοῦ ἀστερόεντος (*Iliad* VI.108). Pope translates the phrase εἰς ἅλα ("into the salt," metonymy for "into the sea," *Iliad* I.314) as "briny Wave" (*Iliad* I.412); and for the recurring phrase ὀλέθρου πείραθ᾽ ("the brink of destruction [or death]," *Iliad* VI.143) Pope writes "the dark Gates of Death" (*Iliad* VI.178). All of these phrases—"liquid Road," "wat'ry Way," "starry Sky," "briny Wave," "the dark Gates of Death"— attempt to create the illusion, in a written medium, of Homer's unmannered and spontaneous skiagraphic boldness.

It is largely because of his use of this kind of predictable diction in his *Iliad* that many of Pope's detractors have criticized both the translation and its influence. Coleridge, pointing to Pope's use of such a diction in his translation of Homer's moonlight simile at the end of *Iliad* VIII, says that he is not alone in regarding Pope's Homeric translations as "the main source of our pseudo-poetic diction."[54] Coleridge's remarks were to become a commonplace. A little more than a decade later Robert Southey would write that "Pope's Homer has done more than . . . all other books, towards the corruption of our poetry."[55] Coleridge implies that the alleged mannerisms are examples of the translator's meticulous refinement of Homer's style. This is, however, only partially true; as I have tried to show, Pope's strategy for transforming a poem originally designed for the ear into a poem which he knew would have to bear the close scrutiny of the eye

[54] *Biog. Lit.*, 1:26.
[55] From a letter dated March 26, 1831, and cited from *The Correspondence of Robert Southey with Caroline Bowles*, ed. Edward Dowden (Dublin: Hodges, Figgis, & Co., 1881), p. 224.

as well as the ear did indeed demand that he make use of precisely the same sort of *diligentia* which Virgil employed in his adaptation of Homer. But Pope was very much on his guard against indulging in what Boivin called "the modern Principle of Variety," a principle to which he felt his great poetic model and predecessor in the field of Homeric translation, John Dryden, too often adhered. And so Pope tried to "preserve the Antiquities" and to maintain as many of Homer's repetitions and epithets—in short, his stock phrases—as good English would allow. It is one of the ironies of literary history that the alleged mannerisms of Pope's Homer are usually attributed to the translator's refinement of Homer's style; for much of the diction to which critics such as Coleridge object is the direct result of Pope's attempt to avoid what had come to be viewed in the early eighteenth century as the mannered overrefinement, the stylistic fussiness, of the modern age.

CHAPTER FIVE

Pope's *Iliad* and the Longinian Tradition

Thee, bold *Longinus*! all the Nine inspire,
And bless *their Critick* with a *Poet's Fire.*
An ardent *Judge*, who Zealous in his Trust,
With *Warmth* gives Sentence, yet is always *Just*;
Whose *own Example* strengthens all his Laws,
And *Is himself* that great *Sublime* he draws.
[*Essay on Criticism*, ll. 675-680]

These lines about Longinus were written several years before the publication of the first volume of Pope's *Iliad* in 1715. In his treatise *On the Sublime* Longinus discusses the various means by which an author can achieve an elevated style, and one of these means is through what he calls the "variation of person," which will "produce the effect of strong emotion and rapid change of tone" (*Peri Hypsous* 27.3).[1] Pope in this section of the *Essay on Criticism* has been addressing the reader and describing to him the methods and distinctive contributions of ancient critics such as Aristotle ("The mighty *Stagyrite* first left the Shore, / Spread all his Sails, and durst the Deeps explore," ll. 645-646), Horace ("*Horace* still charms with graceful Negligence," l. 653), Dionysius of Halicarnassus ("See *Dionysius Homer*'s Thoughts refine," l. 665), and Quintilian ("In grave *Quintilian*'s copious Work we find / The justest *Rules*, and clearest *Method* join'd,"

---

[1] *"Longinus" on Sublimity*, trans. D. A. Russell (Oxford: Clarendon Press, 1965), p. 34.

ll. 669-670). When Pope comes to discuss Longinus, the voice suddenly switches from the third person singular to the vocative and the poet addresses the great critic directly:

> Thee, bold Longinus! all the Nine inspire,
> And bless *their Critick* with a *Poet's Fire.*
> [ll. 675-676]

That quality Pope praises in Longinus is the ancient critic's capacity to realize, through his style and through the presence which informs the style, the quality of sublimity which is the subject of the treatise itself. In the lines quoted above, by means particularly of the sudden—and therefore sublime and passionate—shift to the vocative, Pope pays homage to Longinus by not only praising the critic but by doing so in a Longinian manner. The style of Longinus is as sublime as his subject, which is sublimity; and Pope's lines about Longinus are themselves an attempt to realize, and not merely to describe, Longinian sublimity.

The author to whom Longinus alludes most often for examples of elevated writing is Homer, and the work of Homer to which he most often alludes is the *Iliad.* It was only natural, then, that Pope, in attempting to render Homer's *Iliad* into an appropriately elevated English style, would turn to Longinus' comments. Just as many readers have not been aware of Pope's appreciation of the skiagraphic effect of Homer's style and of the ways in which the Augustan poet attempts to reproduce this effect in English, so they have not been sufficiently aware of the Longinian influence upon Pope's translation. Pope "made Homer graceful," Samuel Johnson observed, "but lost him some of his sublimity."[2] Johnson's remark is understandable, but it is misleading if we then conclude that it was not Pope's intention to reproduce as much of Homer's sublimity as an English poetic translation could possibly achieve. For Johnson said that *some*—by no means *all*—of Homer's sublimity was lost when the Greek hexameters were turned into English heroic couplets.

With regard to his capacity to understand the nature of Ho-

---

[2] *Lives of the Poets,* 3:223.

meric sublimity, Pope was in fact in a unique position as a Homeric translator, for no poetic translator had ever before made such abundant use of Longinus' treatise *On the Sublime*. One of the most revealing ways, therefore, to distinguish the style of Pope's version from that of his most daunting predecessor, George Chapman, is to observe the manner in which Pope's style attempts to meet the criteria of Longinian elevation, while Chapman's style appears often to subvert these very same criteria. Chapman does, it is true, allude to Longinus at least once; in the dedicatory preface to his *Odyssey* the Elizabethan poet mentions, in order to call into question, the ancient critic's comparison of the *Iliad* and *Odyssey* from chapter nine of the *Peri Hypsous*.[3] But unlike Pope, Chapman—who completed his Homer well before the appearance of the first English translation of Longinus in 1652—does not appear to have been particularly influenced by the critical remarks of Longinus, if indeed he pondered them seriously at all. To the implications of Chapman's apparent lack of familiarity with the *Peri Hypsous* I shall return, but first it will be helpful to review the history of the influence of Longinus in the seventeenth and eighteenth centuries.

The first edition of the treatise was that of Robertello in 1554. An edition was published at Oxford in 1636—to be reprinted twice in 1651—but these editions were obviously printed too late for Chapman to make use of, since his complete version of the *Iliad* was first published in 1609. Except for a passing reference made by Milton in his *Treatise on Education*, no other Elizabethan or Jacobean critic, apart from Chapman, appears ever to have mentioned Longinus, not even the learned Ben Jonson, in whose *Discoveries* appear remarks drawn from so many classical critics and rhetoricians. The first translation of Longinus in English was that done by John Hall in 1652, but Hall's version does not appear to have drawn much attention. I strongly suspect that Hobbes, whose extraordinarily flat version of the *Iliad* (1676)

[3] "Much wonder'd at, therefore, is the Censure of Dionysius Longinus (a man otherwise affirmed, grave and of elegant judgment), comparing Homer in his *Iliads* to the Sunne rising, in his *Odysses* to his descent or setting," *Chapman's Homer*, 2:5.

[103]

was published after the appearance of Hall's translation, did not consult Longinus; even if he had, which is doubtful, his version certainly does not manifest Longinus' influence, for Pope is entirely just in referring to Hobbes's *Iliad* and *Odyssey* as poetic versions "too mean for Criticism."[4]

It is with Boileau's translation of the *Peri Hypsous* in 1674 that Longinus becomes a real force in the English literary world. The first mention we get of Longinus by John Dryden, for example, comes after the appearance of Boileau's translation. In *The Author's Apology for Heroic Poetry and Poetic License* (1677), Dryden says that Longinus "was undoubtedly, after Aristotle, the greatest critic among the Greeks."[5] And Dryden's praise initiates Longinus' fame in neoclassical criticism, from John Dennis and Alexander Pope through Samuel Johnson and Sir Joshua Reynolds. But how did the sudden rise of Longinus' influence affect Homer's reputation—as well as the style of the translation of his works—in the Age of Passion? Several passages from the *Peri Hypsous* are especially relevant to the question.

FLAWED GENIUS VERSUS CAREFUL MEDIOCRITY

First, there is the passage from chapters thirty-two and thirty-three in which Longinus expresses his preference for the great writer who sometimes commits errors to the meticulous craftsman who never rises above mediocrity:

> I am certain . . . that great geniuses are least "pure." Exactness in every detail involves a risk of meanness; with grandeur, as with great wealth, there ought to be something overlooked. It may also be inevitable that low or mediocre abilities should maintain themselves generally at a correct and safe level, simply because they take no risks and do not aim at the heights, whereas greatness, just because it is greatness, incurs danger.

[4] *TE*, 7:22. For my summary of the recovery and the influence of the Longinian text, I am indebted to A.F.B. Clark, *Boileau and the French Classical Critics in England, 1660-1830* (Paris: Librairie Ancienne Édouard Champion, 1925), pp. 361-379.

[5] *Of Dramatic Poesy and Other Critical Essays*, ed. Watson, 1:197.

[104]

It is for this reason, Longinus continues, that he prefers Homer to Apollonius, Archilochus to Eratosthenes, Pindar to Bacchylides, and Sophocles to Ion:

> Apollonius makes no mistakes in the *Argonautica*; Theocritus is very felicitous in the *Pastorals*, apart from a few passages not connected with the theme; but would you rather be Homer or Apollonius? Is the Eratosthenes of that flawless little poem *Erigone* a greater poet than Archilochus, with his abundant, uncontrolled flood, that bursting forth of the divine spirit which is so hard to bring under the rule of law? Take lyric poetry: would you rather be Ion of Chios or Sophocles? Ion and Bacchylides are impeccable, uniformly beautiful writers in the polished manner; but it is Pindar and Sophocles who sometimes set the world on fire with their vehemence, for all that their flame often goes out without reason and they collapse dismally. Indeed, no one in his senses would reckon all Ion's works put together as the equivalent of the one play *Oedipus*.[6]

These remarks were to become commonplace in the later seventeenth and in the eighteenth centuries. The Moderns, from J. C. Scaliger through Charles Perrault, had preferred Virgil to Homer because it was Virgil whom they believed to have been the more diligent and self-conscious artist. And so Pope, in his notes, feels he must defend Homer against the charge of stylistic imprecision brought against his author by Moderns such as Scaliger who, in his *Poetices* (1561), compares—usually to the detriment of the earlier poet—Homeric passages with the corresponding Virgilian imitations. Those passages Scaliger selects from Homer tend invariably to be those which, as Pope observes, are "not so labour'd" as those "that *Virgil* drew out of them."[7] At one point in *Iliad* III Pope is translating a simile that Virgil imitates in the *Aeneid*. In his comparison of the two passages Scaliger had criticized the Homeric model for what he perceived to be a needless repetition of a word; Pope in his translation of

---

[6] *"Longinus" on Sublimity*, 33.2-5, pp. 39-40.
[7] *TE*, 7:16.

the passage avoids the repetition, but he defends Homer nevertheless with the following words, which I quoted in a different context in the previous chapter:

> It must be observed in general, that *little Exactnesses* are what we should not look for in *Homer*; the Genius of his Age was too incorrect, and his own too fiery to regard them.[8]

The implication of this statement is that the truly daring and passionate writer will, almost of necessity, make occasional mistakes. This is the substance of Dryden's first reference to Longinus who, he says, "has judiciously preferred the sublime genius who sometimes errs to the middling or indifferent one which makes few faults, but seldom or ever rises to any excellence."[9] At the conclusion of *Iliad* XVI Pope in fact quotes at length the passage from the *Peri Hypsous* in which Longinus expresses his preference for the great writer who sometimes errs to the meticulous draftsman who never rises above a safe mediocrity. Pope had already expressed this view in *An Essay on Criticism*:

> But in such Lays as neither *ebb*, nor *flow*,
> *Correctly cold*, and *regularly low*,
> That shunning Faults, one quiet *Tenour* keep;
> We cannot *blame* indeed—but we may *sleep*.
> [ll. 239-242]

And he repeats it in the *Iliad* preface when he says that "a cooler Judgment may commit fewer Faults" than does Homer and "be more approv'd in the Eyes of *One* Sort of Criticks," but that "Warmth of Fancy will carry the loudest and most universal Applauses which holds the Heart of a Reader under the strongest Enchantment."[10]

By the early years of the eighteenth century in England, Homer's bold negligence is beginning to be viewed not as a fault but rather as a virtue that reveals him to be a great genius who, along with Pindar and the author of the Old Testament, paid

---

[8] Ibid., 7:191.
[9] *Of Dramatic Poesy and Other Critical Essays*, ed. Watson, 1:197.
[10] *TE*, 7:16.

little attention to the confining rules of art. Addison, for example, in *Spectator* 160 (September 3, 1711) contrasts "the greater and more daring Genius" of the "Ancients" to "the Nicety and Correctness of the Moderns." It is because of the "greater and more daring genius" of the Ancients, Addison says, that the similes in both Homer and in the Old Testament—as well as in all the writings "conformable to this Eastern way of Thinking"—will often appear too bold to the modern reader:

> In short, to cut off all Cavelling against the Ancients, and particularly those of the warmer Climates, who had most Heat and Life in their Imaginations, we are to consider that the Rule of observing what the *French* call the *Bienseance* in an Allusion, has been found out of latter Years and in the colder Regions of the World; where we would make some Amends for our want of Force and Spirit, by a scrupulous Nicety and Exactness in our Compositions.[11]

Pope similarly tells the readers of his translation that they should not, as I mentioned in the previous chapter, expect from Homer

> those minute resemblances in every Branch of a Comparison, which are the pride of modern Similes. If that which one may call the main Action of it, or the principal Point of Likeness, be preserv'd; he affects, as to the rest, rather to present the Mind with a great Image, than to fix it down to an exact one.[12]

In that same *Spectator* paper Addison goes on, as I also mentioned in the previous chapter, to compare the genius of Homer, Pindar, and the author of the Old Testament to "a rich Soil in a happy Climate, that produces a whole Wilderness of noble Plants rising in a thousand beautiful Landskips without any certain Order or Regularity." He then contrasts this kind of genius to the genius of a Virgil and this "second Class of great Genius's" he compares to "the same rich Soil under the same happy Cli-

---

[11] *Spectator*, ed. Bond, 2:127-128.
[12] TE, 7:272.

mate, that has been laid out in Walks and Parterres, and cut into Shape and Beauty by the Skill of the Gardener."[13] Pope in the *Iliad* preface employs this very same garden metaphor—which, in the garbled and inaccurate version I cited in the previous chapter, aroused the ire of Mme. Dacier—in order to describe Homer's style:

> Our Author's Work is a wild Paradise, where if we cannot see all the Beauties so distinctly as in an order'd Garden, it is only because the Number of them is infinitely greater. 'Tis like a copious Nursery which contains the Seeds and first Productions of every Kind, out of which those who follow'd him have but selected some particular Plants, each according to his Fancy, to cultivate and beautify.[14]

Whereas the Moderns preferred Virgil to Homer because of the Roman poet's allegedly superior diligence, Homer's defenders, now with the sanction of Longinus, could prefer their author for what they perceived to be his bolder and more passionate negligence.

THE CIRCUMSTANTIAL AND THE UNIVERSAL

A second passage from the *Peri Hypsous* which was to have a great influence upon Pope's view of Homer occurs in chapter forty-three. Longinus has been discussing those qualities of style that are destructive of sublimity. Among the qualities that detract from sublimity, Longinus says, is the use of words that are insufficiently dignified. As examples of this particular stylistic transgression, Longinus chooses a passage from Herodotus and then one from Theopompus in which the author "first gives a magnificent setting to the descent of the Persian king on Egypt, and then ruins it all with a few words."[15] The passage from Theopompus reads as follows:

> What city or nation in Asia did not send its embassy to the King? What thing of beauty or value, product of the earth or

[13] *Spectator*, ed. Bond, 2:129.
[14] *TE*, 7:3.
[15] *"Longinus" on Sublimity*, 43.2, p. 49.

work of art, was not brought him as a gift? There were many precious coverlets and cloaks, purple, embroidered, and white; there were many gold tents fitted out with all necessities; there were many robes and beds of great price. There were silver vessels and worked gold, drinking cups and bowls, some studded with jewels, some elaborately and preciously wrought. Countless myriads of arms were there, Greek and barbarian. There were multitudes of pack animals and victims fattened for slaughter, many bushels of spice, many bags and sacks and pots of onions and every other necessity. There was so much salt meat of every kind that travellers approaching from a distance mistook the huge heaps for cliffs or hills thrusting up from the plain.

Longinus comments that in this description the author

passes from the sublime to the mean; the development of the scene should have been the other way round. By mixing up the bags and the condiments and the sacks in the splendid account of the whole expedition, he conjures up the vision of a kitchen. . . . It was open to Theopompus to give a general description (ὡς ὁλοσχερῶς ἐπελθεῖν) of the "hills" which he says were raised, and, having made this change, to proceed to the rest of the preparations, mentioning camels and multitudes of beasts of burden carrying everything needed for luxury and pleasure of the table, or speaking of "heaps of all kinds of seeds and everything that makes for fine cuisine and dainty living."[16]

What Longinus is first of all objecting to here is the order in which Theopompus develops the scene, for the elevation evoked by the description of the gifts given to the king slips decidedly in emotional pitch since it proceeds from the sublime (ἐκ τῶν ὑψηλοτέρων) to the mean (εἰς τὰ ταπεινότερα) rather than the other way around. Longinus then suggests that Theopompus could, nevertheless, have sustained the lofty tone of the passage had he eliminated such inappropriately mundane details as "bushels of spice," "bags and sacks and pots of onions," and a supply of

[16] Ibid., p. 50.

"salt meat"; it would have been far better, Longinus says, had Theopompus represented these details ὁλοσχερῶς, that is, "roughly," or "in a general way."

When Pope comes to translate Homer he is faced with the problem of how to render similarly humble details. If he feels that these details would appear too mean to his Augustan audience, he may eliminate them completely or, as Longinus suggests, present them "in a general way." Pope's translation abounds with such examples; one or two will suffice to make the point. Homeric details such as "black-skinned beans" and "chickpeas" (*Iliad* XIII.589), for instance, become in Pope's version the more elevated and generalized "golden grain" (l. 742). And when Ajax in *Iliad* XI is being overpowered by the Trojan troops, but stubbornly resists them, Homer compares the stolid Greek warrior to a "donkey" or an "ass" (ὄνος, l. 558):

ὡς δ' ὅτ' ὄνος παρ' ἄρουραν ἰὼν ἐβιήσατο παῖδας
νωθής, ᾧ δὴ πολλὰ περὶ ῥόπαλ' ἀμφὶς ἐάγη,
κείρει τ' εἰσελθὼν βαθὺ λήϊον· οἱ δέ τε παῖδες
τύπτουσιν ῥοπάλοισι· βίη δέ τε νηπίη αὐτῶν·
σπουδῇ τ' ἐξήλασσαν, ἐπεί τ' ἐκορέσσατο φορβῆς·
ὡς τότ' ἔπειτ' Αἴαντα μέγαν, Τελαμώνιον υἱόν,
Τρῶες ὑπέρθυμοι πολυηγερέες τ' ἐπίκουροι
νύσσοντες ξυστοῖσι μέσον σάκος αἰὲν ἕποντο.

(As when a donkey [ὄνος], sluggish but stubborn, has
   overpowered a group of boys in a field,
while the boys hurl their clubs at him from all sides,
but he manages to make his way into the field
   nevertheless and he eats the abundant corn; the boys
pelt him with their clubs, but their strength seems futile;
with a relentless effort they do finally drive him out, but
   only after he has had his fill;
just so did the high-spirited Trojans and their many allies
pursue great Ajax, son of Telamon,
continually piercing the middle of his shield with their
   spears.)

[ll. 558-565]

[110]

Here is Pope's version:

> As the slow Beast with heavy Strength indu'd,
> In some wide Field by Troops of Boys pursu'd,
> Tho' round his Sides a wooden Tempest rain,
> Crops the tall Harvest, and lays waste the Plain;
> Thick on his Hide the hollow Blows resound,
> The patient Animal maintains his Ground,
> Scarce from the Field with all their Efforts chas'd,
> And stirs but slowly when he stirs at last.
> On *Ajax* thus a Weight of *Trojans* hung,
> The Strokes redoubled on his Buckler rung.
>
> [ll. 682-691]

I mentioned earlier that elevation and liveliness were often seen in the neoclassical period, and even by Pope himself, as mutually exclusive qualities of style. Yet the translation of the specific ὄνος into the generic "Beast" (l. 682) and "Animal" (l. 687) does not sap this passage of its circumstantial liveliness. For Pope has managed to bring out what he considers to be the most important quality of the simile: the aptness of the comparison as a means of describing the character of Ajax, whom he correctly sees in the present context as "a stubborn but undaunted Warrior" and whom he describes in general in the Poetical Index which he published along with his translation as "indefatigable and patient."[17] These qualities Pope emphasizes, in part, by translating ὄνος as "slow Beast" and "patient Animal." The words "Beast" and "Animal" may be more generic and therefore more colorless than the word ὄνος, but the adjectives "slow" and "patient" qualify the nouns "Beast" and "Animal" with a very apt regard for their function in this particular narrative context.

We should not therefore read such a change as a condescending attempt by Pope to make Homer's occasional vulgarities acceptable to an excessively refined eighteenth-century audience, for in his preface Pope criticizes those modern translators who

---

[17] *TE*, 8:63, 595.

have "a chimerical insolent Hope of raising and improving their Author."[18] Pope's translation reflects, rather, the poet's awareness that the connotations of words may change. So in his notes Pope quotes with approval Boileau's remarks, from his *Ninth Reflection upon Longinus*, that while "the word *Asinus* in *Latin*, and *Ass* in *English*, are the vilest imaginable, . . . that which signifies the same Animal in *Greek* and *Hebrew*, is of Dignity enough to be employed on the most magnificent Occasions."[19] By rendering the particular Homeric word ὄνος in his generalized manner, Pope is attempting to maintain that tone of dignity which both he and Boileau believe had never been violated in the original text as it was experienced by Homer's audience.

If, on the one hand, Pope were to translate Homer with too much literal circumstantiality, he would be denying the poem its claim to serious attention by the readers of his own time; he would be denying, that is, the universality of the poem's appeal. The great representation of General Nature would then become a mere archeological artifact, incapable of speaking to the present. If, on the other hand, he were to translate into a diction that was full of currently fashionable idioms, such modern particularities would run the risk of eventually rendering the language of the translation obsolete. This is a point made frequently by Samuel Johnson, but the tradition is initiated by Longinus when he says in the *Peri Hypsous*, in a third passage to which I would now like to draw the reader's attention, that the chief cause of the decadence of contemporary literature is "that desire for novelty of thought which is all the rage today." The pleasure conveyed by such writing will, at best, endure "only for the moment of its hearing," while truly sublime writing is that which will

> please everybody all the time. . . . When people of different training, way of life, tastes, age and manners all agree about something, the judgement and assent, as it were, of so many

---

[18] Ibid., 7:17.
[19] Ibid., 8:65.

distinct voices lends strength and irrefutability to the conviction that their admiration is rightly directed.[20]

So Swift, in the preface to *A Tale of a Tub* (1704), remarks of the transitory quality of modern wit that

> nothing is so very tender as a *Modern* Piece of Wit, and which is apt to suffer so much in the Carriage. Some things are extremely witty *to day*, or *fasting*, or *in this place*, or *at eight a clock*, or *over a Bottle*, or *spoke by Mr. What d'y'call'm*, or *in a Summer's Morning*: Any of which, by the smallest Transposal or Misapplication, is utterly annihilate. Thus, *Wit* has its Walks and Purlieus, out of which it may not stray the breadth of a Hair, upon peril of being lost. The *Moderns* have artfully fixed this *Mercury*, and reduced it to the Circumstances of Time, Place, and Person. Such a Jest there is, that will not pass out of *Covent-Garden*; and such a one, that is no where intelligible but at *Hide-Park* Corner.[21]

Pope applied Swift's principle to his practice of translating Homer into a generalized language that would be appropriate to the work of a poet "whose positions," as Samuel Johnson writes, "are general" and whose "representations" are "natural, with very little dependence on local or temporary customs."[22] Not to translate Homer thus would be to concede victory to those who believed that the ancient poet did, after all, have nothing to say to a contemporary audience. Richard Bentley, for example, was convinced that the Homeric poems could offer no moral instruction to the contemporary reader, since they were in truth a primitive collection of songs designed purely for entertainment. In his belief that the poems were interesting chiefly as historical phenomena, he typifies the positions of the Moderns, who felt that the true value of the poems lay, not in their analysis of the constants of human nature, but in what the poems could tell us

---

[20] *"Longinus" on Sublimity*, 7.4, p. 8.

[21] *A Tale of a Tub*, ed. with an intro. and notes by A. C. Guthkelch and D. Nicol Smith, 2nd ed. (Oxford: Clarendon Press, 1958), p. 43.

[22] *Life of Pope, Lives of the Poets*, 3:114.

about the actual historical conditions of an ancient and primitive culture. The notion that the Homeric poems had no explicitly moral or philosophical content would be developed later in the century by Giambattista Vico, who would claim that the poetic mind, which could not think logically, expressed itself in particulars rather than in universals.[23] Pope's generalized diction suggests his belief in Homer's universality, his ability to speak and to be understood across the centuries. To have translated Homeric Greek into a language of unmediated particulars would be to imply that the poem could not at all be assimilated into contemporary culture; it would be to stress too emphatically the poem's remoteness. And this was a remoteness that was often, in fact, more of an illusion than a reality. While Pope attempted to translate literally as many of Homer's epithets, for example, as good and graceful English would allow, he was also aware that too frequent and too uncompromising attempts to render them literally will "give the Translation an exotic, pedantic, and whimsical Air, which is not to be imagin'd the Original ever had." Pope continues:

[23] On the Moderns' interest in Homer chiefly as an archeological phenomenon, see Kirsti Simonsuuri's useful book *Homer's Original Genius: Eighteenth-Century Notions of Early Greek Epic (1688-1798)* (Cambridge: Cambridge University Press, 1979). On Vico's suggestion, made in *La scienza nuova*, that the poetic mind could not think logically and tended to express itself in particulars rather than in universals, see Simonsuuri, chapter seven ("Vico's Discovery of the True Homer"). The narrowly historical approach to the Homeric poems was most often associated in the later seventeenth and early eighteenth centuries with a condescending progressivism which is distinctively Modern and it is against such an attitude that Pope, as a translator and admirer of Homer, was thoroughly opposed. But, on the other hand, it must be observed that positivism resulted in a more accurate historical understanding of Homeric and other early cultures, an understanding which, if it did not derail into progressivism, could result in the ability to make the crucial distinction between, in Eric Voegelin's terms, the "compact" symbolic form of the myth and the "differentiated" symbolic form of philosophy. On this problem, see the four volumes of Voegelin's *Order and History*, particularly volumes two (*The World of the Polis*) and three (*Plato and Aristotle*). The great quantities of empirical evidence upon which such a distinction could be based were simply not yet available to Pope, who at times introduces into his translation specifically philosophical concepts, such as "soul," when in fact such a concept had not, in Homer, been historically differentiated.

[114]

To call a Hero the *great Artificer of Flight*, the *swift of Foot*, or the *Horse-tamer*, these give us Ideas of little Peculiarities, when in the Author's Time they were Epithets used only in general to signify Alacrity, Agility, and Vigor. A common Reader would imagine from these Versions, that *Diomed* and *Achilles* were Foot Racers, and *Hector* a Horse-Courser, rather than that any of them were Heroes. A man shall be call'ed a faithful Translator for rendering πόδας ὠκύς in *English*, *swift-footed*; but laughed at if he should translate our *English* word *dext'rous* into any other Language, *right-handed*.[24]

LONGINUS AND NEOCLASSICAL CRITICISM

The Longinian suggestion that to represent any subject matter with excessive circumstantiality is to detract from sublimity is, of course, a notion to be found in many of the major critics of the Augustan age. In his *Odyssey* postscript, for example, Pope says that a difficult stylistic problem to resolve is "how far a Poet, in pursuing the description or image of an action, can attach himself to *little circumstances*, without vulgarity or trifling."[25] This is an echo of an allusion Pope had earlier made to Longinus in the notes that accompany his translation of the *Iliad*. In chapter ten of the *Peri Hypsous* Longinus discusses how a fearful action can be represented in as elevated a manner as possible; one of the ways in which an author can spoil the effective representation of such an action is, once again, through a too scrupulous enu-meration of a trivial particular. Longinus selects several passages depicting a group of sailors contending with a storm; he then goes on to suggest that Homer's description is far superior to that of Aratus because the latter poet, by alluding to a trivial particular, defines the danger with excessive and inappropriate circumstantiality. In his commentary upon the passage discussed by Longinus, Pope recalls that the ancient critic shows how "a Poet of less Judgment [than Homer] would amuse himself in less

[24] *TE*, 7:429.
[25] Ibid., 10:387.

[115]

important Circumstances, and spoil the whole Effect of the Image by minute, ill-chosen, or superfluous Particulars."[26] Pope's paraphrase of the Longinian passage, which he included in his notes, reads as follows:

Thus *Aratus* endeavouring to refine upon that line [i.e., of Homer],
> *And instant Death on ev'ry Wave appears!*
He turn'd it thus,—
> *A slender Plank preserves them from their Fate.*
Which, by flourishing upon the Thought, has lost the Loftiness and Terror of it, and is so far from improving the Image, that it lessens and vanishes in his Management. By confining the Danger to a single Line, he has scarce left the Shadow of it; and indeed the word *preserves* takes away even that.[27]

In chapter eight of the *Peri Bathous* (1727), in impersonating what he perceives to be a tasteless modern critic, Pope ironically recommends two passages from the works of Sir Richard Blackmore. The first he considers "cautious" and "particular," the second as "no less remarkable in the Circumstances." The second passage is from Blackmore's description of hell in his epic *Prince Arthur*:

> *In flaming Heaps the raging Ocean rolls,*
> *Whose livid Waves involve despairing Souls;*
> *The liquid Burnings dreadful Colours shew,*
> *Some* deeply red, *and others* faintly blue.

"Could the most minute *Dutch* Painters," Pope asks, "have been more exact?"[28]

That it is the minuteness of the Dutch painters that prevents their works from achieving sublimity is a theme that is sounded again and again later in the century by Sir Joshua Reynolds. The observation is Longinian in the sense that its premise is similar to Longinus' warning that excessive circumstantiality will detract

---

[26] Ibid., 8:225.
[27] Ibid.
[28] *Poetry and Prose of Pope*, ed. Williams, p. 404.

from sublimity. But such an observation must also be viewed in the light of a fifth passage from the *Peri Hypsous*:

It has been remarked that "the failed Colossus is no better than the Doryphorus of Polyclitus.". . . We say that accuracy is admired in art and grandeur in nature. Impeccability is generally a product of art; erratic excellence comes from natural greatness; therefore, art must always come to the aid of nature, and the combination of the two may well be perfection.[29]

As did the passage cited earlier in which Longinus expresses his preference for the great writer who sometimes commits errors to the meticulous craftsman who never rises above mediocrity, so this passage makes clear the proper relationship between Art and Nature as this relationship was to be stated so often during the neoclassical period. It is because he believes that Art must always assist, and must never obscure, Nature, that Longinus expresses his implied preference for the faulty Colossus over the Hellenistic refinement of detail characteristic of Polycleitus' perfectly proportioned spearman. An object rendered ὁλοσχερῶς may achieve sublimity, but an excessive concern with artistic detail will tend to turn the viewer's attention from the object itself by drawing an inordinate amount of attention to the technique with which the object is rendered. Thus the paintings of the Dutch school do not approach elevation, Reynolds writes in his *Seventh Discourse*, because these paintings depict "exact representations of individual objects." "Even in portraits," Reynolds says in his *Fourth Discourse*—and we must recall that portraits were considered a genre that was inherently less elevated than, for example, history painting—"the grace and . . . the likeness consists more in taking the general air, than in observing the exact similitude of every feature." In his *Third Discourse* Reynolds says that the painter of genius will not "waste a moment upon those smaller objects, which only serve to catch the sense, to divide the attention, and to counteract his great design of speaking to the heart." In his *Fourth Discourse* Reynolds praises

[29] *"Longinus" on Sublimity*, 36.3-4, p. 43.

Annibale Carracci for his refusal to clutter his canvases with any more than twelve figures. "It is impossible," Reynolds writes,

> for a picture composed of so many parts to have that effect so indispensably necessary for grandeur, that of one complete whole. However contradictory it may be in geometry, it is true in taste, that many little things will not make a great one. The Sublime impresses the mind at once with one great idea; it is a single blow: the Elegant indeed may be produced . . . by an accumulation of many minute circumstances.[30]

This theme occurs again and again throughout the *Discourses*.

This Longinian tradition is most eloquently represented in neoclassical literary criticism by Samuel Johnson. Just as Reynolds in his *Discourses* expresses his belief that excessive attention 1) to artistic means and 2) to circumstantiality will detract from grandeur, so these are the criteria of Johnson's 1) defense of Shakespeare's reputed ignorance of the unities; "a play written with a nice observation of critical rules," Johnson writes, "is to be contemplated as an elaborate curiosity, as the product of superfluous and ostentatious art."[31] And it is the basis as well of Johnson's 2) famous criticism of the metaphysical poets who, he observes in the *Life of Cowley*, lose the "grandeur of generality" through a too "scrupulous enumeration" of minute particulars:

> The fault of Cowley, and perhaps of all the writers of the metaphysical race, is that of pursuing his thoughts to their last ramifications, by which he loses the grandeur of generality; for of the greatest things the parts are little; what is little can be but pretty, and by claiming dignity becomes ridiculous. Thus all the power of description is destroyed by a scrupulous enumeration; and the force of metaphors is lost, when the mind by the mention of particulars is turned more upon the original than the secondary sense, more upon that from which the illustration is drawn than that to which it is applied.[32]

[30] *Discourses on Art*, ed. Wark, pp. 111, 56-57, 50-51, 62.
[31] *Preface to Shakespeare* (1765), *Yale Johnson*, 7:80.
[32] *Lives of the Poets*, 1:45.

And later in the same *Life* Johnson remarks of Cowley's description, in the *Davideis*, of Gabriel's attire: "What might in general expression be great and forcible, he weakens and makes ridiculous by branching it into small parts."[33]

Johnson's criticism of the metaphysical poets—whose "thoughts," Johnson writes, "are often new, but seldom natural"[34]—was anticipated by Pope in the *Peri Bathous* when he ironically recommends that the poet depict "Circumstances which are most . . . astonishing and peculiar" and that the poet must "above all, preserve a laudable *Prolixity*; presenting the Whole and every Side at once of the Image to view."[35] And what Johnson says of the metaphysical poets' inability to achieve the sublime is analogous, in some important ways, to Pope's criticism of the style of Chapman's *Iliad*. It is commonly assumed that Chapman's *Iliad* is more exuberant, more passionate, more sublime than Pope's version. "If Homer could return from Elysium to read all the English renderings," Douglas Bush, for example, writes, "he would surely find in Chapman his truest son, a man who has fed on lion's marrow."[36] Pope himself, in his review of his predecessors in the field of Homeric translation, speaks in the *Iliad* preface of Chapman's "daring fiery Spirit that animates his Translation, which is something one might imagine *Homer* himself would have writ before he arriv'd to Years of Discretion."[37] Although Pope does indeed praise Chapman's "daring fiery Spirit" in the *Iliad* preface, many of the differences between his own style of translating and that of Chapman suggest that

[33] Ibid., 1:53.

[34] Ibid., 1:20.

[35] *Poetry and Prose of Pope*, ed. Williams, p. 404. Cf. Johnson, *Life of Cowley*: "Those writers who lay on the watch for novelty could have little hope of greatness; for great things cannot have escaped former observation. Their [i.e., the metaphysical poets'] attempts were always analytick: they broke every image into fragments" (p. 21). For Pope's view of the metaphysical style, see his remarks on Crashaw's style in a letter to Cromwell, December 17, 1710. See also Arthur H. Nethercot, "The Reputation of the 'Metaphysical Poets' in the Age of Pope," *Philological Quarterly* 4 (1925):161-179 and Ian Jack, "Pope and 'The Weighty Bullion of Dr. Donne's Satires,' " *PMLA* 66 (December 1951):1009-1022.

[36] *Chapman's Homer*, ed. Nicoll, 1:xiv.

[37] *TE*, 7:21.

Pope felt that the Elizabethan version often lost the grandeur of generality through a too scrupulous enumeration of minute particulars. Samuel Johnson tells us that Pope "perhaps never translated any passage until he had read his [i.e., Chapman's] version, which indeed he has been sometimes suspected of using instead of the original."[38] It is interesting, therefore, to compare their translations of a single Homeric passage and to ask, which of them is the more encumbered with superfluous particulars and which, therefore—by Longinian criteria—is the less elevated?

FROM RENAISSANCE PROLIXITY TO AUGUSTAN ELEVATION

Toward the beginning of Book XVIII occurs the scene in which Achilles, having just learned that Patroclus has been killed, laments to his mother Thetis that it was his own inactivity that precipitated the tragedy of his friend's death. Achilles states his unequivocal desire to avenge Patroclus' death, to which Thetis replies:

"ὠκύμορος δή μοι, τέκος, ἔσσεαι, οἷ' ἀγορεύεις·
αὐτίκα γάρ τοι ἔπειτα μεθ' Ἕκτορα πότμος ἑτοῖμος."
Τὴν δὲ μέγ' ὀχθήσας προσέφη πόδας ὠκὺς Ἀχιλλεύς·
"αὐτίκα τεθναίην, ἐπεὶ οὐκ ἄρ' ἔμελλον ἑταίρῳ
κτεινομένῳ ἐπαμῦναι· ὁ μὲν μάλα τηλόθι πάτρης
ἔφθιτ', ἐμεῖο δὲ δῆσεν ἀρῆς ἀλκτῆρα γενέσθαι.
νῦν δ' ἐπεὶ οὐ νέομαί γε φίλην ἐς πατρίδα γαῖαν,
οὐδέ τι Πατρόκλῳ γενόμην φάος οὐδ' ἑτάροισι
τοῖς ἄλλοις, οἳ δὴ πολέες δάμεν Ἕκτορι δίῳ,
ἀλλ' ἧμαι παρὰ νηυσὶν ἐτώσιον ἄχθος ἀρούρης,
τοῖος ἐὼν οἷος οὔ τις Ἀχαιῶν χαλκοχιτώνων
ἐν πολέμῳ· ἀγορῇ δέ τ' ἀμείνονές εἰσι καὶ ἄλλοι."

"What you have said means that your own death is very
    near, my son,
Since it is decreed that your death will quickly follow
    upon Hector's."

[38] *Life of Pope, Lives of the Poets,* 3:115.

[120]

Sighing deeply swift-footed Achilles responded:
"Then let my death come quickly, since I did not
come to the defense of my friend who was killed, my
    friend who far from his native land
died, when he needed my fighting strength to defend
    him;
since now I shall not return to my beloved homeland,
since I was no light of deliverance to Patroclus
nor to my other companions, who in great numbers
    went down before divine Hector,
while I sat by the ships, a useless burden on the land,
I, who am surpassed by none of the other bronze-
    armored Achaeans
in battle, although there are those who are more
    accomplished speakers."

                                  [ll. 95-106]

Here is Chapman's version:

She weeping, said: 'That houre is neare, and thy death's
    houre then nie,
Which in thy wish serv'd of thy foe succeedeth instantly.'
    'And instantly it shall succeed,' he answerd, 'since my
    fate
Allow'd not to my will a powre to rescue (ere the date
Of his late slaughter) my true friend. Farre from his
    friends he died,
Whose wrong therein my eyes had light and right to see
    denied.
Yet now I neither light my selfe, nor have so spent my
    light,
That either this friend or the rest (in numbers infinite
Slaughterd by Hector) I can helpe, nor grace with wisht
    repaire
To our deare country, but breathe here unprofitable aire,
And onely live a lode to earth with all my strength,
    though none
Of all the Grecians equall it. In counsell many a one

Is my superiour; what I have, no grace gets; what I
want,
Disgraceth all.'

[ll. 85-98]

And here is Pope's:

A Flood of Tears, at this, the Goddess shed;
Ah then, I see thee dying, see thee dead!
When *Hector* falls, thou dy'st.—Let *Hector* die,
And let me fall! (*Achilles* made reply)
Far lyes *Patroclus* from his native plain!
He fell, and falling wish'd my Aid in vain.
Ah then, since from this miserable Day
I cast all hope of my Return away,
Since unreveng'd, a hundred Ghosts demand
The Fate of *Hector* from *Achilles*' hand;
Since here, for brutal Courage far renown'd,
I live an idle Burden to the Ground,
(Others in Council fam'd for nobler Skill,
More useful to preserve, than I to kill)
Let me—

[ll. 123-137]

There is no question that Chapman's fourteener lends to the
English line a sense of spaciousness that approximates in its
grandeur the Homeric dactyllic hexameter. And there is a re-
flective pathos in this passage from Chapman's version which
the passage from Pope's does not quite convey. But the faults of
Chapman's version, I would like to suggest, are those of the
metaphysical style as described by Samuel Johnson.

"I was no φάος to Patroclus or to my other companions" (l.
102), Homer says. The word φάος means simply "light" and in
this context must be taken as a brief metaphor meaning "that
which can offer deliverance from impending disaster." In some
canceled lines which appear in the original manuscript of his
translation it can be seen that Pope did at first try to include the

word,[39] but he apparently decided in the end that what was important to preserve was its metaphorical meaning, and so for Homer's phrase "since I was no light to my other companions" Pope freely substitutes the lines "Since unreveng'd, a hundred Ghosts demand / The Fate of *Hector* from *Achilles*' hand." This rendering attempts to heighten the image of Achilles to heroic proportions at this point in the action, and such heightening is wholly appropriate to the context. Achilles is here breaking out of the closed circle of his merely private suffering and, by asserting his desire to avenge Patroclus' death as well as the deaths of his other companions, he is now assuming the public responsibility that he had been previously shirking.

In his interpretation of this scene, Pope is at one with Plato. For Socrates, in the *Apology*, points to this very speech as a model for his own refusal, in response to the coercions of the Athenian government, to abandon the philosophical life. To the hypothetical question "Are you not afraid, Socrates, of leading a life which is very likely now to cause your death?" Socrates answers:

> If you think that a man of any worth at all ought to reckon the chances of life or death when he acts, or that he ought to think of anything but whether he is acting justly or unjustly, and as a good or a bad man would act, you are mistaken. According to you, the demigods who died at Troy would be foolish, and among them Achilles, who thought nothing of danger when the alternative was disgrace. For when his mother— and she was a goddess—addressed him, when he was resolved to slay Hector, in this fashion, " 'My son, if you avenge the death of your comrade Patroclus and slay Hector, you will die yourself, for fate awaits you next after Hector.' When he heard this, he scorned danger and death; he feared much more to live a coward and not to avenge his friend. 'Let me punish the evildoer and afterwards die,' he said, 'that I may not remain here by the beaked ships jeered at, encumbering the earth.' "

[39] The canceled lines read "Till I revenge him I detest the light, / Time hangs upon me, and I walk in night" (British Museum Add. MS. 4808, 64v).

[123]

Do you suppose that he thought of danger or of death? For this, Athenians, I believe to be the truth. Wherever a man's station is, whether he has chosen it of his own will, or whether he has been placed at it by his commander, there it is his duty to remain and face the danger without thinking of death or of any other thing except disgrace.[40]

Chapman is certainly aware of the heroic grandeur of Achilles' speech. This he conveys in a later part of the speech when he translates Achilles' words

> Now I shall go, so that I might overcome Hector, that
>   destroyer of a life so dear to me,
> And I shall accept death, whenever
> Zeus and the other immortals wish to bring it about
> [ll. 114-116]

with the following lines, which border on the histrionic but which are grand nevertheless:

> And when the loser of my friend his death in me shall
>   find,
> Let death take all. Send him, ye gods; I'le give him my
>   embrace.
> [ll. 109-110]

But in his pursuit of verbal quibbles earlier in the speech, Chapman has managed to distract the reader's attention from experiencing the pathos he should feel here. One reason Pope chose not to translate literally the φάος of line 102 may have been his awareness of the problems it created for Chapman. Homer's Achilles says that Patroclus died "far from his native land" and that "I was no light [i.e., of deliverance] to Patroclus / or to my other companions, who in great numbers went down before divine Hector." This Chapman renders as follows:

> . . . Farre from his friends he died,
> Whose wrong therein my eyes had light and right to see
>   denied.

[40] *Plato: Euthyphro, Apology, Crito*, trans. F. J. Church (Indianapolis: Bobbs-Merrill, 1948), p. 34.

Yet now I neither light my selfe, nor have so spent my
   light,
That either this friend or the rest (in numbers infinite
Slaughterd by Hector) I can helpe. . . .

"If the father of criticism has rightly denominated poetry τέχνη
μιμητική, an imitative art," Johnson wrote of the metaphysical
poets in the Life of Cowley, "these writers will, without great
wrong, lose their right to the name of poets, for they cannot be
said to have imitated anything." They have not imitated or rep-
resented anything, according to Johnson, because in their search
for far-fetched conceits, they leave behind the particular subject
matter, that is, the experience, which they were at first attempting
to represent. Nor, Johnson writes, was "the sublime . . . within
their reach" since "sublimity is produced by aggregation, and
littleness by dispersion." The metaphysical poets "broke every
image into fragments; and could no more represent, by their
slender conceits and laboured particularities, the prospects of
nature, or the scenes of life, than he who dissects a sunbeam
with a prism can exhibit the wide effulgence of a summer noon."[41]
Precisely the same criticisms may be made of Chapman's conceits
in this moving passage from the Iliad. Chapman saw the Greek
word φάος—or the Latin lumen in the translation of Spondanus
which we know he used—and this apparently suggested to him
the strangely unidiomatic phrase "whose wrong my eyes had
light . . . to see denied." The word "light" probably suggested
the internal rhyme with "right." And "light" is repeated twice
in the following line. "And now I neither light my selfe" is, again,
not idiomatic English; "nor have so spent my light" is idiomatic,
but because this is the third time Chapman uses the word in the
space of two lines, its appearance seems gratuitous and man-
nered. And so with the phrase "what I have no grace gets; what
I want / Disgraceth all" (ll. 97-98). The phrase "what I have no
grace gets" is unidiomatic and one suspects that Chapman wrote
it because he was taken with the alliteration of "grace" and "get"
as well as with the play on words between "grace" and "dis-
graceth" in the following line.

[41] Lives of the Poets, 1:19, 20-21.

[125]

The use of this kind of wit was deemed out of place in Augustan epic theory. Dryden, for example, believed that Tasso's *Gerusalemme Liberata* was too full of "conceits, points of epigram, and witticisms; all of which are not only below the dignity of heroic verse, but contrary to its true nature: Virgil and Homer have not one of them."[42] And although Pope is often accused of introducing too much Ovidian wit into his translation, with Dryden he was in complete agreement. In his personal copy of Chapman's *Iliad*, for example, Pope wrote in the margin beside a passage in which Chapman introduced an element of witty conceit not present in the original: "Vd. Dryden / Wt [i.e., wit] is markd not in Homer."[43] And at one point in his commentary Pope goes so far as to express his suspicion that a line of Homer's, which he considers gratuitously witty, must be an interpolation, since "we may indeed meet with such little Affectations in Ovid, ... but the Taste of the Ancients in general was too good for these Fooleries."[44]

To a classical and Augustan sensibility, then, conceits were thought to be out of place in serious epic. And even if conceits are occasionally permissible, it is often the case that Chapman's handling of them, in this speech and elsewhere in his translation, is questionable not so much on the grounds that they violate decorum by introducing a note of inappropriate levity, but rather that such witticisms, such labored particularities, tend to obscure the sense and thus to dissipate sublimity; they distract the attention of the reader from Nature to Art and thus the passions will not be moved. So Pope, again in his copy of Chapman's *Iliad*, objects to a play on words which the Elizabethan poet had introduced into one of Homer's scenes depicting the death of a warrior in battle. This warrior, Chapman writes,

[42] *A Discourse Concerning the Original and Progress of Satire, of Dramatic Poesy and Other Critical Essays*, ed. Watson, 2:82.

[43] Appendix E ("Markings and Marginalia in Pope's Copy of Chapman's *Iliad*"), TE, 10:475.

[44] Ibid., 7:466.

... (taking chariot) tooke his wound and tumbl'd with
   the same
From his attempted seate. The lance through his right
   shoulder strooke
And horrid darknesse strooke through him. The spoile
   his souldiers tooke.

[V.50-52]

Pope underlined the phrase "(taking chariot) tooke" as well as
the word "strooke" in both lines 51 and 52, suggesting his dis-
approval of a gratuitous play on words at precisely the sort of
moment he considered especially marked by tragic pathos.[45] So
Pope finds fault, as Samuel Johnson will after him, with Shake-
speare's excessive use of metaphorical language in "the speeches
of his kings and great men" in his tragedies since, as he told
Spence, such metaphors generally "stiffen his style"; the use of
such "forced language," he continues, was "the way of Chapman
... and all the tragic writers of those days."[46]
    It is just this kind of affectation that Longinus, as Pope says
at one point in his observations, criticizes in the poem the *Ari-
maspeia*, which is attributed to Aristeas of Proconnesus. The
lines cited by Longinus from the *Arimaspeia*, which Pope says

---

[45] In his *Essay on Homer's Battles* Pope praises "the Poet's wonderful Art of
introducing many pathetick Circumstances about the Deaths of the Heroes"
(Ibid., 7:255).

[46] *Anecdotes, Observations, and Characters of Books and Men*, ed. James M.
Osborn, 2 vols. (Oxford: Clarendon Press, 1966), 1:183. Cf. Johnson's remarks
from the *Preface to Shakespeare*: "He is not long soft and pathetick without
some idle conceit, or contemptible equivocation. He no sooner begins to move,
than he counteracts himself; and terrour and pity, as they are rising in the mind,
are checked and blasted by sudden frigidity" (*Yale Johnson*, 7:74). The Yale
editor points us to the last sentence of Johnson's general observations on *Romeo
and Juliet*: "His persons, however distressed, 'have a conceit left them in their
misery, a miserable conceit' " (*Yale Johnson*, 8:957; Johnson is quoting from
Dryden's preface to *Fables Ancient and Modern*). Cf. also, of course, Johnson's
famous observation about Shakespeare that "a quibble was to him the fatal
Cleopatra for which he lost the world, and was content to lose it" (*Yale Johnson*,
7:74).

[127]

are "affected Verses" written in a "false Taste," read as follows in Pope's translation:

> Ye Pow'rs! What Madness! How, on Ships so frail,
> (Tremendous Thought!) can thoughtless Mortals sail?
> For stormy Seas they quit the pleasing Plain,
> Plant Woods in Waves, and dwell amidst the Main.
> Far o'er the Deep (a trackless Path) they goe,
> And wander Oceans, in pursuit of Woe.
> No Ease their Hearts, no Rest their Eyes can find,
> On Heav'n their Looks, and on the Waves their Mind;
> Sunk are their Spirits, while their Arms they rear;
> And Gods are weary'd with their fruitless Pray'r.[47]

The balanced couplets into which Pope translates the Greek lines are more reminiscent of early eighteenth-century verse, it is true, than of Chapman's spacious fourteener. But the gratuitous play on words and parenthetical prolixity ("[Tremendous Thought!] ... thoughtless") as well as the gratuitous conceit ("Plant Woods in Waves, and dwell amidst the Main") recall precisely those elements of Chapman's style to which Pope objected in the marginalia written in his copy of Chapman's *Iliad*. And it was Pope's intention, following the advice of Longinus, consistently to exclude from his translation just such qualities of style in order to achieve a tone of elevation worthy of his sublime original.[48]

---

[47] *TE*, 8:225.

[48] Pope's reasons for "revising" Chapman's Homer are analogous to his reasons for reworking the satires of Donne, which he began to do (1713) at about the time he started to translate Homer. It was not Pope's intention simply to make Donne more "correct"; for Pope, as I have mentioned, was well aware, from the time of his early published writings, that to be "correctly cold" (*Essay on Criticism*, l. 240) was certainly not a virtue in an author. Pope, it is true, sees his relationship to Donne as analogous to Horace's relationship to Lucilius, as the epigraph to Pope's *The Second Satire of Dr. Donne, Dean of St. Paul's, Versify'd* suggests: in the lines from Horace's *Satires* I.x, which Pope chose for the epigraph, Horace says it must be admitted that Lucilius' verses are neither sufficiently polished (*magis factos*) nor "easy" (*mollius*). But polish and ease need not be hindrances to achieving sublimity, for it is in fact their very lack of ease that prevents Donne's satires, in their tendency to fragment the subject matter they try to represent, from sufficiently moving the passions. And the same may be said of the style of much of Chapman's *Iliad*.

PART III: VERSIFICATION

CHAPTER SIX

The Heroic Couplet

RHYME, ELEVATION, AND PERSPICUITY

So far I have been arguing that, when rightly understood, it was Pope's intention to make Homer appear as elevated, as fiery an author as good English would allow. In order to achieve this end, Pope drew upon the traditional means of elevating poetic style as this was described by Aristotle in chapter twenty-two of the *Poetics* and restated in the eighteenth century by Addison in *Spectator* 285. He was sensitive to, and attempted to simulate in a written medium, the oral, "skiagraphic" nature of Homer's style as this style was described by Aristotle in *Rhetoric* III.12. And he tried further to elevate the style of his translation by following the Longinian suggestion, which was to become a commonplace in neoclassical criticism, that too scrupulous an enumeration of minute particulars will only detract from sublimity.

More difficult to defend on the basis of its capacity to evoke sublimity, especially in comparison with blank verse, is Pope's choice of the rhyming couplet as an appropriate means of translating Homer's stately dactyllic hexameters. William Cowper, for example, remarked that Pope, "who managed the bells of rhyme with more dexterity than any man, tied them about Homer's neck."[1] Part of our contemporary resistance to the Popean couplet as an appropriate response to the Homeric hexameter can be explained in terms of our modern assumption, descending

---

[1] *The Gentleman's Magazine* (London, 1785), p. 610.

from Cowper's of the later eighteenth century, that the greatest and most "sublime" art is the least confined, and that the couplet is therefore perhaps too severely restricting a medium. But the greater capacity of blank verse to achieve sublimity was enunciated by an influential figure as early as the beginning of the English Augustan period. In his famous prefatory note to *Paradise Lost* (1674) John Milton, in response to those who he anticipates may well wonder "why the Poem Rimes not," argues that rhyme is

> trivial and of no true musical delight; which consists only in apt Numbers, fit quantity of Syllables, and the sense variously drawn out from one Verse into another, not in the jingling sound of like endings, a fault avoided by the learned Ancients both in Poetry and all good Oratory. This neglect then of Rime so little is to be taken for a defect, though it may seem so perhaps to vulgar Readers, that it rather is to be esteem'd an example set, the first in *English*, of ancient liberty recover'd to Heroic Poem from the troublesome and modern bondage of Riming.[2]

It is for this reason, Milton says, that he chooses to write *Paradise Lost* in "*English* Heroic Verse without Rime, as that of *Homer* in *Greek*, and of *Virgil* in *Latin*."[3] And at the close of the Augustan period Samuel Johnson in *The Life of Milton*, after extolling the virtues of rhyme in comparison with those of blank verse, admits nevertheless that "I cannot prevail on myself to wish that Milton had been a rhymer" and concludes: "He that thinks himself capable of astonishing may write blank verse, but those that hope only to please must condescend to rhyme."[4]

Now it must be admitted that for Alexander Pope to have translated the *Iliad* into blank verse was not a realistic possibility. Pope's aborted epic the *Brutus*, it is true, was written in blank verse, but this may be one of the very reasons it was aborted.

---

[2] *John Milton: Complete Poems and Major Prose*, ed. Merritt Y. Hughes (New York: Odyssey Press, 1957), p. 210.

[3] Ibid.

[4] *Lives of the English Poets*, 1:94.

Pope's genius as a poet cannot be separated from his genius as a master of the rhyming couplet. When asked by Lyttleton why he did not translate the *Iliad* into blank verse, for instance, Pope is reported by Stockdale to have said that he "could translate it more easily into rhyme." This remark, as Dr. Johnson has pointedly observed, is something of an understatement.[5]

To translate Homer into rhyming couplets, then, was for Pope to exploit one of his greatest strengths as a poet, but rhyme had other distinct advantages for effectively simulating, in English, Homeric elevation. Although to a modern ear rhyme might seem less elevated—or, certainly, less "sublime"—than blank verse, this was not necessarily the case in the Augustan period. That which distinguished poetry from prose since antiquity was the fact that prose was generally straightforward, plain, and ordinary, while poetry employed a diction that was figurative and unusual. Aristotle's remarks in the *Rhetoric* are as succinct as they are representative:

> People do not feel towards strangers as they do towards their own countrymen, and the same thing is true of their feeling for language. It is therefore well to give everyday speech an unfamiliar air: people wonder at what is far off and remote (θαυμασταὶ γὰρ τῶν ἀπόντων εἰσίν) and all that is wonderful is agreeable (ἡδὺ δὲ τὸ θαυμαστόν). In verse such effects are common, and they are fitting (ἁρμόττει ἐκεῖ): the persons and things there spoken of are comparatively remote from ordinary life. In prose passages they are far less often fitting because the subject-matter is less exalted.[6] [3.2.1404b8-15]

The distinction is repeated by Cicero in both the *De Oratore* and the *Orator*. While an orator may occasionally embellish his diction by the use of rare words, newly coined words, or words used in a metaphorical sense, Cicero says, "these are more freely

---

[5] "When I communicated this anecdote to Dr. Johnson," Stockdale reports, his response was "Sir, when Pope said that, he knew that he lied," *Johnsonian Miscellanies*, ed. G. B. Hill, 2 vols. (Oxford: Clarendon Press, 1897), 2:332.

[6] Trans. Roberts, p. 167. I have made slight alterations in the translation.

allowed to the license of poets than to ourselves" (*De Oratore* III.xxxviii.153). For while the orator may occasionally employ some of the qualities of poetry, it is nevertheless important that "in prose we avoid the semblance of poetry" (*Orator* LX.202).[7]

One means by which English verse could readily distinguish, itself from prose and thereby elevate itself above the everyday was through rhyme. The problem with blank verse, to an Augustan ear, was precisely that the endings of the lines were blank; or, as Dr. Johnson said, quoting a contemporary critic, "Blank verse is verse only to the eye."[8] Blank verse, that is, might very well appear indistinguishable from prose to an eighteenth-century ear. So indistinguishable from prose might it appear that, were there to occur even the slightest departures from the iambic pentameter norm, such blank verse might well be printed as prose. And so, perhaps because there were some occasional metrical irregularities in it—and perhaps because it was itself a rendition of a prose version (that of Mme. Dacier)—the translation of the *Iliad* done in 1711 by John Ozell (Books I-VI), William Broome (Books VII-XV), and William Oldisworth (Books XVI-XXIV) was in fact printed as prose. Here is a passage—which I shall cite as if it had been printed as blank verse—from that translation: Iris, in Book XV, has been sent by Zeus to persuade Poseidon to cease at once from giving his powerful aid to the Greeks, and the god of the sea responds:

[7] *De Oratore*, trans. E. W. Sutton and H. Rackham, 2 vols., LCL (Cambridge, Mass. and London: Harvard University Press and William Heinemann, 1947), p. 121; *Orator*, trans. G. L. Hendrickson and H. M. Hubbell, LCL (Cambridge, Mass. and London: Harvard University Press and William Heinemann, 1942), p. 477. Cf. Isocrates, *Evagoras* 8-10: poets are "granted the use of many embellishments of language" and "can treat their lofty subjects not only in conventional expressions, but in words now exotic, now newly coined, and now in figures of speech, neglecting none, but using every kind with which to embroider their poesy. Orators, on the contrary, are not permitted the use of such devices; they must use with precision only words in current use and only such ideas as bear upon the actual facts" (*Isocrates*, trans. L. Van Hook, 3 vols., LCL [London and Cambridge, Mass.: William Heinemann and Harvard University Press, 1954], 3:9).

[8] The critic whom Johnson is quoting, according to G. B. Hill, is one "Mr. Locke of Norbury Place" (*Life of Milton*, *Lives of the Poets*, 1:193, n. 2).

Three are the Sons of *Saturn, Jove,* and I,
And *Pluto,* Ruler of the dark Abodes:
By Lot we hold our Empires, at my Nod
The roaring Billows of the Ocean sleep,
And *Pluto* rules the Kingdom of the Night.
Jove o'er the Heavens stretches his Domain,
[O'er the wide Clouds, and the ethereal Plains.]
[*Olympus* and the Earth in common lie,]
Therefore I'll not obsequiously obey
The will of *Jove*; let him command above,
And leave to me the Empire of the Deep.
Nor let him think to fright me with his Threats;
Let him reserve such Language for his Sons
And Daughters, whom he forces to obey.
    To whom the Messenger of *Jove* reply'd:
Must I, O potent Ruler of the Main,
Bear this fierce Answer to the King of Heaven?
Does Nought deserve a Change? to change sometimes
Speaks Wisdom; and a Guardian Fury waits
On elder Brothers, to revenge their Wrongs.
To whom the Sov'reign of the Floods thus spoke:
Your words have Reason, and it much avails,
[When Messengers are blest with prudent Minds.][9]

In spite of the fact that this passage was originally printed as
prose, it scans without the least difficulty as iambic pentameter
blank verse: the endings of the lines are generally clearly enun-
ciated and the caesura remains near the medial position in a
sufficient number of lines so that a norm is established from
which the less regular lines may be perceived to vary. Except
insofar that the endings of these lines do not rhyme, so closely
do their metrical characteristics resemble those of the heroic
couplet, that Pope was in fact able to transfer four of these lines,
virtually intact, into his own rendition of the passage. I have

---

[9] *TE*, 10:582. The Twickenham editors indicate in their text—which they also
print as verse—the words, phrases, and lines which Pope took over or adapted
in his translation.

placed in brackets those lines which Pope took over: 1) the line "O'er the wide Clouds, and the ethereal Plains" from the Ozell-Broome-Oldisworth *Iliad* becomes, in Pope's version, "O'er the wide clouds and o'er the starry plain" (l. 214); 2) "*Olympus* and the Earth in common lie" becomes "*Olympus*, and this earth, in common lie" (l. 218); 3) "Bear this fierce Answer to the King of Heaven" becomes "Bear this fierce answer to the King of Gods" (l. 225); and 4) "When Messengers are blest with prudent Minds" becomes "When Ministers are blest with prudent Mind" (l. 231).

It is instructive to compare this passage from the early eighteenth-century "prose" translation of Ozell, Broome, and Oldisworth with a modern "poetic" version of the very same passage from the *Iliad* (1974) of Robert Fitzgerald (I have numbered the lines so that they can be easily referred to in the discussion which follows):

1   . . . "Sons of Kronos
    all of us are, all three whom Rhea bore,
    Zeus and I and the lord of those below.
    All things were split three ways, to each his honor,
5   when we cast lots. Indeed it fell to me
    to abide forever in the grey sea water;
    Hades received the dark mist at the world's-end,
    and Zeus the open heaven of air and cloud.
    But Earth is common to all, so is Olympos.
10 No one should think that I shall live one instant
    as he thinks best! No, let him hold his peace
    and power in his heaven, in his portion,
    not try intimidating me—
    I will not have it—as though I were a coward.
15 Better to roar and thunder at his own,
    the sons and daughters he himself has fathered!
    They are the ones that have to listen to him."

    Wind-swift Iris answered:

                                        "Shall I put it
    just that way, god of the dark blue tresses,

[136]

20 bearing this hostile message back to Zeus?
    Or will you make some change? All princely hearts
    are capable of changing. And, you know,
    the Furies take the part of elder brothers!"[10]

Whereas all the lines in the passage from the Ozell-Broome-
Oldisworth *Iliad*, even though they were printed as prose, can
be scanned as examples of iambic pentameter, of the twenty-two
complete lines cited here perhaps fifteen can be so scanned with-
out question. The second line, allowing for the common inversion
of the first foot, scans with perfect ease:

    áll of us áre, all thrée whom Rhéa bóre, . . .

But the third line is already problematic. It might best be de-
scribed as a beheaded iambic pentameter—such nine-syllable lines
are common in Fitzgerald's Homeric translations (see, for ex-
ample, lines 18 and 19 of this passage)—with a trisyllabic sub-
stitution in the third foot ("and the lord"). Line 13 ("not try
intimidating me") lacks a foot and thus cannot truly be scanned
as a pentameter. And the use of feminine endings in this passage
is so pervasive—such endings occur in lines 1, 4, 6, 7, 9, 10, 12,
14, 16, 17, 18, 19, and 23—that this, too, prevents the iambic
pentameter norm from being firmly established.

Now Robert Fitzgerald has a far surer sense of the English
poetic line, it should be made clear, than most contemporary
translators of ancient Greek poetry. If one leafs through, for
example, the University of Chicago series of the complete Greek
tragedies and picks almost any passage at random the truth of
this statement will be hard to deny. Listen to the speech of
Aphrodite which opens the *Hippolytus* of Euripides:

    I am called the Goddess Cypris:
    I am mighty among men and they honor me by many
        means.
    All those that live and see the light of sun

---

[10] *The Iliad of Homer* (Garden City, N.Y.: Anchor Press/Doubleday, 1974),
pp. 355-356.

[137]

from Atlas' Pillars to the tide of Pontus
are mine to rule.
Such as worship my power in all humility,
I exalt in honor.
but those whose pride is stiff-necked against me
I lay by the heels.
There is joy in the heart of a God also
when honored by men.[11]

[ll. 1-11]

It would be very difficult indeed to identify the metrical norm in these lines, which are a translation of Greek lines in which the metrical scheme—the iambic trimeter—is plainly obvious and wholly conventional. So that, while one must praise, in contrast, the more clearly enunciated metrical norm which is to be found in the Homeric translations of Robert Fitzgerald, it must also be pointed out, as has at least one contemporary critic, that the blank verse of his translations seems at times as much the result of typographical layout as of clearly realized metrical principles.[12] When, for example, the following passage from Fitzgerald's *Odyssey* is printed as prose, is it possible to identify the poetic lines? The scene is from the twenty-third book; Eurycleia has just told Penelope the miraculous news that Odysseus has at last returned and that he and Telemachus have just taken their revenge upon the evil suitors, and Penelope replies:

"Nurse dear, though you have your wits about you, still it is hard not to be taken in by the immortals. Let us join my son, though, and see the dead and that strange one who killed them." She turned then to descend the stair, her heart in tumult. Had she better keep her distance and question him, her husband? Should she run up to him, take his hands, kiss him now? Crossing the door sill she sat down at once in firelight,

[11] Trans. David Grene, *The Complete Greek Tragedies*, ed. David Grene and Richmond Lattimore, 4 vols. (Chicago: University of Chicago Press, 1959-1960), 3:163.

[12] H. A. Mason, *To Homer Through Pope*, pp. 198-200. Mason's remarks originally appeared in *The New York Review of Books*, May 9, 1968.

against the nearest wall, across the room from the lord Odysseus.[13]

That "blank verse is verse only to the eye" may have been a questionable pronouncement in the eighteenth century; for I have tried to show that, even when printed as prose, the qualities of the pentameter line manage to articulate themselves in the Ozell-Broome-Oldisworth *Iliad*. But the pronouncement is perhaps less questionable today. For if, when regarding the passage from Fitzgerald's version of *Odyssey* XXIII cited above, the eye were denied the luxury of typography and thus of perceiving the endings of the lines, would these endings in all probability be perceptible to even the most discriminating ear?

The problem with blank verse, then, is that, especially to an Augustan ear, it may appear indistinguishable from prose. It is for this reason that Neander, in Dryden's *Essay of Dramatic Poesy* (1668), says that in serious plays rhyme is preferable to blank verse. Earlier in the famous dialogue Crites had argued that blank verse was closer to "nature" and was therefore a more suitable poetic instrument. But one must distinguish, Neander says, between

> what is nearest to the nature of comedy, which is the imitation of common persons and ordinary speaking, and what is nearest the nature of a serious play: this last is indeed the representation of nature, but 'tis nature wrought up to an higher pitch. The plot, the characters, the wit, the passions, the descriptions, are all exalted above the level of common converse, as high as the imagination of the poet can carry them with proportion to verisimility. Tragedy, we know, is wont to image to us the minds and fortunes of noble persons, and to portray these exactly: heroic rhyme is nearest nature, as being the noblest kind of modern verse.

> indignatur enim privatis et prope socco
> dignis carminibus narrari caena Thyestae

---

[13] *The Odyssey of Homer* (1961; reprint ed. New York: Anchor Press/Doubleday, 1963), pp. 431-432.

(For Thyestes' supper scorns to be treated in the language of common life, language unworthy of the tragic style),

(says Horace). And in another place,

effutire leves indigna tragoedia versus

(Tragedy thinks it unworthy to chatter silly verses).

Blank verse is acknowledged to be too low for a poem, nay more, for a paper of verses; but if too low for an ordinary sonnet, how much more for tragedy, which is by Aristotle, in the dispute betwixt the epic poesy and the dramatic, for many reasons he there alleges, ranked above it?[14]

Tragedy, Neander says, is a representation of "nature wrought up to an higher pitch"; and the same is even truer of the epic, which Dryden considered—at odds with Aristotle's preference but at one with the critics and writers of the Renaissance—as "the greatest work of human nature."[15] Through his use of rhyme, then, Pope could exalt his translation "above the level of common converse" and as high as his imagination could carry him "with proportion to verisimility."

But rhyme had another distinct and, in fact, contrary advantage. "Style to be good must be clear," Aristotle recommended in the *Rhetoric* (III.1.1404b); "it must also be appropriate ($\pi\rho\acute{\epsilon}$-$\pi o \upsilon \sigma \alpha \nu$), avoiding the extremes of meanness and undue elevation."[16] And in the *Poetics* he says that while the inclusion of unusual words, metaphors, and poetic embellishments will raise a style "above the commonplace and mean, the use of proper words will make it perspicuous ($\sigma \alpha \phi \acute{\eta} \nu \epsilon \iota \alpha \nu$)." Aristotle continues:

For by deviating in exceptional cases from normal idiom, the language will gain distinction; while, at the same time, the

[14] *Of Dramatic Poesy*, ed. Watson, 1:86-87.
[15] *The Author's Apology for Heroic Poetry and Poetic License* (1677), *Of Dramatic Poesy*, 1:198.
[16] Trans. Roberts, p. 167.

partial conformity with usage will give perspicuity (τὸ σα-
φές).[17] [XXII. 1458b]

Joseph Addison restates Aristotle's recommendation for the early
eighteenth century in the *Spectator* paper I have previously dis-
cussed. "The language of an heroic Poem," Addison writes, should
be not only "Sublime" but it should be "Perspicuous"[18] as well.
The use of rhyme will contribute to sublimity by virtue of its
remoteness from normal usage. But it also has the potential of
enabling an elevated style to achieve perspicuity.

Here is how Pope, as presented by Thomas Parnell in that
author's prefatory remarks to his translation of *Homer's Battle
of the Frogs and Mice* (1717), answers those who might suggest
to him that he should have translated the *Iliad* into blank verse:

> Some may fancy, a Poet of the greatest Fire wou'd be imitated
> better in the Freedom of Blank Verse, and the Description of
> War sounds more pompous out of Rhime. But, will the Trans-
> lation . . . be thus remov'd from Prose, without greater In-
> conveniences? What Transpositions is *Milton* forc'd to, as an
> Equivalent for Want of Rhime, in the Poetry of a Language
> which depends upon a Natural Order of Words? And even
> this wou'd not have done his Business, had he not given the
> fullest Scope to his Genius, by choosing a Subject upon which
> there could be no Hyperboles.[19]

The point Pope is making is that English word order is more
difficult to tamper with than—it is implied—the word order of
Greek and Latin; and therefore to lend to a poetic style that air
of foreignness which will help it achieve elevation, it is necessary,
if one is writing blank verse, to distort English syntax to such a
degree that the language will no longer be "perspicuous." Even
such distortions, however, may not sufficiently distinguish a style

[17] Trans. Butcher, p. 83.
[18] *Spectator*, ed. Bond, 3:11.
[19] Thomas Parnell, *Homer's Battle of the Frogs and Mice with the Remarks
of Zoilus*, London, 1717. Douglas Knight cites this passage and discusses it in
Pope and the Heroic Tradition, pp. 62-63.

VERSIFICATION

from prose, unless the subject matter is as astounding and as
marvelous as is Milton's in *Paradise Lost*. But the presence of
rhyme will immediately suggest to an audience that what it is
experiencing is uncommon, out of the ordinary. Once this air of
foreignness is conveyed, the poet is no longer forced to depart
so violently from idiomatic usage: he is then free to achieve the
perspicuity that is, for Aristotle and for Addison, together with
sublimity a necessary quality of style in a heroic poem. Pope
would later in his life repeat his criticism of Milton's style. In
the *Odyssey* postscript he says that Milton should have at-
tempted to copy Homer's "plainness and perspicuity in the *Dra-
matic* parts" of *Paradise Lost*, for in the speeches of that poem
"there is frequently such transposition and forced construction,
that the very sense is not to be discover'd without a second or
third reading."[20] And in 1739 Pope told Spence that he "doubted
whether a poem could sustain itself" in English without rhyme,
"unless it be stiffened with such strange words as are like to
destroy our language itself. The high style that is affected so
much in blank verse would not have been borne even in Milton,
had not his subject turned so much on such strange out-of-the-
world things as it does."[21]

"Milton's style in his *Paradise Lost* is not natural; 'tis an exotic
style."[22] This observation made by Pope to Spence in 1736 was
restated by Samuel Johnson later in the century. So unidiomatic
did Milton's style appear to Johnson that it led him to reach his
now famous conclusion that the great poet "had formed his style
by a perverse and pedantick principle. He was desirous to use
English words with a foreign idiom. . . . Of him, at last, may be
said what Jonson says of Spenser, that 'he wrote no language,'
but has formed what Butler calls 'a Babylonish Dialect.' "[23] The
reference to Butler is suggestive. In *Hudibras* (1667), from which
this last phrase is drawn, Butler portrays Sir Hudibras as a rep-

[20] *TE*, 10:391.
[21] *Anecdotes, Observations, and Characters of Books and Men*, ed. Osborne,
1:173.
[22] Ibid., 1:197.
[23] *Life of Milton, Lives of the Poets*, ed. Hill, 1:190-191.

resentative Puritan, a man much taken with his own private view
of the world as well as with his Greek, Latin, and Hebrew learn-
ing which, like Milton, he did not hesitate to conceal. His manner
of speech, Butler says,

> In loftiness of sound was rich,
> A *Babylonish* dialect,
> Which learned Pedants much affect.
> It was a particolour'd dress
> Of patch'd and pyball'd Languages:
> 'Twas *English* cut on *Greek* and *Latin*,
> Like Fustian heretofore on Sattin.
> It had an odde promiscuous Tone,
> As if h' had talk'd three parts in one.
> Which made some think, when he did gabble,
> Th' had heard three Labourers of *Babel*;
> Or *Cerberus* himself pronounce
> A Leash of Languages at once.[24]
>
> [I.i.92-104]

What Butler most objects to in the Puritans is their fanatical
desire to impose their will upon a recalcitrant reality. As a Puritan
revolutionary, Milton, in Johnson's view, attempted to do just
this in the political sphere. And as a poet, according to Johnson,
Milton similarly attempted to impose a recalcitrantly foreign
syntax onto English. As the Puritans' rigidly subjective view of
the world has a questionable relation to empirical reality, so
Milton's style, Johnson suggests, "was not modified by his sub-
ject."[25] Certainly the tone of revolutionary pathos is unmistak-
able in the concluding sentence from Milton's prefatory note to
Paradise Lost:

> This neglect then of Rime so little is to be taken for a defect,
> though it may seem so perhaps to vulgar Readers, that it rather
> is to be esteem'd an example set, the first in *English*, of ancient

[24] *Hudibras*, ed. with intro. and comm. by John Wilders (Oxford: Clarendon
Press, 1967), p. 4.
[25] *Lives of the Poets*, 1:190.

liberty recover'd to Heroic Poem from the troublesome and modern bondage of Riming.[26]

If Milton freed the heroic poem from the "modern bondage of Riming," he did so, according to Pope and Johnson, at the expense of violently distorting the natural contours of the English language; he did so, in other words, at the expense of "perspicuity."

POETIC DICTION AND THE VERSE LINE

I would like finally to address another objection to the style of Pope's Homer, one which may seem harder to answer. Leigh Hunt (1784-1859), a poet who was to influence Keats, is an early exponent of this critical view. In an issue of *The Reflector* (2 [1812]:314), Hunt objects to what he perceives to be the tiring regularity of the eighteenth-century heroic couplet and advises that poets should attempt to "bring back the real harmonies of the English heroic, and to restore to it the true principles of its music—variety." He continues:

> Let the reader take any dozen or twenty lines from Pope at a hazard, or if he pleases, from his best and most elaborate passages, and he will find that they have scarcely any other pauses than at the fourth or fifth syllable, and both with little variation of accent. Upon these the poet is eternally dropping his voice, line after line, sometimes upon only one of them for eight or ten lines together. . . . See, for instance, the first twenty lines of Windsor Forest, the two first paragraphs of Eloisa to Abelard, and that gorgeous misrepresentation of the exquisite moonlight picture in Homer. The last may well be quoted:—

> As when the moon—refulgent lamp of night,
> O'er Heav'ns clear azure—spreads her sacred light,
> When not a breath—disturbs the deep serene,
> And not a cloud—o'ercasts the solemn scene;
> Around her throne—the vivid planets roll,

---

[26] *Milton: Poems*, ed. Hughes, p. 210.

And stars unnumber'd—gild the glowing pole,
O'er the dark trees—a yellower verdure shed,
And tip with silver—ev'ry mountain's head;—
Then shine the vales—the rocks in prospect rise,
A flood of glory—bursts from all the skies:
The conscious swains—rejoicing in the sight,
Eye the blue vault—and bless the useful light.

Of the justice of these remarks with regard to *Windsor Forest* and *Eloisa to Abelard* I shall not concern myself here. Let it suffice to say that Pope was very much aware, as he remarked in a letter to his friend William Walsh, that it was precisely "the judicious Change and Management" of the caesura upon which "the Variety of Versification" depends; for if the placement of the caesura does not vary, Pope continues, "it will be apt to weary the Ear with one continu'd Tone."[27] In defense of the moonlight passage it must be said, first of all, that "the *Sound* must seem an *Echo* to the *Sense*": Pope is in this particular passage describing a hauntingly silent scene and the couplets should therefore be perfectly balanced and regular so as to convey as little nervously animated movement as possible. And it must also be said that in an English translation of a heroic poem too great a variety in the placement of the caesura might, unless the poet happens to be John Milton, well create an impression of inappropriate prosiness. A strong break in the middle of the line happens, in fact, to be a characteristic of orally composed poetry in general. This is true of Old English verse, in which each distinct half of the poetic line is strongly enunciated by two stressed syllables, a pattern which is made even more conspicuous through alliteration; and it is true of Homeric verse in which, while enjambement and secondary pauses are frequent, there is one clear break in every line. And it must further be said that a chief characteristic of the oral style of presentation, as Aristotle suggests in *Rhetoric* III.12, is a certain unsubtle obviousness; for

---

[27] *The Correspondence of Alexander Pope*, 1:23. The letter is dated October 22, 1706. Leigh Hunt's remarks in *The Reflector* are discussed by Geoffrey Tillotson, *Pope and Human Nature* (Oxford: Clarendon Press, 1958), pp. 182ff.

Pope to be overly subtle in his attempt to simulate Homeric verse would thus be a misrepresentation of his author.

It may well be that Pope, by placing the caesura at or near the medial position in the lines in this passage and elsewhere in his *Iliad*, is trying to avoid a tone of relaxed prosiness and thus to help simulate Homer's quality of poetic fire which he so eloquently describes in the *Iliad* preface. For when Pope comes to translate the *Odyssey*—a work which, in contrast to the supremely sublime *Iliad*, Pope, following Longinus, believes "sometimes descends into the plainer Narrative, and sometimes even to that familiar dialogue essential to Comedy"[28]—he often tends to vary much more significantly the placement of the caesura.

In the twenty-sixth chapter of his *De Compositione Verborum*, Dionysius of Halicarnassus discusses the ways in which verse can be made to resemble prose. This can be achieved, Dionysius says, if the poet will

> make the clauses begin and end at various places within the lines, not allowing their sense to be self-contained in separate verses, but breaking up the measure. He must make the clauses vary in length and form, and will often also reduce them to phrases which are shorter than clauses, and will make the periods—those at any rate which adjoin one another—neither equal in size nor alike in construction; for an elastic treatment of rhythms seems to bring verse quite near to prose.[29]

Although this may come as a surprise to Leigh Hunt and his followers, Pope was well aware of these remarks of Dionysius, whose "Treatise of the *Composition of Words*"[30] he praises in the *Iliad* preface and refers to frequently in his notes. But Pope was more than well aware of these remarks, for he (or one of his auxiliaries) in fact translated them in the notes which accompany his version of the *Odyssey*. "Whoever would write ele-

[28] *TE*, 10:386.

[29] *Dionysius of Halicarnassus on Literary Composition*, ed. with intro., trans., notes, glossary, and appendices by W. Rhys Roberts (London: Macmillan and Co., 1910), p. 271.

[30] *TE*, 7:11.

gantly," Pope says in his transcription of Dionysius' observations,

> must have regard to the different turn and juncture of every period, there must be proper distance and pauses; every verse must be a compleat sentence, but broken and interrupted, and the parts made unequal, some longer, some shorter, to give a variety of cadence to it. Neither the turn of the parts of the verse, nor the length, ought to be alike. This is absolutely necessary: For the Epic or Heroic verse is of a fix'd determinate length, and we cannot, as in the Lyric, make one longer, and another shorter; therefore to avoid an identity of cadence, and a perpetual return of the same periods, it is requisite to contract, lengthen, and interrupt the pause and structure of the members of the verses, to create an harmonious inequality, and out of a fix'd number of syllables to raise a perpetual diversity.[31]

Dionysius goes on to show how Homer, in the first lines of *Odyssey* XIV, manages to achieve the effect just described. Here are the Homeric lines:

> Αὐτὰρ ὁ ἐκ λιμένος προσέβη τρηχεῖαν ἀταρπὸν
> χῶρον ἀν' ὑλήεντα δι' ἄκριας, ᾗ οἱ Ἀθήνη
> πέφραδε δῖον ὑφορβόν, ὅ οἱ βιότυυ μάλιστα
> κήδετο οἰκήων, οὓς κτήσατο δῖος Ὀδυσσεύς.
>
> Τὸν δ' ἄρ' ἐνὶ προδόμῳ εὗρ' ἥμενον, ἔνθα οἱ αὐλὴ
> ὑψηλὴ δέδμητο, περισκέπτῳ ἐνὶ χώρῳ,
> καλή τε μεγάλη τε, περίδρομος.

> Then Odysseus left the harbor and set out along a
>   rugged path,
> up the woodland and through the hills, to the place
>   where Athena
> had said he would find the godlike swineherd, the man
>   who, more than any of the others in Odysseus'
>   household,

---

[31] Ibid., 10:33.

VERSIFICATION

made it his concern to look after his master's land and
possessions.

He found him sitting on the porch in front of his house
where the lofty courtyard was built, in a place which
commanded a wide view,
a courtyard large and beautiful, and built in a circular
fashion.

[*Odyssey* XIV.1-7][32]

Dionysius' stylistic analysis of the Homeric passage reads, in
Pope's transcription, as follows:

Αὐτὰρ ὁ ἐκ λιμένος προσέβη τρηχεῖαν ἀταρπόν.

Here one line makes one sentence; the next is shorter,

Χῶρον ἀν' ὑλήεντα—

The next is still shorter,

—δι' ἄκριας—

The next sentence composes two Hemystics [*sic*],

—ἢ οἱ 'Αθήνη
Πέφραδε δῖον ὑφορβόν—

and is entirely unlike any of the preceding periods.

—ὅ οἱ βιότοιο μάλιστα
Κήδετο οἰκήων, οὓς κτήσατο δῖος 'Οδυσσεύς.

Here again the sentence is not finished with the former verse,
but breaks into the fourth line; and lest we should be out of
breath with the length of the sentence, the period and the verse
conclude together at the end of it.

Then *Homer* begins a new sentence, and makes it pause
differently from any of the former.

Τὸν δ' ἄρ' ἐνὶ προδόμῳ εὗρ' ἥμενον

Then he adds,

32 My own translation.

[148]

—ἔνθα οἱ αὐλὴ
Ὑψηλὴ δέδμητο—

This is perfectly unequal to the foregoing period, and the pause
of the sentence is carry'd forward into the second verse; and
what then follows is neither distinguish'd by the pauses nor
parts periodically, but almost at every word there is a stop.

—περισκέπτῳ ἐνὶ χώρῳ
Καλή τε μεγάλη τε.

Here now is Pope's version of the Homeric passage:

> But He, deep-musing, o'er the mountains stray'd,
> Thro' mazy thickets of the woodland shade,
> And cavern'd ways, the shaggy coast along,
> With cliffs, and nodding forests over-hung.
> *Eumaeus* at his Sylvan lodge he sought,
> A faithful servant, and without a fault.
> *Ulysses* found him, busied as he sate
> Before the threshold of his rustic gate;
> Around the mansion in a circle shone
> A rural Portico of rugged stone.
>
> [ll. 1-10]

Pope's lines are, it is true, less freely enjambed than are Homer's,
but two of the ten lines—lines 7 ("*Ulysses* found him, busied as
he sate / Before the threshold of his rustic gate") and 9 ("Around
the mansion in a circle shone / A rural Portico of rugged stone")—
are enjambed very conspicuously. In the moonlight simile from
the *Iliad*—a work which is marked by consistent elevation and
is thus far removed from prose—the caesura falls in every line
after either the fourth or fifth syllable. But in this passage from
the more relaxed and proselike *Odyssey* the pauses are much
more varied. A caesura falls after the second syllable, for ex-
ample, in lines 1 ("But He, deep-musing, o'er the mountains
stray'd") and 4 ("With cliffs, and nodding forests over-hung")
and after either the third or eighth syllable, or perhaps after both,
in line 5 ("*Eumaeus* at his Sylvan lodge he sought"); in line 9
("Around the mansion in a circle shone") the caesura falls, if

indeed it falls at all, just before the final syllable. In line 8 ("Before the threshold of his rustic gate"), where the caesura does appear to fall in the medial position, the pause is so faint as to be almost indistinct; and the same may be said of the pause that appears to be placed after the sixth syllable in the final line ("A rural Portico of rugged stone"). Lest the reader suspect that the variety in the placing of the pauses in this passage points to an authorship other than Pope's, it should be mentioned that Book XIV is one of those books that is certainly the work of Pope and not of his assistants Fenton and Broome.[33]

It must be admitted, on the other hand, that Pope's usual handling of the pentameter line and of the couplet, particularly in his *Iliad*, does tend to make more conspicuous the traditional elements of epic diction that are less obvious in, for example, the more relaxed couplets of Dryden and in Milton's blank verse. It may well be for this reason that Samuel Johnson, in the *Idler* paper I discussed earlier, singled out the opening lines of Pope's *Iliad* for exhibiting qualities of epic style which were in fact thoroughly traditional. And so it may be for this reason as well that Coleridge was later to single out Pope's Homer, in a manner that would become commonplace in the nineteenth century, for its allegedly corrupting influence upon contemporary poetic style. "His translation of Homer," Coleridge said in his famous and influential remark, "I do not stand alone in regarding as the main source of our pseudo-poetic diction."[34]

The lines that provoked Coleridge's critical disapproval happen to be the very ones that Leigh Hunt only a few years earlier had chosen to discuss in his attack upon Pope's prosody. Here again is the passage, which appears at the conclusion of *Iliad* VIII, cited this time at greater length and without the prejudicial dashes inserted by Hunt at the medial position of the lines;

---

[33] See George Sherburn, *The Early Career of Alexander Pope* (Oxford: Clarendon Press, 1934), p. 260. The preceding passages from Pope's *Odyssey* and from Pope's transcription of the remarks of Dionysius are cited from *TE*, 10:32-35.

[34] *Biographia Literaria*, 1:26.

Homer is comparing the fires kindled in the Trojan camp to the
shining of the moon and stars on a clear night:

> The Troops exulting sate in order round,
> And beaming Fires illumin'd all the Ground.
> As when the Moon, refulgent Lamp of Night!
> O'er Heav'ns clear Azure spreads her sacred Light,
> When not a Breath disturbs the deep Serene;
> And not a Cloud o'ercasts the solemn Scene;
> Around her Throne the vivid Planets roll,
> And Stars unnumber'd gild the glowing Pole,
> O'er the dark Trees a yellower Verdure shed,
> And tip with Silver ev'ry Mountain's Head;
> Then shine the Vales, the Rocks in Prospect rise,
> A Flood of Glory bursts from all the Skies:
> The conscious Swains, rejoicing in the Sight,
> Eye the blue Vault, and bless the useful Light.
> So many Flames before proud *Ilion* blaze,
> And lighten glimm'ring *Xanthus* with their Rays.
> The long Reflections of the distant Fires
> Gleam on the Walls, and tremble on the Spires.
> A thousand Piles the dusky Horrors gild,
> And shoot a shady Lustre o'er the Field.
> Full fifty Guards each flaming Pile attend,
> Whose umber'd Arms, by fits, thick Flashes send.
> Loud neigh the Coursers o'er their Heaps of Corn,
> And ardent Warriors wait the rising Morn.
>
> [ll. 685-708]

Of these lines Coleridge writes:

> In the course of my lectures, I had occasion to point out the
> almost faultless position and choice of words, in Mr. Pope's
> *original* compositions, particularly in his Satires and moral
> Essays, for the purpose of comparing them with his translation
> of Homer, which I do not stand alone in regarding as the main
> source of our pseudo-poetic diction.... Among other passages,

I analyzed sentence by sentence, and almost word by word, the popular lines,

> "As when the moon, resplendent [sic] lamp of light [sic]," &c. . . .

The impression on the audience in general was sudden and evident: and a number of enlightened and highly educated persons, who at different times afterwards addressed me on the subject, expressed their wonder, that truth so obvious should not have struck them *before*; but at the same time acknowledged . . . that they might in all probability have read the same passage again twenty times with undiminished admiration, and without once reflecting, that "ἄστρα φαεινὴν ἀμφὶ σελήνην φαίνετ᾽ ἀριπρεπέα" (i.e. the stars around, or near the full moon, shine preeminently bright) conveys a just and happy image of a moonlight sky: while it is difficult to determine whether in the lines,

> "Around *her throne* the vivid planets *roll*,
> And stars *unnumber'd gild* the *glowing pole*,"

the sense or the diction be the more absurd.[35]

That the diction of Pope's translation is considerably more elaborate than that of the original there is no doubt, but it must be pointed out once again that Pope did not invent this diction. Milton spoke of the "Rising Sun" as a gilding agent in *Paradise Lost* III.551[36] and he spoke of the planet Venus in a similar sense

---

[35] Ibid., 1:26-27.

[36] Milton is comparing Satan, as he looks down at earth from Heaven Gate, to a "Scout" who

> Through dark and desert ways with peril gone
> All night; at last by break of cheerful dawn
> Obtains the brow of some high-climbing Hill,
> Which to his eye discovers unaware
> The goodly prospect of some foreign land
> First seen, or some renown'd Metropolis
> With glistering Spires and Pinnacles adorn'd,
> Which now the Rising Sun gilds with his beams.
> [ll. 544-551]

[152]

in *Paradise Lost* VII.366.[37] The entire metaphor, moreover (which is not present in the original), appears to have been adapted by Pope from Dryden's *Aeneis* VII.188; among the deities to whom Aeneas is praying in this passage is "Night, and all the Stars that guild her sable Throne."[38] "Rolling" heavenly bodies are not an invention of Pope's; in *Paradise Lost* VIII.20 Milton spoke of "number'd Stars, that seem to roll." Nor is the diction of the phrase "glowing pole" any more pseudo-poetic than Milton's "starrie Pole" which appears in *Paradise Lost* IV.724. In fact, almost all of the elements of diction which Coleridge would have considered as pseudo-poetic can be traced back directly to Milton or to Dryden.[39]

Just as the elements of style to which Johnson objects in *Idler* 77 had been recommended by both Aristotle in the *Poetics* and Addison in *Spectator* 285 and realized by Milton in *Paradise Lost*, so the words and phrases with which Coleridge finds fault can be found in Milton and in Dryden. But poetry is not written

---

Cited from *Milton: Poems*, ed. Hughes, p. 271. The verbal parallels between this passage and Pope's translation of the moonlight simile suggest that Pope may well have had the Miltonic passage in mind when he came to translate the Homeric simile.

[37] Milton is describing the creation of the heavenly bodies. In the "Light" of the "sun's Orb" "the Morning Planet gilds her horns" (*Milton: Poems*, ed. Hughes, p. 355). A few lines later Milton refers to the sun as "the glorious Lamp" (l. 370), which Pope's "Lamp of Night" (*Iliad* VIII.687) may be modeled upon.

[38] *The Poems of John Dryden*, ed. Kinsley, 3:1238.

[39] The word "exulting" (Pope's *Iliad* VIII.685) was bequeathed to Pope by Dryden, who uses "exulting" in his *Aeneis* as a translation of the Latin *exsultare* and its cognates (see, e.g., Dryden's "exulting" in *Aeneis* XII.700). The adjective "conscious" in Pope's "conscious Swains" (*Iliad* VIII.697) was likewise bequeathed to Pope by Dryden, who uses "conscious" as a translation of the Latin *conscius* (Dryden's "conscious virtue" in *Aeneis* V.607, for example, translates Virgil's *conscia virtus* in *Aeneid* V.455). Pope's "blue Vault" (*Iliad* VIII.698) is perhaps indebted to Milton's "Vault of Heaven" (*P.L.*I. 669). Pope's "dusky Horrors" (*Iliad* VIII.703) may likewise be indebted to Milton, who in *Paradise Regained* speaks of "dusk with horrid shades" (*P.R.* I.296). The adjective "dusky" can be found throughout *Paradise Lost* (I.226, II.488, V.186, 677, VI.58) and Dryden's *Aeneis* (III.663, VI.382, 395, 614, VII.569, IX.20, XII.685). H. A. Mason, in *To Homer Through Pope*, discusses Pope's moonlight simile and mentions Pope's indebtedness to Milton and Dryden (pp. 67-68).

[153]

in words and phrases alone: it is written in lines, the endings of
which may either rhyme or not rhyme, and it is written in meter;
and the amount of attention a poet draws to any particular word
or phrase will be determined, to a large degree, by his handling
of the line and, if the endings of the lines rhyme, of the couplet.
It is because of Pope's handling of the pentameter line and of
the couplet that the traditional elements of epic diction often
become conspicuous in his translation. None of the couplets in
the moonlight simile quoted above, for example, is enjambed,
and every line but one is clearly end-stopped.[40] Thus in the cou-
plet

> As when the Moon, refulgent Lamp of Night!
> O'er Heav'ns clear Azure spreads her sacred Light
> [ll. 687-688]

the emphatic caesura which occurs after the fourth syllable in
line 687 draws attention to the phrase "refulgent Lamp of Night"
which immediately follows the caesura, and the similarly em-
phatic caesura which occurs in the medial position in the fol-
lowing line—and which breaks the line into distinct halves—
draws attention to the phrase "Heav'ns clear Azure." Such em-
phatic pauses occur in or very near the middle of almost every
line in this passage. The Latinate adjective "refulgent" appears
in *Paradise Lost* VI.527 and Dryden uses it continuously
throughout his *Aeneis*;[41] Milton refers to the heavenly bodies as

---

[40] Pope's tendency to end-stop his lines and couplets and to break his lines
into balanced halves is more pronounced in the earlier poetry (the first volume
of the *Iliad* translation was published as early as 1715), as John A. Jones argues:
"The balanced line is the basic feature of the couplet upon which Pope based
his stylistic developments. Generally he used less balance in the later poems. . . .
By the time of the *Dunciad Variorum* in 1728, Pope embodied complex satire
in a more direct and proselike syntax than is characteristic of the earlier poems;
and though his antithetic parallels are still at work, they are not as closely confined
in separate couplets as earlier, and are subordinated to the designs of the enclosing
passages" (*Pope's Couplet Art* [Athens: Ohio University Press, 1969], pp. 200-
201).

[41] "Refulgent" appears in Dryden's *Aeneis* I.557, II.834, VI.660, VIII.697,
XI.1238, and XII.637.

"lamps" in *Paradise Lost*;[42] and the phrase "Heav'ns Azure" comes directly from *Paradise Lost* I.297. Such characteristics of epic diction are far less conspicuous in the typical line of Milton because it is unrhymed and because there is a great flexibility in the position of the caesura; they are also less conspicuous in the line of Dryden because of the almost as great flexibility in the position of the caesura, a flexibility which tends to increase the number of run-on lines and open couplets.

Pope attempts to heighten the style of his *Iliad* by incorporating what Addison in *Spectator* 285 refers to as "the Transposition of Words," but this device is also at times rendered conspicuous because of Pope's handling of the pentameter line and of the couplet. Andromache in Book VI of Pope's translation, for example, fears for Hector's life and asks him to withdraw from battle before he is killed; Hector replies:

> Me glory summons to the martial Scene,
> The Field of Combate is the Sphere for Men.
>
> [ll. 634-635]

The Miltonic inversion "Me glory summons" is made conspicuous here by the end-stopped quality of both the line and the couplet as well as by the placement of the caesura, which falls after the phrase "Me glory summons" and which appears in precisely the same medial position in the following line. And similar observations can be made of the couplet which introduces Hector's angry speech to the indolent Paris earlier in Book VI:

> Him thus unactive, with an ardent Look
> The Prince beheld, and high-resenting spoke.
>
> [ll. 404-405]

Pope himself believed, as I have mentioned, that Milton's choice of rhymeless verse in *Paradise Lost* forced him to employ just such inversions of normal word order as "Me glory summons"

---

[42] *P.L.* III.581, VII.370, IX.104. To speak of the heavenly bodies as "lamps" is, of course, a commonplace in western literature and is ultimately derived from the Latin *lampas* ("torch"), which is used in Latin literature as a metaphor for the sun or moon (e.g., Virgil in *Aeneid* III.67 refers to the sun as *Phoebea lampas*).

and "Him thus unactive" in order to distinguish his blank verse from prose. But if such inversions are conspicuous in Milton's blank verse, they are at times rendered even more so in the often symmetrically balanced and regularly end-stopped couplets of Pope's *Iliad*.

In *Idler* 77 Johnson objected to the superfluous epithet "gloomy" from line three of the first book of Pope's *Iliad*, but Pope was not the first English poet to have used that particular epithet in a context in which it was superfluous. "Gloomy" is a favorite epithet of Milton's in *Paradise Lost*[43] and it appears, in a context analogous to Pope's, as an epithet of Pluto in Book IV. Milton is describing the Garden of Eden and declares that its beauty cannot be surpassed by the beauty of any comparable garden or grove from the ancient world:

> Not that fair field
> Of *Enna*, where *Proserpin* gath'ring flow'rs,
> Herself a fairer Flow'r by gloomy *Dis*
> Was gather'd, which cost *Ceres* all that pain
> To seek her through the world; nor that sweet Grove
> Of *Daphne* by *Orontes*, and th' inspir'd
> *Castalian* Spring might with this Paradise
> Of *Eden* strive.
>
> [ll. 268-275][44]

The epithet "gloomy" in the phrase "gloomy *Dis*" (l. 270) is as superfluous here as it is in Pope's "Pluto's gloomy Reign." But because the basic rhythmical and syntactical unit is the extended period or verse paragraph rather than the individual line or couplet; because the position of the caesura is so extremely flexible, a flexibility which is characteristic of Miltonic blank verse; and because the verses do not rhyme, the phrase "gloomy *Dis*" is not conspicuous, despite the fact that it occurs at the end of a

---

[43] Aside from its appearance in *P.L.* IV.270, it occurs in *P.L.* I.152, II.976, III.242, and VI.832, as well as in *Comus* 470, *Paradise Regained* I.42, and *Samson Agonistes* 161.

[44] *Milton: Poems*, ed. Hughes, p. 284.

line. The phrase is relatively inconspicuous for one other important reason: in these lines, as in Miltonic blank verse in general, there is a great variety in the degree of stress between accented and unaccented syllables. The stress on the word "where" in line 269, for example, is very light, as is the stress on the word "which" in line 271; and in that same line the word "that," although unaccented, is raised almost to the level of the accented syllable, thus simulating the spondaic foot of the ancient hexameter line and offering yet another variation upon the iambic norm.[45]

It should not be inferred from what I have said about Pope's management of the couplet in his *Iliad*, however, that the pentameter couplet is by its very nature incapable of simulating the frequently enjambed hexameter of Homeric verse and of the more extended periods of Virgil. It is true that Milton, in his prefatory note to *Paradise Lost*, argues that rhyme is "trivial and of no true musical delight; which consists only in apt Numbers, fit quantity of Syllables, and the sense variously drawn out from one Verse into another, not in the jingling sound of like endings."[46] As Ben Jonson suggests in the *Conversations with Drummond*, however, the couplet will not be "jingling" so long as the pentameter line is "broken, like Hexameters," that is, if there is a good deal of the kind of caesural variation and frequent enjambement that is characteristic of the ancient hexameter line. Ben Jonson's projected epic was to be written "all in Couplets"

---

[45] It is largely through his allowing for there to be a great variety in the degree of stress between accented and unaccented syllables that Milton is able, in his accentual-syllabic iambic pentameter line, to approximate the rhythmical subtlety of the quantitative hexameter line. Milton's line also approximates the flexibility in the position and frequency of the caesura in the ancient hexameter. Thus William Cowper, in the preface to the first edition of his blank-verse translation of the *Iliad* and *Odyssey*, writes of the relation of Milton's style to Homer's: "It is in those breaks and pauses, to which the numbers of the English poet are so much indebted both for their dignity and variety, that he chiefly copies the Grecian" (*The Iliad of Homer, Translated into Blank Verse*, 2 vols. [1791; reprint ed. London, 1802], 1:xxix).

[46] *Milton: Poems*, ed. Hughes, p. 210.

which, Drummond reports, Jonson felt "to be the bravest sort of Verses."[47] And one twentieth-century critic, himself a master of the couplet, considered the heroic couplet "the most flexible of forms: it can suggest . . . the effects of nearly any other technique available."[48] I would now like to suggest that Dryden's efforts at Homeric translation often more nearly simulate than do Pope's the "broken" hexameter of Homer and Virgil, and that while there are elements in Dryden's diction which Coleridge would surely have considered as pseudopoetic, these tend to be submerged in the larger unit of the verse paragraph.

Dryden completed a version of the entire first book of the *Iliad* which he included in his *Fables Ancient and Modern; Translated into Verse, from Homer, Boccace and Chaucer: With Original Poems* (1700). His first attempt to translate Homer is "The Last Parting of Hector and Andromache from the Sixth Book of Homer's *Iliads*" which was published in a miscellany of poems entitled *Examen Poeticum* in 1693, and it is to the opening lines of this excerpt that I wish now to turn. The "Argument," in Dryden's words, is this:

> *Hector*, returning from the Field of Battel, to visit *Helen* his Sister-in-Law, and his Brother *Paris*, who had fought unsuccessfully hand to hand, with *Menelaus*, from thence goes to his own Palace to see his Wife *Andromache*, and his Infant Son *Astyanax*. The description of that Interview, is the Subject of this Translation.

Here is the text:

---

[47] Drummond reports that Jonson "had ane jntention to perfect ane Epick Poem jntitled Heroologia of the Worthies of his Country, rowsed by fame, and was to dedicate it to his Country, it is all jn Couplets, for he detesteth all other Rimes, said he had written a discourse of Poesie both against Campion and Daniel especially this Last, wher he proves couplets to be the bravest sort of Verses, especially when they are broken, like Hexameters" (*Ben Jonson: Works*, ed. Herford and Simpson, 1:132).

[48] Yvor Winters, "The Influence of Meter on Poetic Convention," *In Defense of Reason* (New York: The Swallow Press and William Morrow and Company, 1947), p. 14.

Thus having said, brave *Hector* went to see
His Virtuous Wife, the fair *Andromache*.
He found her not at home; for she was gone
(Attended by her Maid and Infant Son,)
To climb the steepy Tow'r of *Ilion*.
From whence with heavy Heart she might survey
The bloody business of the dreadful Day.
Her mournful Eyes she cast around the Plain,
And sought the Lord of her Desires in vain.
  But he, who thought his peopled Palace bare,
When she, his only Comfort, was not there;
Stood in the Gate, and ask'd of ev'ry one,
Which way she took, and whither she was gone:
If to the Court, or with his Mother's Train,
In long Procession to *Minerva*'s Fane?
The Servants answer'd, neither to the Court
Where *Priam*'s Sons and Daughters did resort,
Nor to the Temple was she gone, to move
With Prayers the blew-ey'd Progeny of *Jove*;
But, more solicitous for him alone,
Than all their safety, to the Tow'r was gone,
There to survey the Labours of the Field;
Where the *Greeks* conquer, and the *Trojans* yield.
Swiftly she pass'd, with Fear and Fury wild,
The Nurse went lagging after with the Child.

                                        [ll. 1-25]⁴⁹

This passage surely contains some elements of style and of diction
to which both Johnson and Coleridge would have objected. But
because the placement of the caesura is so varied and the lines
so frequently enjambed, most of the devices of epic diction, such
as inversions of normal word order and the insertion of super-
fluous epithets, are barely noticeable. Dryden refers to Athena
in line 19, for example, as "the blew-ey'd Progeny of *Jove*," a

---

⁴⁹ *Examen Poeticum: Being the Third Part of Miscellany Poems Containing
New Translations of the Ancient Poets. Together with many Original Copies by
the Most Eminent Hands* (London, 1693).

VERSIFICATION

periphrastic epithet which could pose the danger of drawing
more attention to itself than the context might be able to bear.
But because the position of the caesura in the lines surrounding
it is so varied, and because the first line of both the couplet in
which it appears and of the preceding couplet are enjambed, the
epithet seems to be a relatively inconspicuous element in one
extended verse paragraph, beginning with line 10 ("But he, who
thought his peopled Palace bare"), rather than a curiosity too
cumbersome for a single pentameter line or couplet. And so with
the inversion of normal word order in line 8 ("Her mournful
Eyes she cast around the Plain"); this, too, is scarcely noticed,
largely because the caesura in the following line is withheld until
it falls, finally, after the eighth syllable.[50] In the opening lines of
Pope's *Iliad*, in his version of the moonlight simile, and in the
two couplets I quoted from *Iliad* VI, the caesura falls after the
fourth, fifth, or sixth syllable in every line but two, thus tending
to break the lines into distinct halves. While there are a sufficient
number of Dryden's lines in which the caesura falls after the
fourth or fifth syllable in order to establish a norm from which
the other lines may be perceived to vary, the caesura in these
other lines falls in almost every possible position; and in some
lines—in line 11, for example—there are clearly two caesurae
rather than one. Also contributing to the periodic movement of
Dryden's lines is the fact that there are five enjambed lines com-
pared with just one in Pope's moonlight simile.[51]

[50] In his "Epistle Dedicatory to the *Rival Ladies*" (1664), Dryden expresses
his views on the desirability of avoiding inversions of normal word order when
writing English rhyming verse. See *Of Dramatic Poesy*, ed. Watson, 1:6-7. For
Dryden's views on how rhyming verse can be made "natural" and "easy" and
thus approach "the negligence of prose" through the poet's avoiding unnatural
word order, varying the position of the caesura, and frequently enjambing his
lines, see Neander's comments in *Of Dramatic Poesy: An Essay* (1668), *Of
Dramatic Poesy*, 1:82 and 84.
[51] Samuel Johnson concludes his famous comparison between Dryden and Pope
in the *Life of Pope* by stating that "Dryden is read with frequent astonishment,
and Pope with perpetual delight" (*Lives of the English Poets*, 3:223). Later in
the *Life of Pope* Johnson writes that Pope, in his *Iliad* translation, made Homer

[160]

In Milton and in Dryden, then,—as in Homer and in Virgil—
the characteristics of epic diction, such as the inclusion of su-
perfluous epithets and inversions of normal word order, tend to
be submerged in more or less extended periods. In Pope's *Iliad*,
however, these same characteristics are often made conspicuous
by the poet's handling of the pentameter line, which is often end-
stopped and breaks into balanced halves, and of the couplet,
which tends to be closed.

In his treatise *On the Sublime*, Longinus discusses the proper
use of rhetorical figures (τὰ σχήματα) in speeches:

> Playing tricks by means of figures is a peculiarly suspect
> procedure. It raises the suspicion of a trap, a deep design, a
> fallacy. It is to be avoided in addressing a judge who has power
> to decide, and especially in addressing tyrants, kings, governors
> or anybody in a high place. Such a person immediately be-
> comes angry if he is led astray like a foolish child by some
> skilful orator's figures. He takes the fallacy as indicating con-
> tempt of himself. He becomes like a wild animal. Even if he
> controls his temper, he is now completely conditioned against
> being convinced by what is said. A figure is therefore generally

"graceful, but lost him some of his sublimity" (ibid., 240). In his comparison
between Dryden and Pope, Johnson is associating Dryden with the "sublime"
and Pope with the "graceful." Johnson's distinction between the "sublime" and
the "graceful" reflects directly the distinctions between the "sublime" and the
"beautiful" as these were developed by Edmund Burke in *A Philosophical En-
quiry into the Origin of Our Ideas of the Sublime and the Beautiful* (1757). For
both Burke and Johnson clarity, proportion, and the bounded would be char-
acteristic of the "beautiful," while obscurity, vastness, and the infinite would
evoke the "sublime." I believe that Johnson is suggesting, in the final sentence
of the comparison between Pope and Dryden, that while Pope's couplets are
balanced and regularly closed and therefore produce "delight" (a psychological
experience which Burke associates with the "beautiful"), Dryden's couplets more
closely approximate the freedom of blank verse and thus produce "astonishment"
(an emotion which Burke associates with the "sublime"). Johnson clearly as-
sociates rhyme with "delight" and blank verse with "astonishment" in the *Life
of Milton*: "He that thinks himself capable of astonishing, may write blank verse,
but those that hope only to please must condescend to rhyme" (*Lives of the
English Poets*, 1:194).

thought to be best when the fact that it is a figure is concealed.[52][1.7.1]

A speaker should avoid the gratuitous use of figures, Longinus advises, when he is addressing a truly authoritative judge (κριτὴν κύριον); and when such figures are used, they must at all costs be made to appear inconspicuous. Pope did not invent the figures of speech to which Johnson and Coleridge objected; he simply brought to the discriminating attention of two arbiters of literary taste the artifice which Milton and Dryden had managed largely to conceal.

In spite of this problem, however, it would be difficult to refute Johnson's claim that Pope's *Iliad* is "the noblest version of poetry the world has ever seen"; it remains, certainly, the greatest verse translation of the *Iliad* in English. The poem and its translator were, it is true, not quite a perfect match: Pope, as it turned out, would become a master not of the lofty epic but of the mock epic and of his own brilliantly pointed renditions of Horatian satire. But in terms of subject matter and of style, the meeting of the man and the task occurred at a strikingly fortuitous moment in literary history. As I have shown in chapters one and two, Achilles' ungovernable wrath was for centuries an embarrassment to moralistic critics, to their beneficiaries among writers

---

[52] Trans. D. A. Russell, *"Longinus" on Sublimity*, p. 26. This is by no means the only Longinian echo in *Idler* 77. The similarities between many of the details of Johnson's criticism of the opening lines of Pope's *Iliad* and Longinus' criticism of a passage which he considered "turbid" (τεθόλωται . . . τῇ φράσει) and "pseudo-tragic" (παρατράγῳδα) from the now lost Greek play, *Orithya*, are striking. See *Peri Hypsous* 3.1. It is not entirely unlikely that Johnson was thinking of the comments of Longinus, who was very much on the minds of the writers of the *Idler* at this time. Sir Joshua Reynolds, who contributed *Idler* 76, makes a number of Longinian references in that *Idler* paper. And in *Idler* 61 Johnson may well be echoing William Smith's translation of the *Peri Hypsous* (1739), as the editors of the *Yale Johnson* suggest (see 2:192). Johnson could have recalled Longinus' criticism of the passage from the *Orithya* through Dryden. In *The Grounds of Criticism in Tragedy* (1679), an essay which Johnson refers to in the *Life of Dryden* (*Lives of the Poets*, 1:356), Dryden alludes directly to *Peri Hypsous* 3.1.

and critics of Renaissance epic, and to the translator—such as George Chapman—working in this tradition; its accurate representation was now, in an age fascinated with the depiction of the passions, eminently achievable. And for perhaps the last time in the history of English poetry, appropriate stylistic resources were available to the translator of the *Iliad*: he could still eschew the constraints of literalness and, at the same time, be considered a faithful translator by most members of his audience; and, as I have demonstrated in chapter three, he could still draw upon the traditional means of elevating style as recommended by Aristotle in the *Poetics*, as achieved by Milton in *Paradise Lost*, and as restated by Addison in the *Spectator*. In addition, as I have pointed out in chapter four, Pope was sympathetic to the intentions of Aristotle's description of the bold and spontaneous skiagraphic style, a style which Aristotle associates with the oral recitation of Homeric epic, and as a translator he tried to simulate this quality in a written medium in ways that are analogous to Virgil's adaptation of Homer. And Pope, as I have suggested in chapter five, attempted to heighten the style of his *Iliad* in accordance with the advice given by Longinus, advice which Chapman, Pope's Elizabethan predecessor, appears either to have ignored or not to have seriously considered.

Not long after Pope completed his versions it would become increasingly difficult for the translator to recreate the disciplined energy of Homeric verse, as English poetry would become increasingly stripped of many of its traditional resources. First to disappear would be the diction associated with the elevated style, a diction which would come to be seen as "artificial." And next to go would be the integrity of the poetic line itself. Blank verse would, for a while, replace the couplet as a means of translating the Homeric hexameter, but Cowper's Homeric versions (1791), to name just one attempt, would come off as flat in comparison with Pope's and would not stand the test of time. Then blank verse would be further diluted to prose, resulting in readable versions, such as that of Samuel Butler (1898); but prose is, by its very nature, incapable of simulating what Pope described in the *Iliad* preface as "that unequal'd Fire and Rapture, which is

[163]

so forcible in *Homer*, that no Man of true Poetical Spirit is Master of himself while he reads him."[53] And when modern verse translations would appear in the latter half of our own century, so profound would be the lack of consensus as to what constituted the poetic line that the approximation of Homer's formal grandeur would be beyond the resources of English poetry. But in Pope's version we find, for the last and perhaps the only time in the history of English verse, a traditional and viable poetic style that can be held answerable to the demands of the Homeric hexameter. And it was a style that was managed by a poet—great imitator and verbal genius that he was—who was very nearly equal to the impossible task.

[53] *TE*, 7:4.

Pope and Horace's Implied Distinction
Between the Oral and the Written Styles

Aristotle's distinction in *Rhetoric* III.12 between the oral and the written styles is strongly implied by Horace in the famous *ut pictura poesis* passage from the *Ars Poetica*, which Pope alludes to in *An Essay on Criticism* (ll. 169-180). As does Aristotle in *Rhetoric* III.12, Horace in *A.P.* 361-365 is contrasting two kinds of style, the less exact style, which is again associated with Homeric epic, and the more refined style, characteristic perhaps of the shorter literary genres. The *ut pictura poesis* analogy appears in the context of Horace's discussion of the responsibilities of the literary critic:

> sunt delicta tamen quibus ignovisse velimus:
> nam neque chorda sonum reddit, quem volt manus et
>   mens,
> poscentique gravem persaepe remittit acutum;
> nec semper feriet quodcumque minabitur arcus.
> verum ubi plura nitent in carmine, non ego paucis
> offendar maculis, quas aut incuria fudit
> aut humana parum cavit natura. quid ergo est?
> ut scriptor si peccat idem librarius usque,
> quamvis est monitus, venia caret, et citharoedus
> ridetur, chorda qui semper oberrat eadem:
> sic mihi, qui multum cessat, fit Choerilus ille,
> quem bis terve bonum cum risu miror; et idem

indignor quandoque bonus dormitat Homerus,
verum operi longo fas est obrepere somnum.
ut pictura poesis: erit quae, si propius stes,
te capiat magis, et quaedam, si longius abstes.
haec amat obscurum, volet haec sub luce videri,
iudicis argutum quae non formidat acumen;
haec placuit semel, haec deciens repetita placebit.

[ll. 347-365]

Yet there are faults which we can gladly pardon; for the
string does not always yield the sound which hand and heart
intend, but when you call for a flat often returns you a sharp;
nor will the bow always hit whatever mark it threatens. But
when the beauties in a poem are more in number, I shall not
take offense at a few blots which a careless hand has let drop,
or human frailty has failed to avert. What, then, is the truth?
As a copying clerk is without excuse if, however much warned,
he always makes the same mistake, and a harper is laughed
at who always blunders on the same string: so the poet who
often defaults, becomes, I think, another Choerilus, whose one
or two good lines cause laughter and surprise; and yet I also
feel aggrieved whenever good Homer "nods," but when a
work is long, a drowsy mood may well creep over it. A poem
is like a picture: one strikes your fancy more the nearer you
stand; another, the farther away. This courts the shade, that
will wish to be seen in the light, and does not fear the sharp
insight of the judge. This pleased but once; that, though ten
times called for, will always please.[1]

As Wesley Trimpi has demonstrated ("The Meaning of Horace's
Ut Pictura Poesis," "Horace's '*Ut Pictura Poesis*': The argument
for Stylistic Decorum"), when one views the *ut pictura poesis*
analogy as a transposition of Aristotle's distinctions (in *Rhetoric*
III.12) into an Augustan literary setting, the following interpre-
tation emerges. Corresponding to Aristotle's written style is the

---

[1] The Latin text and the translation, which I have adapted slightly, are cited
from *Horace: Satires, Epistles, and Ars Poetica*, trans. H. R. Fairclough, pp.
478-481.

kind of picture and poem which is seen better the nearer to it one stands (*si propius stes / te capiat magis*), which loves the shade (*haec amat obscurum*), and which pleased once (*haec placuit semel*). Corresponding to Aristotle's description of the style of oratory addressed to public assemblies is the kind of picture and poem which must be seen at a distance (*si longius abstes*), which wishes to be seen in the light and "does not fear the sharp insight of the judge" (*volet haec sub luce videri / iudicis argutum quae non formidat acumen*), and which will always please (*haec deciens repetita placebit*). Aristotle's distinctions between the oral and the written styles were chiefly descriptive, except in so far that deliberative subjects and occasions were more important than forensic and ceremonial subjects and occasions. Horace's distinctions—made in the context of the stylistic concerns of the Augustan period—between the less exact and the more refined styles have evaluative connotations which may be summarized as follows. The more meticulous style, characteristic perhaps of the Roman schools of declamation, must be observed near at hand if the details—often approaching preciosity—of stylistic refinement are not to be lost; such a style "loves the shade" not in the literal sense, but it prefers the *obscurum*, where *obscurum* is taken to be a metaphor for the shaded protectiveness of the scholastic environment; such a style pleases only once because it depends so greatly upon stylistic novelty which, it is suggested, may lose its effectiveness upon repeated readings. The less refined style, characteristic of actual public debate in the forum, must be experienced "at a distance," since its power does not depend exclusively upon details of stylistic refinement which must be viewed near at hand; it prefers to be experienced in the sunlight in the sense that debate in the forum did not take place in the shaded and private confines of the academic garden, but rather in the midst of the heat and noise of a public assembly; it need not fear—i.e., be *meticulous* about—criticism of detail where rhetorical artifice is not expected to be exact; it is a style which will continue to please because, again, it does not depend exclusively for its effectiveness upon stylistic refinement. It should be pointed out that the negative connotations associated with the

[167]

refined style in this particular passage may simply be "foil" for Horace's defense of the less exact style characteristic of Homeric epic. Horace was, of course, himself a master of the highly refined style and never attempted the longer literary genres. It is unlikely, therefore, that he intended these lines to be taken as a blanket condemnation of the very style that he defends so vigorously and explicitly in so many of his poems.

Two passages from Pope's poems appear to draw upon important aspects of the Horatian analogy. The first, from *An Essay on Criticism*, employs the metaphor of distance; and the second, from *Epistle II* ("To a Lady: Of the Characters of Women"), employs the association of brightness with the openness of public display and of shade with the intricacies of the private world.

The lines from *An Essay on Criticism* (169-180) appear in the context of Pope's defense of those authors who seem to transgress the rules:

> I know there are, to whose presumptuous Thoughts
> Those *Freer Beauties*, ev'n in *Them* [the ancient masters],
>   seem Faults:
> Some Figures *monstrous* and *mis-shap'd* appear,
> Consider'd *singly*, or beheld too *near*,
> Which, but *proportion'd* to their *Light*, or *Place*,
> Due Distance *reconciles* to Form and Grace.
> A prudent Chief not always must display
> His Pow'rs in *equal Ranks*, and *fair Array*,
> But with th'*Occasion* and the *Place* comply,
> *Conceal* his Force, nay seem sometimes to *Fly*.
> Those oft are *Stratagems* which *Errors* seem,
> Nor is it *Homer Nods*, but *We* that *Dream*.

Where Horace, it is true, was comparing two kinds of styles, Pope is here recommending that the viewer (the reader becomes a viewer by virtue of the analogy between poetry and painting) must gauge for himself the "Due Distance" (l. 174) from any single work of art at which he must stand if the various elements in that single work are to be seen properly. But there are striking resemblances between the two passages, for Pope, in his notes,

says that line 180 ("Nor is it *Homer Nods*, but *We* that *Dream*")
is an allusion to *Ars Poetica*, line 359 (*indignor quandoque bonus
dormitat Homerus*); and both authors associate Homer with the
kind of work from which one should stand at a distance if the
"*Freer Beauties*" of such a work are to be fully appreciated.

In his *Epistle to a Lady*, Pope makes the following distinctions
between the characters of men and women:

> But grant, in Public Men sometimes are shown,
> A Woman's seen in Private life alone:
> Our bolder Talents in full light display'd,
> Your Virtues open fairest in the shade.
> Bred to disguise, in Public 'tis you hide;
> There, none distinguish 'twixt your Shame or Pride,
> Weakness or Delicacy; all so nice,
> That each may seem a Virtue, or a Vice.
>
> [ll. 199-206]

Horace contrasted the bolder style of the painting which wishes
to be seen in the light of day (*sub luce videri*) with the more
meticulous, even precious, style of the picture which courts the
shade (*amat obscurum*); and if we recall Aristotle's distinction
in *Rhetoric* III.12, Horace's painting which wishes to be seen in
the light of day is an adaptation, it will be remembered, of the
"skiagraphic" painting which Aristotle likens to the bold and
public style of deliberative oratory as opposed to the more refined
and private written style. Pope in the passage cited above says
that what he perceives to be the "bolder Talents" of men are
best "display'd" in "Public" and "in full light," while a woman's
"Virtues," which are "all so nice"—that is, tender, delicate, overly
refined—"open fairest in the shade." It should also be pointed
out that Pope may well be implicitly comparing the characters
of men and women—as Aristotle and Horace had compared the
characteristics of literary styles—to styles of painting, for Pope's
poem is organized as a series of verbal portraits and the poet
very self-consciously uses the vocabulary of painting to describe
the various types of women he presents. On Pope's "picture-
gallery manner of proceeding" in this poem, see Jean H. Hag-

[169]

strum, *The Sister Arts: The Tradition of Literary Pictorialism and English Poetry from Dryden to Gray.*[2]

Pope, then, if we are to judge from the passages cited above from the *Essay on Criticism* and the *Epistle to a Lady*, would appear to have sympathized with the positive connotations Horace associates with the picture that asks to be seen at a distance. He was sympathetic, that is, with the quality of unmannered boldness characteristic of the skiagraphic style—the style which Aristotle associates with Homeric epic—and we can assume that it was Pope's aim, as a translator of Homer, to simulate this quality of style in English.

[2] (Chicago: University of Chicago Press, 1958), pp. 236-241.

Selected Bibliography

I. EDITIONS OF HOMER

Barnes, Joshua. *Homeri Ilias et Odyssea, et in easdem Scholia, sive Interpretatio Veterum. Item Notae Perpetuae in Textum et Scholia, Variae Lectiones etc. . . . accedunt Batrachomyomachia, Hymni et Epigrammata, una cum Fragmentis, et Gemini Indices.* 2 vols. Cambridge, 1711.
Munro, David B. and Allen, Thomas W. *Tomi I et II, Iliadis Libros I-XXIV Continentes.* 1902. Reprint. Oxford: Oxford University Press, 1966.
Sponde, Jean de. *Homeri quae extant Omnia, Ilias, Odyssea, Batrachomyomachia, Hymni, Poematia aliquot, Pindari Thebani Epitome Iliados et Daretes Phrygii de Bello Troiano Libri, Indices Locupletissimi.* Basel, 1583.
Stanford, W. B. *The Odyssey of Homer.* 2 vols. London: Macmillan, 1947.

II. TRANSLATIONS OF HOMER

Butler, Samuel. *The Iliad of Homer Rendered into English Prose for those who cannot read the Original.* London, New York, and Bombay, 1898.
Chapman, George. *Chapman's Homer: The Iliad, The Odyssey and The Lesser Homerica.* Edited, with introduction, textual notes, commentaries and glossaries by Allardyce Nicoll. 2 vols. Vol. 1: *The Iliad.* Bollingen Series XLI. New York: Bollingen Foundation, 1956. Vol. 2: *The Odyssey and The Lesser Homerica.* London: Routledge & Kegan Paul, 1957.
Cowper, William. *The Iliad of Homer, Translated into Blank Verse.* 2 vols. 2nd edition. London, 1802.
Dacier, Anne. *L'Iliade d'Homère, traduite en François avec des Remarques.* 3 vols. Paris, 1711.

Dryden, John. *The First Book of Homer's Ilias.* In *Fables Ancient and Modern; Translated into English Verse, from Homer, Ovid, Boccace, and Chaucer: with Original Poems. The Poems of John Dryden.* Edited by James Kinsley. Vol. 4:1583-1604. Oxford: Clarendon Press, 1958.

———. "The Last Parting of Hector and Andromache from the Sixth Book of Homer's *Iliads.*" *Examen Poeticum: Being the Third Part of Miscellany Poems Containing New Translations of the Ancient Poets. Together with Many Original Copies by the Most Eminent Hands.* London, 1693.

Hobbes, Thomas. *The English Works of Thomas Hobbes.* Edited by Sir William Molesworth. Vol. 10: *The Iliads and Odysses of Homer Translated out of Greek into English.* London, 1884.

Fitzgerald, Robert. *The Iliad of Homer.* Garden City, N.Y.: Anchor Press/Doubleday, 1963.

———. *The Odyssey of Homer.* 1961. Reprint. New York: Anchor Press/Doubleday, 1963.

Lattimore, Richmond. *The Iliad of Homer.* 1951. Reprint. Chicago and London: University of Chicago Press, 1971.

Ogilby, John. *Iliads translated, adorn'd with sculpture, and illustrated with annotations.* London, 1669.

Pope, Alexander. *The Iliad.* 6 vols. London, 1715-1720.

———. *The Iliad of Homer.* Translated by Alexander Pope. Edited by Gilbert Wakefield. 6 vols. London, 1796.

———. *The Odyssey.* 5 vols. London, 1725-1726.

———. *The Twickenham Edition of the Poems of Alexander Pope.* General editor, John Butt. 11 vols. London and New Haven: Methuen & Co. Ltd. and Yale University Press, 1961-1967. Vols. 7-10: *The Iliad* and *The Odyssey.* Edited by Maynard Mack. Associate editors Norman Callan, Robert Fagles, William Frost, and Douglas M. Knight.

III. OTHER SOURCES

Addison, Joseph and Steele, Richard. *The Spectator.* Edited by Donald F. Bond. 5 vols. Oxford: Clarendon Press, 1965.

Aquinas, St. Thomas. *Summa Theologiae.* Vol. 25. Latin text and English translation, Introduction, Notes, Appendices, and Glossaries by John Fearon, O.P. New York and London: Blackfriars in conjunction with McGraw-Hill and Eyre & Spottiswoode, 1968.

Aristotle. *Aristotle's Art of Poetry. Translated from the Original Greek, according to Mr. Goulston's Edition, Together with Mr. D'Acier's Notes Translated from the French.* London, 1705.

――――. *Aristotle's Poetics: The Argument.* Commentary by Gerald F. Else. Cambridge, Mass.: Harvard University Press, 1967.

――――. *Aristotle's Theory of Poetry and Fine Art.* Translated and with critical notes by S. H. Butcher. New York: Dover Publications, Inc., 1951.

――――. *The Basic Works of Aristotle.* Edited and with an Introduction by Richard McKeon. New York: Random House, 1941.

――――. *Nichomachean Ethics.* Translated by H. Rackham. Loeb Classical Library. Cambridge, Mass. and London: Harvard University Press and William Heinemann, 1926.

――――. *On the Soul, Parva Naturalia, On Breath.* Translated by W. S. Hett. Loeb Classical Library. 1936. Reprint edition. Cambridge and London: Harvard University Press and William Heinemann, 1964.

――――. *Posterior Analytics and Topics.* Translated by H. Tredennick (*Posterior Analytics*) and E. S. Forster (*Topics*). Loeb Classical Library. Cambridge, Mass. and London: Harvard University Press and William Heinemann, 1960.

――――. *The Rhetoric of Aristotle with a Commentary by Edward Meredith Cope.* Edited by J. E. Sandys. 3 vols. Cambridge: Cambridge University Press, 1877.

――――. *Rhetoric and Poetics.* Translated by W. R. Roberts (*Rhetoric*) and I. Bywater (*Poetics*). New York: The Modern Library, 1954.

Arnold, Matthew. *On Translating Homer.* Introduction and notes by W.H.D. Rouse. London: John Murray, Albemarle Street, 1905.

Arthos, John. *The Language of Natural Description in Eighteenth-Century Poetry.* Ann Arbor: University of Michigan Press, 1949.

Aubignac, François Hédelin d'. *La Pratique du Théâtre.* Edited by Pierre Martino. Alger: Carbonel; Paris: Champion, 1927.

Auerbach, Erich. *Literary Language and its Public in Late Latin Antiquity and in the Middle Ages.* Translated by Ralph Manheim. Bollingen Series LXXIV. New York: Bollingen Foundation, 1965.

――――. *Mimesis: The Representation of Reality in Western Literature.* Translated by Willard Trask. Princeton: Princeton University Press, 1953.

Bartlett, Phyllis B. "The Heroes of Chapman's Homer." *The Review of English Studies* 17 (1941):257-280.

[173]

Bate, Walter Jackson, ed. *Criticism: The Major Texts.* 1952. Reprint. New York: Harcourt Brace Jovanovich, Inc., 1970.

Battestin, Martin C. *The Providence of Wit: Aspects of Form in Augustan Literature and the Arts.* Oxford: Clarendon Press, 1974.

Bentley, Richard. *Remarks upon a late Discourse of free-thinking.* London, 1713.

Boethius. *The Theological Tractates and The Consolation of Philosophy.* Translated by H. F. Stewart (*Theological Tractates* and *The Consolation of Philosophy*) and E. K. Rand (*Theological Tractates*). Loeb Classical Library. 1918. Reprint. Cambridge and London: Harvard University Press and William Heinemann, 1936.

Boswell, James. *The Journal of a Tour to the Hebrides with Samuel Johnson.* London and Toronto: J. M. Dent & Sons, 1909.

——. *The Life of Samuel Johnson.* 2 vols. London and Toronto: J. M. Dent & Sons, 1906.

Boyd, John D. *The Function of Mimesis and its Decline.* Cambridge, Mass.: Harvard University Press, 1968.

Bray, René. *La Formation de la Doctrine Classique en France.* Paris: Hachette, 1927.

Brink, C. O. *Horace on Poetry: The "Ars Poetica."* Cambridge: Cambridge University Press, 1971.

Brower, Reuben A. *Alexander Pope: The Poetry of Allusion.* Oxford: Clarendon Press, 1959.

——. "Dryden's Poetic Diction and Virgil." *Philological Quarterly* 18 (April 1939):211-217.

——. *Hero and Saint: Shakespeare and the Graeco-Roman Tradition.* Oxford: Clarendon Press, 1971.

Burke, Edmund. *A Philosophical Enquiry into the Origin of Our Ideas of the Sublime and the Beautiful.* Edited by James T. Boulton. London and Notre Dame: University of Notre Dame Press, 1968.

Butler, Samuel, *Characters and Passages from Note-Books.* Edited by A. R. Waller. Cambridge: Cambridge University Press, 1908.

——. *Hudibras.* Edited with introduction and commentary by John Wilders. Oxford: Clarendon Press, 1967.

Campbell, Lily B. *Shakespeare's Tragic Heroes: Slaves of Passion.* 1930. Reprint. New York: Barnes and Noble, Inc., 1968.

Carne-Ross, D. S. "Guslar with Rose-Tipped Fingers." *Arion* 1 (Spring 1962):118-125.

——. "A Mistaken Ambition of Exactness." *Delos* 2 (1968):171-195.

————. "Structural Translation: Notes on Logue's *Patrokleia*." *Arion* 1 (Summer 1962):27-38.

Chapman, George. *Bussy D'Ambois* and *The Revenge of Bussy D'Ambois*. Edited by Frederick S. Boas. Boston and London: D. C. Heath and Co., 1905.

————. *The Poems of George Chapman*. Edited by Phyllis Brooks Bartlett. New York: Oxford University Press, 1941.

Cicero. *De Finibus*. Translated by H. Rackham. Loeb Classical Library. London and New York: William Heinemann and the Macmillan Co., 1914.

————. *De Natura Deorum*. Translated by H. Rackham. Loeb Classical Library. 1933. Reprint. Cambridge, Mass. and London: Harvard University Press and William Heinemann, 1967.

————. *De Officiis*. Translated by Walter Miller. Loeb Classical Library. Cambridge, Mass. and London: Harvard University Press and William Heinemann, 1951.

————. *De Oratore*. Translated by E. W. Sutton and H. Rackham. 2 vols. Loeb Classical Library. Cambridge, Mass. and London: Harvard University Press and William Heinemann, 1947.

————. *Orator*. Translated by G. L. Hendrickson and H. M. Hubbell. Loeb Classical Library. 1939; reprint Cambridge, Mass. and London: Harvard University Press and William Heinemann, 1971.

————. *Tusculan Disputations*. Translated by J. E. King. Loeb Classical Library. London and New York: William Heinemann and G. P. Putnam's Sons, 1927.

Clark, A.F.B. *Boileau and the French Classical Critics in England, 1660-1830*. Paris: Librairie Ancienne Edouard Champion, 1925.

Clark, H. W. "In Praise of Pope's Notes." *College Literature* 3 (1976):203-218.

Clarke, M. L. *Greek Studies in England 1700-1830*. Cambridge: Cambridge University Press, 1945.

Coleridge, Samuel Taylor. *Biographia Literaria*. Edited with his aesthetical essays by J. Shawcross. 2 vols. Oxford: Clarendon Press, 1907.

Collins, Anthony. *A Discourse of Free-Thinking Occasioned by the Rise and Growth of a Sect call'd Free-Thinkers*. London, 1713.

Coolidge, John S. "Fielding and the 'Conservation of Character.' " *Modern Philology* 57 (1960):245-259.

Corneille, Pierre. *Théâtre Complet*. 2 vols. Paris: Bibliothèque de la Pléiade, 1950.

Crane, R. S. "Suggestions Towards a Genealogy of the Man of Feeling." *Journal of English Literary History* 1 (1934):205-230.

Crossley, Robert. "Pope's *Iliad*: The Commentary and the Translation." *Philological Quarterly* 56 (1977):339-357.

Cunningham, J. V. *The Collected Essays of J. V. Cunningham.* Chicago: Swallow Press, 1976.

———. *Tradition and Poetic Structure.* Denver: Alan Swallow Press, 1960.

———. "Tragic Effect and Tragic Process in Some Plays of Shakespeare, and their Background in the Literary and Ethical Theory of Classical Antiquity and the Middle Ages." Ph.D. dissertation, Stanford University, 1945.

———. *Woe or Wonder: The Emotional Effect of Shakespearean Tragedy.* Denver: University of Denver Press, 1951.

Curry, Walter Clyde. *Shakespeare's Philosophical Patterns.* Baton Rouge: Louisiana State University Press, 1937.

Curtius, Ernst Robert. *European Literature and the Latin Middle Ages.* Translated by Willard R. Trask. 1953. Reprint. New York and Evanston: Harper & Row, 1963.

Dacier, André. *La Poëtique d'Aristote avec des Remarques.* Paris, 1692.

Davie, Donald. *Purity of Diction in English Verse.* London: Chatto and Windus, 1952.

Demetrius. *On Style (Peri Hermēneias).* Translated by W. Rhys Roberts. Loeb Classical Library. 1927. Reprint. Cambridge, Mass. and London: Harvard University Press and William Heinemann, 1965.

Dennis, John. *The Critical Works of John Dennis.* Edited by Edward Niles Hooker. 2 vols. Baltimore: The Johns Hopkins University Press, 1939-1943.

Descartes, René. *Discours de la Méthode, Les Passions de l'Âme, Lettres.* Paris: Les Grandes Classiques Illustrés, Editions du Monde Moderne, n.d.

Dionysius of Halicarnassus. *Dionysius of Halicarnassus: The Critical Essays in Two Volumes.* Translated by Stephen Usher. Loeb Classical Library. Cambridge, Mass. and London: Harvard University Press and William Heinemann, 1974.

———. *Dionysius of Halicarnassus on Literary Composition.* Edited with introduction, translation, notes, glossary, and appendices by W. Rhys Roberts. London: Macmillan and Co., 1910.

Dio Chrysostom. *Discourses.* Translated by J. W. Cohoon. 5 vols. Loeb

Classical Library. London and Cambridge, Mass.: William Heinemann and Harvard University Press, 1939.

Doran, Madeleine. *Endeavors of Art: A Study of Form in Elizabethan Drama*. Madison, Milwaukee, and London: The University of Wisconsin Press, 1954.

Dryden, John. *Essays of John Dryden*. Selected and edited by W. P. Ker. 2 vols. Oxford: Clarendon Press, 1926.

————. *Of Dramatic Poesy and Other Critical Essays*. Edited with an introduction by George Watson. 2 vols. London and New York: Everyman's Library, 1962.

————. *The Poems of John Dryden*. Edited by James Kinsley. 4 vols. Oxford: Clarendon Press, 1958.

Edinger, William. *Samuel Johnson and Poetic Style*. Chicago and London: University of Chicago Press, 1977.

Elledge, Scott. "The Background and Development in English Criticism of the Theories of Generality and Particularity." *PMLA* 62 (1947):147-182.

Eliot, T. S. "Virgil and the Christian World." *On Poetry and Poets*. London: Faber and Faber, 1957.

Epictetus. *Epictète: Entretiens, Livre IV*. Paris: Association Guillaume Budé, 1965.

Ewing, S. Blaine. *Burtonian Melancholy in the Plays of John Ford*. Princeton: Princeton University Press, 1940.

Felton, Henry. *A Dissertation on Reading the Classics and Forming a Just Style*. 5th ed. London, 1753.

Foerster, D. M. *Homer in English Criticism: The Historical Approach in the Eighteenth Century*. New Haven: Yale University Press, 1947.

Friedländer, Paul. *Plato: An Introduction*. 1958. Reprint. Princeton: Princeton University Press, 1973.

Frost, William. *Dryden and the Art of Translation*. New Haven: Yale University Press, 1955.

————. "*The Rape of the Lock* and Pope's Homer." *Modern Language Quarterly* 8 (1947):342-354.

Gellius, Aulus. *The Attic Nights of Aulus Gellius*. Translated by J. C. Rolfe. 3 vols. Loeb Classical Library. Cambridge, Mass. and London: Harvard University Press and William Heinemann, 1927.

The Gentleman's Magazine. London, 1785.

Gibbon, Edward. *The History of the Decline and Fall of the Roman Empire*. Edited by J. B. Bury. 7 vols. London and New York: Methuen and Co., Macmillan and Co., 1896.

[177]

Goldgar, Bertrand A., ed. *Literary Criticism of Alexander Pope.* Lincoln: University of Nebraska Press, 1965.

Greene, Donald. *The Age of Exuberance: Backgrounds to Eighteenth-Century English Literature.* New York: Random House, 1970.

Grene, David and Lattimore, Richmond, eds. *The Complete Greek Tragedies.* 4 vols. Chicago: University of Chicago Press, 1959-1960.

Gustafson, Richard C. "The Perspicuous and the Sublime: A Historical Study of the Language of Pope's *Iliad.*" Ph.D. dissertation, University of Kansas, 1960.

Hagstrum, Jean H. *Samuel Johnson's Literary Criticism.* 1952. Reprint. Chicago and London: University of Chicago Press, 1967.

———. *The Sister Arts: The Tradition of Literary Pictorialism and English Poetry from Dryden to Gray.* Chicago: University of Chicago Press, 1958.

Havens, R. D. "Simplicity, A Changing Concept." *Journal of the History of Ideas* 14 (1953):3-32.

Herington, C. J. "The New Homer." *The Yale Review* 64 (Summer 1975):568-579.

Herrick, Marvin T. "The Early History of Aristotle's *Rhetoric* in England." *Philological Quarterly* 5 (1926):242-257.

———. "Some Neglected Sources of *Admiratio.*" *Modern Language Notes* 62 (1947):222-226.

Hill, George Birkbeck, ed. *Johnsonian Miscellanies.* 2 vols. Oxford: Clarendon Press, 1897.

Hobbes, Thomas. *Aristotle's Treatise on Rhetoric Literally Translated with Hobbes' Analysis, Examination Questions and an Appendix Containing the Greek Definitions.* Edited by Theodore Buckley. London: George Bell and Sons, 1890.

Horace. *Satires, Epistles, and Ars Poetica.* Translated by H. Rushton Fairclough. Loeb Classical Library. 1926. Reprint. Cambridge, Mass. and London: Harvard University Press and William Heinemann, 1970.

Hume, Robert D. *Dryden's Criticism.* Ithaca and London: Cornell University Press, 1970.

Isocrates. *Isocrates.* Translated by L. Van Hook. 3 vols. Loeb Classical Library. London and Cambridge, Mass.: William Heinemann and Harvard University Press, 1954.

Jack, Ian. *Augustan Satire: Intention and Idiom in English Poetry 1660-1750.* Oxford: Clarendon Press, 1952.

———. "Pope and 'The Weighty Bullion of Dr. Donne's Satires.' " *PMLA* 66 (December 1951):1009-1022.

Jaeger, Werner. *Paideia: The Ideals of Greek Culture*; Volume I: *Archaic Greece; The Mind of Athens*. Translated by Gilbert Highet. 1939. Reprint. New York: Oxford University Press, 1965.

Johnson, Samuel. *Dictionary of the English Language*. 2 vols. 1st and 2nd eds. London, 1755.

———. *Lives of the English Poets*. Edited by George Birkbeck Hill. 3 vols. Oxford: Clarendon Press, 1905.

———. *The Yale Edition of the Works of Samuel Johnson*. Edited by W. J. Bate, Bertrand H. Bronson et al. 9 vols. New Haven and London: Yale University Press, 1958-1971.

Jones, John A. *Pope's Couplet Art*. Athens: Ohio University Press, 1969.

Jonson, Ben. *The Works of Ben Jonson*. Edited by C. H. Herford and Percy and Evelyn Simpson. 11 vols. Oxford: Clarendon Press, 1925-1952.

Keast, W. R. "The Theoretical Foundations of Johnson's Criticism." In *Critics and Criticism*, edited by R. S. Crane. Chicago and London: University of Chicago Press, 1952.

Knight, Douglas M. "The Development of Pope's *Iliad* Preface." *Modern Language Quarterly* 16 (1955):237-246.

———. *Pope and the Heroic Tradition: A Critical Study of his Iliad*. New Haven: Yale University Press, 1951.

La Roche, J. "Zahlenverhältnisse im homerischen Vers." *Wiener Studien* 20 (1898):1-69.

Long, William J. *English Literature: Its History and Significance for the Life of the English-Speaking World: A Textbook for Schools*. Boston: Ginn and Company, 1909.

Longinus. *"Longinus" On the Sublime*. Translated by W. Hamilton Fyfe. Loeb Classical Library. 1927. Reprint. Cambridge, Mass. and London: Harvard University Press and William Heinemann, 1965.

———. *"Longinus" On the Sublime*. Edited with an introduction by D. A. Russell. Oxford: Clarendon Press, 1964.

———. *"Longinus" On Sublimity*. Translated by D. A. Russell. Oxford: Clarendon Press, 1965.

Lord, Albert B. *The Singer of Tales*. Cambridge, Mass.: Harvard University Press, 1960.

Lord, George deF. *Homeric Renaissance: The "Odyssey" of George Chapman*. New Haven: Yale University Press, 1956.

Mace, Dean T. "Dryden's Dialogue on Drama." *Journal of the Warburg and Courtauld Institutes* 25 (1962):87-112.

Mack, Maynard, ed. *Essential Articles for the Study of Alexander Pope.* Hamden, Conn.: Archon Books, 1964.

McKenzie, Alan T. "The Countenance You Show Me: Reading the Passions in the Eighteenth Century." *The Georgia Review* 33 (Winter 1978):758-773.

MacLean, Kenneth. *John Locke and English Literature of the Eighteenth Century.* New Haven: Yale University Press, 1936.

Macrobius. *Macrobius: The Saturnalia.* Translated with introduction and notes by Percival Vaughan Davies. New York and London: Columbia University Press, 1969.

Margliouth, D. S. *The Homer of Aristotle.* Oxford: Basil Blackwell, 1923.

Mason, H. A. *To Homer Through Pope: An Introduction to Homer's Iliad and Pope's Translation.* London: Chatto & Windus, 1972.

Mazon, Paul. *Madame Dacier et les traductions d'Homère en France.* Oxford: Clarendon Press, 1936.

Mesnardière, Jules de la. *La Poétique.* Paris, 1640.

Miller, Henry Knight. *Henry Fielding's* Tom Jones *and the Romance Tradition.* English Literary Studies Monograph Series, no. 6. Victoria: University of Victoria, 1976.

————. "The 'Whig Interpretation' of Literary History." *Eighteenth-Century Studies* 6 (Fall 1972):60-84.

Milton, John. *John Milton: Complete Poems and Major Prose.* Edited by Merritt Y. Hughes. New York: Odyssey Press, 1957.

Monk, Samuel H. *The Sublime: A Study of Critical Theories in XVIII-Century England.* 1935. Reprint. Ann Arbor: University of Michigan Press, 1962.

Moore, C. A. "Shaftesbury and the Ethical Poets in England, 1700-1760." *PMLA* 31 (1916):264-325.

Nethercot, Arthur H. "The Reputation of the 'Metaphysical Poets' in the Age of Pope." *Philological Quarterly* 4 (1925):161-179.

Palisca, Claude V. *Baroque Music.* Englewood Clliffs, N.J.: Prentice-Hall, Inc., 1968.

Parnell, Thomas. *Homer's Battle of the Frogs and Mice with the Remarks of Zoilus.* London, 1717.

Parry, Adam. "The Language of Achilles." In *The Language and Background of Homer,* edited by G. S. Kirk. Cambridge: W. Heffer, 1964.

Parry, Milman. *L'Epithète traditionelle dans Homère: Essai sur un problème de style homérique.* Paris: W. Heffer, 1928.

―――. *The Making of Homeric Verse.* Edited by Adam Parry. London: Oxford University Press, 1971.

Perrault, Charles. *Parallèle des Anciens et des Modernes.* Edited by H. R. Jauss and M. Imdahl. Munich: Eidos, 1964.

Piper, William Bowman. *The Heroic Couplet.* Cleveland and London: The Press of Case Western Reserve University, 1969.

Plato. *The Collected Dialogues of Plato.* Edited by Edith Hamilton and Huntington Cairns. Bollingen Series LXXI. 1961. Reprint. Princeton: Princeton University Press, 1971.

―――. *Plato: Euthyphro, Apology, Crito.* Translated by F. J. Church. Indianapolis: Bobbs-Merrill, 1948.

―――. *Platonis Opera.* Edited by J. Burnett. 5 vols. Oxford: Clarendon Press, 1905.

Pope, Alexander. *The Correspondence of Alexander Pope.* Edited by George Sherburn. 5 vols. Oxford: Clarendon Press, 1956.

―――. *Poetry and Prose of Alexander Pope.* Edited by Aubrey Williams. Boston: Houghton Mifflin, 1969.

―――. *The Prose Works of Alexander Pope.* Edited by Norman Ault. Vol. I: *The Earlier Works, 1711-20.* Oxford: Basil Blackwell, 1936.

―――. *The Twickenham Edition of the Poems of Alexander Pope.* General editor, John Butt. 11 vols. London and New Haven: Methuen & Co. Ltd. and Yale University Press, 1961-1967.

―――. *The Works of Alexander Pope.* Edited by Whitwell Elwin and J. C. Courthope. 10 vols. London, 1871-1889.

Quintilian. *Institutio Oratoria.* Translated by H. E. Butler. 4 vols. Loeb Classical Library. 1921-1922. Reprint. Cambridge, Mass. and London: Harvard University Press and William Heinemann, 1953.

Racine, Jean. *Théâtre Complet.* Edited by Maurice Rat. Paris: Editions Garnier Frères, 1960.

Rader, Ralph, "The Concept of Genre and Eighteenth-Century Studies." In *New Approaches to English Literature,* edited by Phillip Harth. New York and London: Columbia University Press, 1974.

Rapin, René. *Monsieur Rapin's Reflections on Aristotle's Treatise of Poesie.* Translated by Thomas Rhymer. London, 1694.

―――. *Reflections on Aristotle's Treatise of Poesie.* Translator anonymous. London, 1674.

Redfield, James. *Nature and Culture in the Iliad: The Tragedy of Hector.* Chicago: University of Chicago Press, 1975.

The Reflector. Vol. II. London, 1812.

Reynolds, Sir Joshua. *Discourses on Art.* Edited and with an introduction by Robert R. Wark. London: Collier Books, 1969.

Richardson, Jonathan. *An Essay on the Theory of Painting.* London, 1715.

Rogerson, Brewster. "The Art of Painting the Passions." *Journal of the History of Ideas* 14 (January, 1953):68-94

Rose, H. J. *A Handbook of Greek Literature.* New York: E. P. Dutton & Co., Inc., 1960.

Saint-Evremond, Charles de Marquetel de Saint-Denis, seigneur de. *Oeuvres Mêlées de Saint-Evremond.* Examined, annotated, and preceded by a history of the life and works of the author by Charles Giraud. 3 vols. Paris, 1865.

Sandys, J. E. *A History of Classical Scholarship.* 3 vols. Cambridge, 1908.

Scaliger, J. C. *Poetices Libri Septem.* Lyon, 1561.

Schoell, F. L. *Etudes sur L'Humanisme Continental en Angleterre à la Fin de la Renaissance.* Paris: Librairie Ancienne Honoré Champion, 1926.

Sensabaugh, G. F. *The Tragic Muse of John Ford.* Stanford: Stanford University Press, 1944.

Shaftesbury, Third Earl of (Anthony Ashley Cooper). *Characteristics of Men, Manners, Opinions, Times, etc.* Edited with an introduction and notes by John M. Robertson. 3 vols. London: Grant Richards, 1900.

Sherburn, George. *The Early Career of Alexander Pope.* Oxford: Clarendon Press, 1934.

Simonsuuri, Kirsti. *Homer's Original Genius: Eighteenth-Century Notions of Early Greek Epic (1688-1798).* Cambridge: Cambridge University Press, 1979.

Smalley, Donald. "The Ethical Bias of Chapman's *Homer.*" *Studies in Philology* 36 (1939):169-191.

Smith, G. Gregory, ed. *Elizabethan Critical Essays.* 2 vols. 1904. Reprint. London: Oxford University Press, 1971.

Southey, Robert. *The Correspondence of Robert Southey with Caroline Bowles.* Edited by Edward Dowden. Dublin: Hodges, Figgis, & Co., 1881.

Spence, Joseph. *Anecdotes, Observations, and Characters of Books and Men.* Edited by James M. Osborne. 2 vols. Oxford: Clarendon Press, 1966.

———. *An Essay on Mr. Pope's Odyssey in Five Dialogues.* 2nd ed. London, 1737.

Spingarn, Joel E. *Critical Essays of the Seventeenth Century.* 3 vols. 1908. Reprint. London: Oxford University Press, 1957.

———. *A History of Literary Criticism in the Renaissance.* 1898. Reprint. New York: Harcourt, Brace & World, Inc., 1963.

Spitzer, Leo. *Linguistics and Literary History: Essays in Stylistics.* 1948. Reprint. Princeton: Princeton University Press, 1970.

Sprat, Thomas. *History of the Royal Society.* 2nd ed. London, 1702.

Steadman, John M. "Achilles and Renaissance Epic: Moral Criticism and Literary Tradition." In *Lebende Antike: Symposion für Rudolf Sühnel.* Berlin: Erich Schmidt Verlag, 1967.

Suetonius. *Suetonius.* Translated by J. C. Rolfe. 2 vols. Loeb Classical Library. Cambridge, Mass. and London: Harvard University Press and William Heinemann, 1914.

Sühnel, Rudolf. *Homer und die englische Humanität: Chapmans und Popes Übersetzungskunst im Rahmen der humanistischen Tradition.* Tübingen: Max Niemeyer Verlag, 1958.

Sutherland, James. *A Preface to Eighteenth Century Poetry.* Oxford: Clarendon Press, 1948.

Swedenberg, H. T., Jr. *The Theory of Epic in England, 1650-1800.* University of California Publications in English, Vol. 15. 1944. Reprint. New York: Russell & Russell, 1972.

Swift, Jonathan. *Gulliver's Travels, 1726.* Edited by Herbert Davis with an introduction by Harold Williams. 1941. Reprint. Oxford: Basil Blackwell, 1965.

———. *A Tale of a Tub.* Edited with an introduction and notes by A. C. Guthkelch and D. Nichol Smith. 2nd ed. Oxford: Clarendon Press, 1958.

Tasso, Torquato. *Prose.* Edited by Ettore Mazzali. Vol. 22: *La Letteratura Italiana: Storia e Testi.* Milan, Naples: Riccardo Ricciardi Editore, 1959.

Terrason, Jean. *A Critical Dissertation Upon Homer's Iliad.* Translator anonymous. 2 vols. London, 1722-1725.

Tillotson, Geoffrey. *On the Poetry of Pope.* 1938. Reprint. Oxford: Clarendon Press, 1959.

———. *Pope and Human Nature.* Oxford: Clarendon Press, 1958.

Trimpi, Wesley. *Ben Jonson's Poems: A Study of the Plain Style.* Stanford: Stanford University Press, 1962.

Trimpi, Wesley. "Horace's 'Ut Pictura Poesis': The Argument for Stylistic Decorum." *Traditio* 34 (1978):29-73.

―――. "Knowledge and Representation: The Origins of Renaissance Neoclassicism." Paper read at Dominican College, San Rafael, California, November 10, 1973.

―――. "The Meaning of Horace's *Ut Pictura Poesis.*" *Journal of the Warburg and Courtauld Institutes*, 36 (1973):1-34.

Tuveson, Ernest Lee. *The Imagination as a Means of Grace: Locke and the Aesthetics of Romanticism.* Berkeley and Los Angeles: University of California Press, 1960.

Vicaire, Paul. *Platon Critique Littérairie.* Paris: Libraire C. Klingcksieck, 1960.

Vico, Giambattista. *The New Science of Giambattista Vico.* Translated from the third edition (1744) by Thomas Goddard Bergin and Max Harold Fisch. Ithaca, N.Y.: Cornell University Press, 1948.

Virgil. *P. Virgilii Maronis Opera, interpretatione et notis illustravit Carolus Ruaeus.* Amsterdam, 1690.

―――. *P. Virgilii Maronis Opera.* Edited by F. A. Hirtzel. 1900. Reprint. Oxford: Clarendon Press, 1966.

―――. *Virgil: Eclogues, Georgics, Aeneid I-VI.* Translated by H. Rushton Fairclough. Loeb Classical Library. 1916. Reprint. Cambridge, Mass. and London: Harvard University Press and William Heinemann, 1965.

Voegelin, Eric. *Order and History.* 4 vols. Baton Rouge: Louisiana State University Press, 1956-1974.

Warren, Austin. *Alexander Pope as Critic and Humanist.* Princeton Studies in English, No. 1. 1929. Reprint. Gloucester, Mass.: Peter Smith, 1963.

Wasserman, Earl W., ed. *Aspects of the Eighteenth Century.* Baltimore: The Johns Hopkins University Press, 1965.

Weinberg, Bernard. *A History of Literary Criticism in the Italian Renaissance.* 2 vols. Chicago: University of Chicago Press, 1961.

Whitaker, Virgil. "Philosophy and Romance in Shakespeare's 'Problem' Comedies." In *The Seventeenth Century: Studies in the History of English Thought and Literature from Bacon to Pope*, by Richard Foster Jones and others writing in his honor. 1951. Reprint. Stanford: Stanford University Press, 1969.

Williams, Aubrey L. *Pope's Dunciad: A Study of its Meaning.* Baton Rouge: Louisiana State University Press, 1955.

Wimsatt, William K., Jr. "One Relation of Rhyme to Reason." *Modern Language Quarterly* 5 (1944):323-338.

—— and Brooks, Cleanth. *Literary Criticism: A Short History*. New York: Alfred A. Knopf, 1957.

Winters, Yvor. *In Defense of Reason*. New York: The Swallow Press and William Morrow and Company, 1947.

Zimmermann, Hans-Joachim. *Alexander Popes Noten zu Homer: Eine Manuskript- und Quellenstudie*. Heidelberg: Carl Winter, 1966.

Index

Achilles, as problematic epic hero, 4-8; wrath of, 8-18

Addison, Joseph, 83; language of heroic poem discussed, 61-62, 92, 107-108, 131, 141-142, 153, 155, 163

admiration, *see* wonder

Age of Reason, appropriateness as designation of English Augustan period questioned, xv-xviii

Alamanni, Luigi, 7

Ancients and Moderns, dispute between in controversy over Homer, 79-85, 105-108

Apollonius, 105

Aquinas, St. Thomas, moral choice discussed by, 20-21n. 5, 28

Aratus, excessive circumstantiality of style of criticized by Longinus and Pope, 115-116

Archilochus, 105

Ariosto, Ludovico, 7

Aristeas of Proconnesus, his "affected Verses" criticized by Longinus and Pope, 127-128

Aristotle: best literary style defined by, 60; elevated style discussed by, 61, 131, 140-142, 153, 163; Homer's ability to represent everyday subject matter praised by, 64; *Iliad* and *Odyssey*, distinguishes between, 63n. 21; incorporation of the astonishing or wonderful in epic, 36, 86n. 26; intellectualist

view of moral choice subscribed to by, 20-21n. 5; "moral" and "poetical" treatment of character, distinguishes between, 19-20, 20n. 3; objects of knowledge and representation discussed by, 57-59; oral and written styles, distinguishes between, 76-99, 131, 145, 165-170; perspicuous style discussed by, 140-142; poetry and prose, stylistic qualities of distinguishes between, 133; primacy of plot over character in literary theory of, 6, 29-32; responds to Plato's demand that literature should offer moral exempla, 6; tragic and epic genres compared by, 140; the wonderful as effect of poetic diction, on, 59n. 11; the wonderful in tragedy, on, 31-32n. 31, 36

Aubignac, François Hedelin d', 33

Auerbach, Erich: elevation and verisimilitude discussed by, 63n. 21; *passio* in Augustine discussed by, 27-28n. 24

Augustine, 27-28n. 24

Bachyllides, 105

Balzac, Honoré de, 63n. 21

Bartlett, Phyllis B., 12n. 14

Battestin, Martin C., 74n. 1

Bentley, Richard, 78; his estimate of moral intention of Homeric poems, 81-82, 113

INDEX

Blackmore, Sir Richard, 116
blank verse, 131-144, 155-157, 161, 163
Boas, George, xv
Boethius, 27
Boileau-Despréaux, Nicolas, 31-32n. 31; dignified language, on, 112; translator on Longinus, 104
Boivin de Villeneuve, Jean, 96-97
Boswell, James, 82
Bray, René, 32n. 31
Bridges, Ralph, 64n. 23, 76
Brooks, Cleanth, 63
Broome, William, 150; prose translation of *Iliad*, 134-136, 139
Brower, Reuben A., xiv
Burke, Edmund, "sublime" and "beautiful" distinguishes between, 161n. 51
Bush, Douglas, discusses Chapman's Homer, xvii, 119
Butler, Samuel (author of *Hudibras*), 142-143
Butler, Samuel (translator of Homer), 163

Campbell, Lily B., 27
Chapman, George, xvii-xviii, 71-72; idealized representation of Achilles' wrath in *Iliad* of, 10-18, 163; Longinus, his knowledge of, 103, 163; "perturbation" defined by, 21-29; Pope discusses *Iliad* of, 95, 119, 126-127; style of his *Iliad* judged by Longinian criteria, 120-128
character (*ēthos*), representation of in relation to plot (*mythos*), 34-36
Chaucer, Geoffrey, archaic diction in, 93-95
Choerilus, 64
Chrysostom, Dio, 86n. 26
Cicero: *perturbatio* defined by, 25-27; plain style discussed by, 68-69;

poetry and prose, language of distinguishes between, 133-134
Clark, A.F.B., 104n. 4
Coleridge, Samuel Taylor: perceptual standard of criticism as developed by, 75n. 1; "pseudo-poetic" diction of Pope's Homer objected to by, 56, 65n. 24, 99-100, 150-153, 162
Collins, Anthony, 81
Congreve, William, 48
conservation of character, 38-48
Coolidge, John S., 39n. 42
Cope, E. M., 78
Corneille, Pierre, 33
couplet, *see* heroic couplet
Cowley, Abraham, 118-119
Cowper, William, 157n. 45, 163; on use of rhyme in Pope's Homer, 131-132
Crashaw, Richard, 119n. 35
Cromwell, Henry, 119n. 35
Crousaz, Jean Pierre de, 29
Cunningham, J. V., 20-21n. 5, 32n. 31, 59n. 11, 60n. 15
Curtius, Ernst Robert, 48

Dacier, André, "moral" and "poetic" treatment of character, distinguishes between, 20
Dacier, Anne, 78; her quarrel with Pope, 83-84, 108
Dante, 63n. 21
Davenant, Sir William, 30
decorum, 57-62, 72-73
Demetrius, 59n. 11, 80
Dennis, John, 104
Descartes, René, *Traité des passions de l'âme*, 21
Dionysius of Halicarnassus, 100; graceful style, austere style, and mixture of the two discussed by, 64-65; how verse can be made to resemble prose, on, 146-149

Donne, John, 60; Pope's reworking of satires of, 128n. 48

Dryden, John: *All for Love*, 33; archaisms, on use of, 92-94; as Homeric translator, 70-72, 89, 95-96, 100, 153-155, 158-162; *Iliad* and *Aeneid*, conclusions of discussed by, 33-34; Longinus, on, 104, 106, 162n. 52; moral and poetic treatment of character, distinguishes between, 20; "poetic diction" in couplets of, 150, 153, 158-161; "poetic diction" of bequeathed to Pope, 153-155; plot over character, questions primacy of, 30-32; preference for idiomatic word order in rhymed verse, 160n. 50; rhyme preferred to blank verse by Necader in *Essay of Dramatic Poesy*, 66n. 28, 139-140; verisimilitude and elevation, antagonism between discussed in *Essay of Dramatic Poesy*, 66; witty style in epic poetry disapproved of by, 126

Drummond, William, of Hawthorndon, 157-158

Edinger, William, 75n. 1
Eliot, T. S., 6n. 8
Ennius, 93n. 40
Epictetus, 24-25
Eratosthenes, 105
Euripides, 137-138
Ewing, S. Blaine, 21n. 5

Felton, Henry, 81
Fenton, Elijah, 69, 150
Fielding, Henry: compared with Richardson by Samuel Johnson, 74n. 1; conservation of character in *Tom Jones* and *Amelia*, 39n. 42
Fitzgerald, Robert, his blank verse translations of Homer, 136-139
Friedländer, Paul, 5-6n. 6

Gellius, Aulus, 90-91
Gibbon, Edward, 70
Greene, Donald, xv
Grene, David, xv-xvi
Gustafson, Richard C., 61n. 17

Hagstrum, Jean H., 57n. 6, 169-170
Hall, John, translator of Longinus, 103
Handel, George Frederick, xvin. 6
Herodotus, 108
heroic couplet, 131-164
Herrick, Marvin T., 32n. 31, 79
Hobbes, Thomas: Aristotle's *Rhetoric* adapted by, 79-80; Pope's estimation of as Homeric translator, 95, 103-104
Hogarth, William, 21
Homer: hexameter of, 157-158; ideal hero described by, 49-51; *Iliad*, subject of, 8; moral choice in, 42; Plato's criticism of, 4-6; "skiagraphic" style of as described by Aristotle, 76-78, chapter four *passim*; unity of poems disputed, 34, 81-82. *See also* Aristotle; Johnson; and Pope
Horace, 62n. 20: Aristotle's distinction between the oral and written styles as adapted by, 165-170; astonishing events should be narrated rather than acted, recommends that, 86n. 26; conservation of character discussed by, 38-39; lofty and common poetic styles, distinguishes between, 139-140; Lucilius, his stylistic relationship to, 128-129n. 48; plain style discussed by, 59
Hume, Robert D., 66n. 28
Hunt, Leigh, 144-146, 150

intellectualism, *see* moral choice
Ion (of Chios), 105

Isadore of Seville, 48-49
Isocrates, distinguishes between stylistic qualities of poetry and oratory, 134n. 7

Jack, Ian, 119n. 35
Johnson, Samuel: antiquated diction, comments on use of, 95n. 40; blank verse discussed by, 132-134; Homer and nature equated by, 113; Milton's style discussed by, 132, 142-144, 161n. 51; modern tendencies in criticism of, 56-57, 74-75; Pope and Dryden, styles of compared by, 160-161n. 51; Pope's Homer discussed by, xiii-xiv, 55-57, 59, 62, 74-76, 78, 82, 102, 120, 133, 150, 153, 156, 159, 162; Pope's theory of the ruling passion, objects to, 28; "scrupulous enumeration" of particulars in poetry censured by, 118-119, 125; Shakespeare's "conceited" style criticized by, 127n. 46; translation, history of art of discussed by, xiii; unity of Homeric poems defended by, 82
Jones, John A., 154n. 40
Jonson, Ben, 60, 103; archaisms, on use of, 93-94; couplet, discussed by, 157-158

Keast, W. R., 57n. 6
Keats, John, 144
Knight, Douglas M., xiv, 141n. 19

Lattimore, Richmond, 42
Le Bossu, Rene: characteristics of ancient epics distinguished between, 34-36; moral and poetic treatment of character distinguished between, 20; political dimension of *Iliad*, recognized by, 8-9
Le Brun, Charles, 21

Locke (Mr., of Norbury Place), 134n. 8
Longinus, xvi, 59n. 11, chapter five *passim*, 131, 162-163; circumstantiality and generality, on, 108-115, 127-128; English criticism, in, 101-104, 115-120; flawed genius to careful mediocrity preferred by, 104-108; *Iliad* and *Odyssey* compared by, 35-36, 63n. 21, 65, 146; Johnson and, 162n. 52
Lyttleton, George, 133

Mace, Dean T., 30n. 27, 33
Maclean, Kenneth, xvi
Macrobius, 91
Margoliouth, D. S., 42n. 45
Mason, H. A., xiv-xvn. 3, 138
Miller, Henry Knight, xviin. 9, 74-75n. 1
Milton, John: archaic diction, his use of, 92, 93-94n. 40; blank verse of, 132, 145, 155, 156-157, 162; lack of perspicuity in style of, 141-144, 155-156; Longinus, his knowledge of, 103, "poetic diction" of bequeathed to Pope, 152-157
Minturno, Antonio Sebastiano, 32n. 31
moral choice: in Homer, 42; intellectualist and voluntarist traditions of distinguished between, 20-21n. 5

Nethercot, Arthur H., 119n. 35
Nicoll, Allardyce, xviin. 9

Oldisworth, William, prose translation of *Iliad*, 134-137, 139
Ozell, John, prose translation of *Iliad*, 134-137, 139

Palisca, Claude V., xvin. 6
Panaetius, 26
Parnell, Thomas, 9, 80, 141

Parry, Milman, 85-86
passions: increasing interest in their analysis and representation in the seventeenth and eighteenth centuries, 20-21, 29-33; perturbations, defined in relation to, 22-28; representation of in baroque music, xvin. 6
Perrault, Charles, 31n. 31, 79, 84; unity of Homeric poems questioned by, 34, 81
Pindar, 91, 105, 106-107
Polyclitus, 117
Pope, Alexander: Achilles' wrath as represented by, xvii-xviii, 12-13, 15-18, 162-163; archaisms, on use of in poetry, 92-95; the *Brutus*, projected epic of, 19, 72; Chapman, disapproves of conceited style in *Iliad* of, 126-128; Chapman, estimate of *Iliad* of, 95, 119-120; circumstantiality in poetry, criticizes excessive use of, 115-116, 119; conservation of character, problem of in relation to *Iliad* XXIV addressed by, 38-48; Mme. Dacier, his dispute with, 83-84; Dionysius' estimation of Homer's ability to combine austere and graceful styles, concurs with, 64-65; Dionysius on how verse can be made to resemble prose, cites, 146-149; Donne's satires, his reworking of, 128n. 48; freedom of the will, on, 28-29; Homer, advantages of literal translation of discussed by, 95; Homer, commentators of discussed by, 3; Homer, Plato's criticism of discussed by, 4, 50; Homer, previous translators of discussed by, 95-96; Homer, "simplicity" of style of discussed by, 76; Homer, strategy in translating epithets of, 85-90, 114-115; Ho-

mer, Virgil's style seen by as more elevated but less lively than style of, 66-67; Horace's *ut pictura poesis* analogy as adapted by, 168-170; *Iliad*, conclusion of discussed by, 37-38; *Iliad*, generalized diction in translation of, 62-63, 110-115; *Iliad*, opening lines of his translation of criticized by Johnson, 55-57, 59-62, 74-75, 150, 153, 156, 159, 162; *Iliad*, rhyme chosen over blank verse in translation of, 132-133; Milton, on unidiomatic quality of style of, 141-142, 155-156; the passions, his interest in depiction of, 21, 29, 33; perspicuous style discussed by, 141-142; Shakespeare's conceited style criticized by, 127
Poussin, Nicolas, 94n. 40

Quintilian, xiii, 59n. 11, 90, 101; πάθος and ἦθος, on, 63n. 21; use of archaisms, on, 94-95

Racine, Jean Baptiste, 32
Rapin, René, 30
Reason, Age of, appropriateness as designation of English Augustan period questioned, xv-xviii
Reynolds, Sir Joshua: criticizes excessive circumstantiality in painting, 117-118; and Longinus, 162n. 52; on "simplicity," 94n. 40
Richardson, Jonathan, 21
Richardson, Samuel, 74n. 1
Robortello, Francesco, 103
Rogers, Thomas, 27
Russell, D. A., 63n. 21

satire, as preeminently successful poetic genre in English Augustan period, 72-73

Scaliger, Julius Caesar, his criticism of Homer, 84, 89, 105
Schoell, F. L., 25
Sensabaugh, G. F., 21n. 5
Shakespeare, William: "conceited" style of discussed by Pope and Johnson, 127; scenes of moral choice in tragedies of, 20-21n. 5
Sherburn, George, 150n. 33
Sidney, Sir Philip, exemplary hero of epic poem discussed by, 7, 19
Simonsuuri, Kirsti, 114n. 23
skiagraphia, 77-78. See also Aristotle, oral and written styles distinguishes between
Smalley, Donald, 12n. 14, 16n. 17
Sophocles, 105
Southey, Robert, 99
Spence, Joseph, xviii, 29; Essay on Mr. Pope's Odyssey, 67-68
Spens, Janet, 26n. 15
Spenser, Edmund: archaic diction of, 92-94; Renaissance epic hero as conceived of by, 19
Sprat, Thomas, 60-61
Stockdale, Percival, 133
Suetonius, criticizes Virgil's style, 90
Sutherland, James, 69n. 38
Swift, Jonathan, 98, 113

Terrason, Jean, criticizes Achilles' character, 4
Theocritus, 105
Theopompus, 108-110
Tickell, Thomas, rival to Pope as translator of Iliad, 61
Tillotson, Geoffrey, xviii, 145n. 27
translation, literal and poetic forms of defined, xiv

Trimpi, Wesley, 57-58n. 8, 77n. 6, 86n. 26, 91n. 55, 166
Trissino, Giovanni Giorgio, 7

Vico, Giambattista, distinguishes between logical and poetic mind, 114
Virgil: conclusion of Aeneid compared with Iliad, 34; extended periods in hexameter verse of, 157-158, 161; heroism in Aeneid of, 6, 49; Pope views style of his Aeneid as more elevated but less lively than Homer's style, 66-67; responds to demand for exemplary hero, 6; "skiagraphic" stylistic effect achieved by, 102-105
Voegelin, Eric, 8n. 11; "compact" symbolic form of myth and "differentiated" symbolic form of philosophy, distinguishes between, 114n. 23; Plato's criticism of Homer, on, 5-6
voluntarism, see moral choice

Walsh, William, 145
Warburton, William, 29
Whitaker, Virgil, 21n. 5
Wimsatt, William K., 63
Winters, Yvor, on heroic couplet, 158
Wolfius, Hieronymous, translator of Epictetus into Latin, 25
wonder: as effect of poetic diction, 58n. 11, 133; as emotional effect in tragedy and epic, 31-32, 34-36
Wordsworth, William, 65n. 24, 75; perceptual standard of criticism as developed by, 75n. 1

Zimmermann, Hans-Joachim, xvn. 3

PRINCETON ESSAYS IN LITERATURE

January 1983

The Orbit of Thomas Mann.
By Erich Kahler

On Four Modern Humanists:
Hofmannsthal, Gundolf, Curtius, Kantorowicz.
Edited by Arthur R. Evans, Jr.

Flaubert and Joyce: The Rite of Fiction.
By Richard Cross

A Stage for Poets: Studies in the Theatre of Hugo and Musset.
By Charles Affron

Hofmannsthal's Novel "Andreas."
By David H. Miles

Kazantzakis and the Linguistic Revolution in Greek Literature.
By Peter Bien

Modern Greek Writers.
Edited by Edmund Keeley and Peter Bien

On Gide's Prométhée: Private Myth and Public Mystification.
By Kurt Weinberg

The Inner Theatre of Recent French Poetry.
By Mary Ann Caws

Wallace Stevens and the Symbolist Imagination.
By Michel Benamou

Cervantes' Christian Romance: A Study of "Persiles y Sigismunda."
By Alban K. Forcione

The Prison-House of Language:
A Critical Account of Structuralism and Formalism.
By Fredric Jameson

[193]

Ezra Pound and the Troubadour Tradition.
By Stuart Y. McDougal

Wallace Stevens: Imagination and Faith.
By Adalaide K. Morris

On the Art of Medieval Arabic Literature.
By Andras Hamori

The Poetic World of Boris Pasternak.
By Olga Hughes

The Aesthetics of György Lukács.
By Béla Királyfalvi

The Echoing Wood of Theodore Roethke.
By Jenijoy La Belle

Achilles' Choice: Examples of Modern Tragedy.
By David Lenson

The Figure of Faust in Valéry and Goethe.
By Kurt Weinberg

The Situation of Poetry: Contemporary Poetry and Its Traditions.
By Robert Pinksy

The Symbolic Imagination: Coleridge and the Romantic Tradition.
By J. Robert Barth, S.J.

Adventures in the Deeps of the Mind:
The Cuchulain Cycle of W. B. Yeats.
By Barton R. Friedman

Shakespearean Representation:
Mimesis and Modernity of Elizabethan Tragedy.
By Howard Felperin

René Char: The Myth and the Poem.
By James R. Lawler

The German Bildungsroman from Wieland to Hesse.
By Martin Swales

Six French Poets of Our Time: A Critical and Historical Study.
By Robert W. Greene

Coleridge's Metaphors of Being.
By Edward Kessler

[194]

The Lost Center and Other Essays in Greek Poetry.
By Zissimos Lorenzatos

Shakespeare's Revisions of "King Lear."
By Steven Urkowitz

Coleridge and the Language of Poetry.
By Emerson Marks

The Image of the City in Modern Literature.
By Burton Pike

The Imaginary Library: An Essay on Literature and Society.
By Alvin B. Kernan

Steven Shankman is Assistant Professor of English at
Princeton University. He has contributed poems, essays, and reviews
to *Arion, The Southern Review, The Compass, Classical Antiquity,
The Independent Journal of Philosophy,* and
The Eighteenth-Century: A Current Bibliography.

www.ingramcontent.com/pod-product-compliance
Lightning Source LLC
Chambersburg PA
CBHW070839030726
47504CB00005B/1150